Praise for the Bakeshop Mystery Series

Meet Your Baker

"A delectable tale of murder and intrigue . . . This bakeshop mystery is a real page-turner, and we look forward to others in the series, just as tasty."
—*Portland Book Review*

"With plenty of quirky characters, a twisty, turny plot, and recipes to make your stomach growl, *Meet Your Baker* is a great start to an intriguing new series, but what sets this book apart and above other cozy mystery series is the locale. Ashland comes alive under Alexander's skilled hand. The picturesque town is lovingly described in vivid terms, so that it becomes more like a character in the book than just a backdrop to the action."
—*Reader to Reader*

"This debut culinary mystery is a light soufflé of a book (with recipes) that makes a perfect mix for fans of Jenna McKinley, Leslie Budewitz, or Jessica Beck."
—*Library Journal*

"Marvelous . . . All the elements I love in a cozy mystery are there—a warm and inviting atmosphere, friendly and likable main characters, and a nasty murder mystery to solve . . . I highly recommend *Meet Your Baker* and look forward to reading the next book in this new series!"
—*Fresh Fiction*

"*Meet Your Baker* is the scrumptious debut novel by Ellie Alexander, which will delight fans of cozy mysteries with culinary delights." —*Night Owl Reviews*

"Alexander weaves a tasty tale of deceit, family ties, delicious pastries, and murder against a backdrop of Shakespeare and Oregon aflame. *Meet Your Baker* starts off a promising new series."
   —Edith Maxwell, author of *A Tine to Live, A Tine to Die*

"With its likable characters, tightly plotted storyline, and innovative culinary tips, *Meet Your Baker* is sure to satisfy both dedicated foodies and ardent mystery lovers alike."
                  —Jessie Crockett, author of *Drizzled with Death*

A Batter of Life and Death

"Clever plots, likeable characters, and good food . . . Still hungry? Not to worry, because desserts abound in . . . this delectable series."   —*Mystery Scene*

"Readers [who] like their cozys with a bit of competition will want to jump into this mystery."
                                        —*Night Owl Suspense*

"A finely tuned mystery!"   —*Dru's Book Musings*

St. Martin's Paperbacks titles by Ellie Alexander

Meet Your Baker

A Batter of Life and Death

On Thin Icing

Caught Bread Handed

Caught Bread Handed

Ellie Alexander

St. Martin's Paperbacks

This is a work of fiction. All of the characters, organizations, and events portrayed in this novel are either products of the author's imagination or are used fictitiously.

CAUGHT BREAD HANDED

Copyright © 2016 by Kate Dyer-Seeley.
Excerpt from *Fudge and Jury* copyright © 2016 by Kate Dyer-Seeley.

All rights reserved.

For information address St. Martin's Press, 175 Fifth Avenue, New York, NY 10010.

ISBN: 978-1-250-08803-1

Our books may be purchased in bulk for promotional, educational, or business use. Please contact your local bookseller or the Macmillan Corporate and Premium Sales Department at 1-800-221-7945, ext. 5442, or by e-mail at MacmillanSpecialMarkets@macmillan.com.

Printed in the United States of America

St. Martin's Paperbacks edition / July 2016

St. Martin's Paperbacks are published by St. Martin's Press, 175 Fifth Avenue, New York, NY 10010.

10 9 8 7 6 5 4 3 2 1

To Gordy, the leading man in my life.

Acknowledgments

At Torte everyone is family, and bringing Torte to life takes an entire family. Not just my family but friends, neighbors, readers, bookstore owners, librarians, bakers, my publicity team, editors, business owners, and even my friendly mail carrier.

Thank you for sharing recipes, taste testing, editing, reading early drafts, inspiring me in the kitchen, inviting me into your homes, book clubs, and bookstores, and making Torte come to life.

You are all a part of these pages.

And, I have to send a special shout out to Ellen for coming up with the title *Caught Bread Handed*. No title gets more laughs when I'm giving book talks, and that is the way it should be. I hope that along with the title this book brings you a moment of laughter and joy and sends you scurrying to your nearest Torte for a scrumptious pastry.

Chapter One

They say that home is where the heart is. That could be true. But what if my heart was lost? What if my heart couldn't find its way home?

Technically I'd been *home* for six months. Home for me was my childhood town of Ashland, Oregon. It's a magical place with its Elizabethan architecture, charming Shakespearean-themed shops and restaurants, inviting outdoor parks and public spaces, and mild Mediterranean climate. Not to mention the warm and welcoming locals who can make a stranger feel like they've lived in Ashland for decades upon meeting for the first time.

Our family bakeshop, Torte, sits in the center of my hometown. It's located in the downtown plaza just a few hundred feet from Lithia Park and Shakespeare's stairs, a set of cement stairs that lead from the park's expansive lawn to the Oregon Shakespeare Festival's theater complex. Walking around the plaza is like stepping back in time. Storefronts are designed in Tudor style with narrow symmetrical buildings, timber framing, and ornate windows.

Ashland has something for everyone from its world-famous stage productions, to its funky artistic community, and wide open spaces perfect for adventure lovers. The only thing it didn't have at the moment was snow. Usually in January, Mt. Ashland's slopes were coated in deep layers of snow. But not this January.

I looked out Torte's front windows. The sun hung low in the late afternoon sky. A group of musicians with banjos and an accordion were busking in the center of the plaza. Two well-dressed tourists stopped in front of the bubbling fountains to listen to them play. It looked like spring outside. Bistro tables had been set up in front of restaurants and shop doors were propped open. It was hard to believe that people were meandering through downtown without coats in January, especially since winter had begun with an epic storm.

A week ago I had been at Lake of the Woods Resort, a remote alpine lodge, for a catering job and had ended up snowed in. Thick white flakes dumped from the sky for three days. Snow fell in record levels causing power outages and making travel impossible. Ashland had been hit by the blizzard too. Customers had to strap on cross-country skis for their morning coffee fix. After the storm blew over the sun emerged from the clouds. It melted the snow and ushered in a stretch of unseasonably warm weather.

I had to admit that I was a little disappointed. I hadn't experienced a winter in over a decade and I had been looking forward to a change of seasons. My work as a pastry chef for a renowned cruise line had taken me to every corner of the globe. It had been an adventurous ten years. I'd seen nearly every tropical port of call, but the ship always sailed under sunny skies. Winter meant island hopping in the Caribbean and swimming in the Mediterranean Sea. Snow was unheard of in the warm blue waters where tourists took refuge from winter's harsh winds and swirling storms.

In anticipation of the cold-weather months in Southern Oregon, I bought myself a new wardrobe of sweaters, jeans, and thick wool socks. From the looks of the busy plaza outside, I wasn't going to need them anytime soon. People milled around the fountains and information kiosk wearing shorts and thin sweatshirts. Definitely not winter attire. They looked like they belonged on the upper deck of the cruise ship, not Ashland in January. Since I'd returned from Lake of the Woods the temperature in Ashland had been holding in the mid-sixties. At this rate, I was going to have to break out my summer clothes again.

The sound of mixers churning in the background and the smell of sweet rolls rising in the oven made the lack of snow more manageable. Breathing in the comforting scents brought an instant calm to my body. Being home again had been better than I had ever expected. When I returned to Ashland six months ago with a broken heart, I thought it would be a temporary stop until I found my land legs and figured out what was next for me. That quickly changed. The community had welcomed me in, and working at Torte with Mom and our incredible young staff had given me a new sense of purpose and direction. There was just one lingering problem (literally and figuratively)—my estranged husband, Carlos.

I glanced across the plaza and shook my head. Carlos was at the Merry Windsor chatting with a bellboy in a

green-and-gold-stripped uniform. Of course. I couldn't escape him. I wasn't sure I wanted to.

I watched them talk. Carlos's dark hair fell in a soft
wave over one eye. The sleeves of his casual white shirt had
been rolled up to the elbows, revealing his bronzed forearms. He'd been telling everyone in town that he brought
the Spanish sun with him. "You see, this is how we winter in Spain. We drink in the sun along with some lovely
Spanish wine."

Everyone was charmed by Carlos, myself included. It
was impossible not to fall under his spell. His sultry dark
eyes and Spanish accent were practically irresistible, as
was his naturally relaxed personality. He'd been in Ashland a little over a week and had managed to bewitch
everyone in town.

Almost everyone. Richard Lord, the owner of the Merry
Windsor, where Carlos was staying, didn't look pleased
that Carlos was distracting the bellboy from his work. I
shook my head again as I watched his animated speech
and hand motions. The bellboy chatted happily as if he and
Carlos had been friends for years. Carlos had that effect
on people.

My mom, Helen, had the same gift, but she used it dif-
ferently. Her approach was to offer up a hot cup of coffee,
a fresh pastry, and a listening ear. Carlos tended to lure
people in with his witty banter and whimsical pranks. Both
approaches achieved the same result. Mom and Carlos had
a way of putting people at ease. I wasn't sure that I had
the same ability. It's something I've been trying to work
on. I think that I come across as too serious sometimes.

Carlos turned in my direction and caught my eye. He
blew me a kiss and then waved with both hands in an at-

tempt to get me outside. I shook my head and pointed to the kitchen. Heat rose in my cheeks as I left the window and walked back to my workstation. My husband had caught me staring at him. Normally that wouldn't be a bad thing, but right now it was for me. Having Carlos in Ashland for the last week had been equally wonderful and confusing. He was leaving for the ship in three days. I couldn't get distracted now. I had too much to do. Like getting our wholesale orders out the door, I said to myself, focusing on the stack of orders resting on the kitchen island.

I leafed through them, making sure everything was ready for tomorrow morning's shift. Thanks to some new restaurant accounts, Mom and I would finally be able to get the new ovens that Torte so desperately needed. We'd been barely getting by with one functional oven. New kitchen equipment came with a hefty price tag. We had been saving every extra penny for the last six months, and taking on extra wholesale accounts. It had paid off. We were so close that I could almost taste the fresh bread baking in shiny new stainless steel commercial ovens. I'd even gone so far as sketching out how we might make some minor tweaks to the kitchen floorplan and modernize our ordering system.

Having the new wholesale accounts had been great for our bottom line, but it meant that things were very tight in Torte's already small kitchen. I had been coming in earlier than usual in order to bake and deliver bread to our wholesale clients before the morning coffee rush. The long hours were taking a toll on my body. I shifted my weight as I restacked the order forms and surveyed the kitchen. Everything was running smoothly, as usual.

Stephanie, the college student who had been helping

with pastry orders in the back, rolled sugar-cookie dough on the butcher block. "Is this thin enough, Mrs. Capshaw?"

Mom tucked a strand of her brown bobbed hair behind her ear and nodded in approval. "Perfect."

"I'm going to grab a coffee. Need anything?" I asked.

Mom dusted a pan of brownies with powdered sugar. "No, thanks." Her brown eyes narrowed. She caught my apron as I passed. "Hold up there, young lady."

"What?"

"How many cups is that for you today?"

"Uh. I don't know. Not that many. Maybe a couple. I haven't been keeping count." I looked at my feet. If I made eye contact with her I knew that she'd catch me in a lie.

Mom threw her head back and laughed. "Ha!" She turned to Stephanie. "Did you hear that? Not many. By my count you've had at least a gallon."

"A gallon?" I overenunciated my words and played along. "Hardly." Then I folded my arms in front of my chest. "Plus it's my duty to carefully sample our coffee offerings. You wouldn't want us serving bitter coffee to customers, would you?"

Mom flicked my apron and shook her head. "Stephanie, you and I may need to stage a coffee intervention."

Stephanie looked up from the cookie dough and offered us both a rare grin. "I'm in."

I left them brainstorming ways to keep me from the espresso bar and headed for the front of the bakeshop. As I was about to ask Andy, our barista, for a double Americano, a woman's voice called my name.

"Juliet! You are just the person I wanted to see. Can I bother you for moment, dear?" An elderly woman with silver hair stood near the pastry case holding an almond croissant in one hand and clutching the counter with the other.

It was Rosalind Gates, the president of the Ashland Downtown Association. She wore a black T-shirt with the words SOS—SAVE OUR SHAKESPEARE written on the front.

"Sure." I scanned the dining room and pointed to an empty booth near the front windows.

Rosalind looked a bit unsteady on her feet. "Let me help." I offered her my hand and guided her to the booth.

"Thanks, my dear," she said as she carefully lowered herself into the booth. "My hip has been creaky lately."

Before I could ask her what she needed she pointed a bony finger across the street. "Look at that monstrosity. We have to put a stop to this right now. That woman has gone too far this time. Way too far."

My eyes followed Rosalind's quivering finger. She was pointing to ShakesBurgers. The chain restaurant had opened last week. Many local business owners weren't thrilled about it. Downtown Ashland is known for its eclectic shops and restaurants. The plaza is a hub for small, family-owned businesses. ShakesBurgers was the first chain to take owner-ship of a building downtown and most people weren't happy about it. Not only was the neon fast-food burger joint out of place in the historic Shakespearean village, but they had also taken over one of Ashland's beloved restaurants, the Jester.

Alan Matterson had opened the Jester last February. He was an old family friend who had run an extremely success-ful food booth at the farmers' market since I was a kid. His hand-dipped corn dogs were legendary around town, as was Alan's entertaining personality. In any place other than Ashland, Alan might have struggled to find his niche. Here, though, he blended right in. No one gave his black-and-white-checked jester jumpsuits or his zany hats a second look.

Locals flocked to the Jester for Alan's home-style cooking. The restaurant was themed after a medieval court. Tourists loved the restaurant's brocade façade and funky collection of jester hats and scepters that hung from the walls and ceiling. Alan greeted each customer who walked through the door with a goofy joke and a little jig. Kids' meals came with a gag gift—like waxed candy lips or a fake camera that squirted water. The Jester's food was equally irreverent. Alan served his signature corn dogs along with pink-and-blue-swirled cotton candy and banana splits piled high with Umpqua Valley ice cream and topped with sprinkles and maraschino cherries.

It seemed like the Jester would be a lasting success, but in early December right before the holiday season a CLOSED sign was posted on the front door. A week later the building was listed for sale and before anyone could blink, a construction crew ripped down the Shakespearean façade and carted away the cotton candy machine.

One of the issues with running a seasonal business in Ashland is calculating for the slow season. Sadly, many of the shops and restaurants that open in February when OSF kicks off their new season end up closing in November and December when the tourists return home. Watching it happen to a friend like Alan had been devastating. What made it even worse was having a chain like ShakesBurgers move in.

Mindy Nolan, a wealthy real estate developer who owned a number of chain restaurants, swooped in, purchased the building, and gave it an overnight makeover. She opened ShakesBurgers two weeks later. The two restaurants could not have been more different. ShakesBurgers had over thirty stores in eight western states. They specialized in fast food—burgers, fries, anything coated in grease. Unlike the other shops in the plaza, ShakesBurgers had painted the exterior of the building a shocking lime green and installed neon flashing signage that included an animated dancing milkshake and hamburger and a dialogue bubble pulsing their tagline: *Our burgers make your buns shake.*

It all happened so fast. One day the Jester was there and thriving. The next day it was gone. Some of my fellow business owners had expressed concern about Mindy and how she had handled the takeover. The word "hostile" had been tossed around. Rumors tend to spread quickly in a small town. I've learned that it's best not to make assumptions. I hadn't had a chance to talk to Alan, since he'd gone into hiding since ShakesBurgers had opened.

While Mindy was in the middle of renovations, she caught me in the plaza one day and asked if we'd be willing to source all of the bread and buns for ShakesBurgers.

"You're Juliet, right?" She hoisted a box of precut frozen potatoes in one arm and extended her hand. "I'm Mindy Nolan. Word is you bake the best bread in town. I want to source all of our buns from you. We try to partner with local businesses, you know, throw the small guy a bone, when we launch a new store. I don't take no for an answer. You might as well say yes."

Mindy's condescending attitude was off-putting. "I'm not sure," I replied. "We're pretty busy right now."

"A small business owner turning down hundreds—if not thousands—of dollars per month in new revenue before you've even had a chance to hear my pitch, are you crazy?" She set the box of frozen potatoes on the sidewalk and folded her arms across her chest. Her lime-green shirt with a cartoon logo of a burger oozing with melting cheese blended in with the garish color of the building.

I didn't appreciate Mindy's approach. "I'll have to talk it over with my mom," I said, trying to end the conversation.

Mindy continued to press. "I'll make it worth your while. This could be a very lucrative deal for you. ShakesBurgers is one of the fastest growing chains on the West Coast. You're going to want to be in on what we have to offer."

I disagreed. Working with the chain would anger my fellow downtown business owners. I couldn't betray Alan, and I didn't want Torte's products associated with a giant corporation. "Like I said, we'll talk about it, but I don't know that it's going to be a match," I said to Mindy.

My instincts were right. When I told Mom about Mindy's proposition she held up her hand to stop me before I'd even finished speaking. "Juliet, no. No amount of money is worth it. We can't do that to our friends."

"It would be more money, though," I said. My voice didn't sound convincing. "It would get us even closer to new ovens."

Mom was adamant. She stood firm. "No, it's not worth it. She can get her buns from Richard Lord. They seem like a match made in heaven, don't you think?"

I agreed. "Absolutely. I'm glad you think so too. She accosted me with a box of frozen potatoes in her hand. That was my first red flag."

"And Alan." Mom put her hand to her heart. "We couldn't

do that to him. He's still upset about losing the Jester. I saw him the other day and he wasn't even wearing one of his funny hats."

"Juliet, you're not working with the enemy, are you?" Rosalind's voice brought me back into the present moment.

I tore my gaze away from ShakesBurgers. "The enemy?"

She ripped off a bite of flaky croissant. "There's a rumor going around that Torte is supplying ShakesBurgers with buns." Her hands trembled slightly as she spoke.

"That rumor is false. I promise. Mindy approached us about using our products, but Mom and I both declined."

"Thank goodness." Rosalind let out a long sigh. "I told everyone that there was no way that Torte would agree to such a thing." She paused and took another bite. "The rumor mill is working overtime. The latest is that Mindy has hired two OSF actors to dress up in hideous hamburger and milkshake costumes to hand out fliers around town. It's absolutely sacrilegious. The woman is single-handedly destroying Ashland and I intended to put a stop to her."

"How?"

"The city has design standards, but they've become too lax. Mindy might meet the letter of standards on paper, but not the intent."

"I'm not sure I understand."

"Juliet, that thing is an eyesore." Rosalind pointed again. "Look at it. It belongs in a strip mall, not downtown Ashland. ShakesBurgers? What kind of a name is that? Mindy has a blatant disregard for the caliber of development downtown. Neon and, God forbid"—she made a cross in front of her chest and continued—"hamburger mascots prancing around town! Nothing about ShakesBurgers is compliant with the vision of this community."

I had to agree with Rosalind. Everyone was irritated that Mindy had torn down the old façade. Part of downtown's charm is the nod that businesses give to the Bard. Like the flower shop, A Rose by Any Other Name, Puck's Pub, and even the Merry Windsor, the hotel across the street, owned by Richard Lord, my least favorite person in town. Renaissance architecture dominates the plaza. From gables and turrets to elaborately carved porches and staircases, each building downtown is designed in Tudor style.

At Torte, we pay homage to Shakespeare and my father's memory with a rotating quote on our chalkboard menu. It's sort of an unwritten rule that downtown businesses incorporate a touch of whimsy, like our royal-red and teal walls at Torte, which are inspired by Elizabethan art.

"I'm still not clear what you need from me," I said.

"I need the support of all business owners. I've called an emergency meeting tonight. We are going straight to the city council and demand that the design standards be tightened. I've already worked up a rough draft. The new standards will specify materials, quality of finishes, that sort of thing, and trust me, neon-green paint is not on the list." She glared in the direction of ShakesBurgers again.

"Tonight?"

"Yes. At the Black Swan. At five o'clock." Rosalind stuffed half of her croissant into a paper to-go bag and checked the silver watch dangling from her thin wrist. "Oh, dear! It's almost time. You'll be there, won't you, Juliet? We have to put a stop to this."

Before I could reply she was already limping toward the door to catch up with the owner of Puck's Pub. I had a feeling he was going to get an earful about Shakes-Burgers too.

Mom came up behind me with a tray of petit fours as Rosalind left. "What was that about?" she asked.

"Rosalind has called a town meeting tonight to talk about ShakesBurgers."

The smile lines on Mom's cheeks deepened. "Talk, huh?"

I shrugged and helped her arrange the petit fours in the pastry case. They were hand-dipped in pastel-colored white chocolate. Each one looked like a dainty present. "That's what she said."

Mom handed me a pink petit four with a white chocolate heart in the center. "Let me go in your place. You look exhausted, honey."

"No." I took the petit four and bit into it. Layers of vanilla sponge cake, buttercream, and blackberry preserves melted together in my mouth. "You have a date with the Professor. It's fine. I'll make a quick appearance and call it a night."

We walked to the kitchen with the empty tray. "Those are so good," I said. "Are there more?"

Mom pointed to the island where Stephanie was drizzling white chocolate over a tray of petit fours. "Plenty."

Carlos and Sterling had their heads bent over a notebook at the counter. I hadn't noticed them come in while I was talking to Rosalind. Sterling could almost pass for Carlos's younger brother. His black hair matched Carlos's, although he wore his in an intentionally rough cut. When I first met Sterling I judged him based on his skateboarder style and tattoos. What a mistake. He's a wise soul with a kind heart and the most piercing blue eyes.

"It looks like you two are plotting something," I said, interrupting their concentration.

They both looked up.

"Julieta, I have decided tonight I will teach Sterling how to cure meat and make an antipasto. We will serve this as the starter for the Sunday supper, is this good?"

"Great."

"And it is okay that we can have the kitchen tonight?" He sounded surprised.

I picked up another petit four. The chocolate hadn't hardened. It melted onto my fingers. "It's all yours. I have to go to a town meeting."

Mom scowled. "We're not done discussing that."

Carlos clapped Sterling on the back. "Okay. It is decided. We must go to the market."

We'd been hosting specialty dinners affectionately called "Sunday suppers" each week. Customers paid a flat rate for a three-course meal served family style. They'd become so popular around town that we had to start taking reservations. This weekend's supper was already sold out. I had a feeling that it had to do with the fact that rumors had spread that Carlos would be preparing the meal.

Sunday's supper would be his last meal before he had to return to the ship, and everyone wanted a taste of his cuisine. I couldn't blame them. Carlos was the best chef I'd ever met, and not just because I'm biased. His food is simple and elegant. It's an experience. You don't just eat a meal prepared by Carlos, you linger over it, savoring each morsel. He says the secret is infusing his food with love. I'm a believer. In addition to his culinary talents, Carlos is an excellent teacher, a rarity in the world of chefs. While he was in Ashland I had asked him to take Sterling under his wing.

Sterling is our newest hire at Torte, but thanks to a solid work ethic and eagerness to learn, he had quickly become invaluable. Carlos thought so too when they had worked together at the catering event at Lake of the Woods. Carlos had been impressed with Sterling's eagerness to learn and instinct. He was a natural in the kitchen. They hit it off immediately. Carlos loved having a young protégé to nurture. I loved not having to worry about the menu for Sunday and that every seat in the house was taken.

I glanced at the whiteboard hanging on the far wall. It looked like a math equation gone wrong. I had color-coded everyone's schedules along with all of our wholesale orders and custom cakes for the week. It was a jumbled mess.

Stephanie was due in before dawn tomorrow morning. She and I would handle the wholesale bread and pastry orders. Once they were boxed and ready to go, I would deliver them while Mom and Stephanie would swap gears and begin working on stocking Torte's pastry cases. Andy, another college student, would man the espresso bar. So far the system was working, but there was no margin for error. If anyone got behind, or couldn't make it in, it would throw off the entire day.

I yawned and stretched. The clock on the wall ticked in a steady rhythm in the empty room. It was almost five. The long hours had finally been getting to me. I'm usually an early riser. I tend to thrive on little sleep.

Mom noticed. "You're exactly like your father, Juliet," she complained. "He used to work himself sick. He was always the first person here in the morning and the last person to leave at the end of the day."

"I'm fine, Mom," I said. I grabbed a cup of coffee and held it up. "This is all I need."

She frowned. "Juliet, your eyes are bloodshot and you keep staring at that whiteboard in a daze. We need to adjust this schedule."

"No," I protested. "It's okay. I promise. I just need to get through this weekend."

The truth was that having in Carlos in town wasn't helping. We'd been going out each night. In part because Carlos wanted to try every restaurant, and because we had a lot to discuss. Ramiro, Carlos's son, who I had only recently learned about, had been our main topic of conversation. He had failed to mention that he had a son when we got married. I'd been struggling with coming to terms about why he hadn't told me, and Carlos had been doing everything he could to try and regain my trust.

The clock dinged, signaling that it was five. Usually at five, I'd be on my way home, but I'd made a promise to Rosalind. I would have preferred to call it an early night with a glass of wine and the latest issue of *Baker and Spice* magazine, but duty called. It was off to a town meeting for me.

Chapter Two

I figured I could make a quick appearance at the meeting, and then head back to my apartment for a long, hot shower and early bedtime. The warm breeze felt refreshing as I stepped outside. Diners were eating at bistro tables on the sidewalk and a crowd had gathered by the bubblers to watch a magician perform. I smiled to myself and walked toward Lithia Park.

The park is one of my favorite places in town. Since I'd been home I had gotten into a routine of walking the park's wooded pathways in the mornings. My routine had been off for the past couple of weeks and I needed to get back into it. As soon as Carlos leaves, I said to myself as three teenage boys in hockey gear sprinted past me.

In the winter the city erects a temporary ice-skating rink across the street from the park. It's open for skating lessons, hockey games, and for families to play around on the ice. With the warm weather it must be costing a fortune to keep the ice cool.

I walked in the opposite direction of the rink to the Shakespeare stairs. The Black Swan Theater is one of the original buildings on the OSF complex. It's mainly used for workshopping small productions and for lectures and community gatherings these days. I passed the outdoor Elizabethan theater and crossed the street to the Black Swan.

It looked like the entire town was inside. The theater had been set up with rows of chairs facing the stage. Rosalind had done a good job of recruiting business owners. Almost every chair was taken. I found a seat near the back. Hopefully, that way I could duck out early without anyone noticing.

"Juliet, darling, I thought that was you. Not trying to hide, are we?" I heard a voice behind me. It was Lance. Lance is the artistic director for OSF. He and I had become friends since I'd returned to Ashland.

He strolled toward me. Everyone took notice of his catlike walk and signature fashion of a three-piece ivory suit with a scarlet ascot. No one else in Ashland wears an ascot.

Kissing me on both cheeks, he slunk into the empty seat next to me. "Darling, you look terrible. Bags under the eyes. A frazzled ponytail. Do tell, was it a ghastly day at the bakeshop?"

"Thanks a lot, Lance. You sure know how to make a girl feel good." I glanced at my jeans, which were dusted with flour and splattered with chocolate.

He tapped my chin. "Chin up, darling. I know what you need—a stiff drink."

"Right. At the town meeting?"

Lance gave me a devilish grin. He patted his breast pocket. "I always bring a little something to these events. It's better than community theater." He reached in and pulled out a silver flask. "Shall we imbibe?"

I declined. "No, thanks."

He shrugged and drank from the flask. "Suit yourself."

"What's in there?" I asked. The smell was so strong it burned my nostrils.

"Gin, darling. What else?"

"It smells like grain alcohol."

He sniffed it and waved his hand over the flask. "Maybe it is. Oh, dear."

"Lance, you're terrible."

"I am, aren't I?" He winked. "Is there another reason you're looking haggard? Could it be that saucy husband of yours has been keeping our pastry starlet up too late?"

I elbowed him in the ribs.

"Feisty." He pointed to the stage. "Now, shush. The fun is starting."

Rosalind Gates walked with a pronounced limp to the stage and positioned the microphone stand. She could have passed for one of Lance's actors. Her silvery-gray hair fell just above her shoulders. Her features were quite striking. She had enhanced her narrow cheekbones with blush and rimmed her eyes with a charcoal liner.

"She's aging well," Lance whispered.

"How old is she?"

"A lady never reveals her age, Juliet." Lance studied Rosalind's appearance. Then he whispered, "I would bet she's pushing eighty."

"Really?"

Lance nodded. "Look at her hands. They are a dead giveaway."

Rosalind's hands were marked with age spots and wrinkled.

"You should ask her where she got her shirt," Lance said.

I returned my gaze to the stage. She wore a pair of khaki slacks, white tennis shoes, and the black long-sleeved T-shirt that read: SOS—SAVE OUR SHAKESPEARE. I had forgotten to ask her about it earlier.

"What do you think it's supposed to mean? A reference to saving downtown?"

Lance took another swig from the flask. "No idea, darling."

Rosalind tapped on the mic. It cracked, sending a piercing screech through the room. She cleared her throat. "Sorry about that. I guess it's working. Thanks for coming tonight on such short notice. I appreciate your commitment and willingness to support our town during this critical time."

The door to the theater creaked open and slammed shut. Mindy Nolan, the owner of ShakesBurgers, along with two other men, entered the room. They all wore matching eye-shattering-green T-shirts. Mindy wore hers with a simple black skirt. One of the men looked like he belonged in a biker gang. His bald head glistened under the studio lights and he glared at everyone they passed on their way to the stage.

"Who's the Brutus?" Lance said under his breath as the beefy guy stomped past us.

"I've never seen him before," I replied.

Rosalind scowled. "Mindy, I didn't realize that you were coming."

Mindy walked to the front of the room. The two men followed after her. She paused in front of the stage before taking a seat in the front row. "Maybe that's because I wasn't invited."

Rosalind looked flustered, but quickly recovered. "I

wasn't sure you would feel comfortable attending tonight's meeting, since we're all here to discuss your restaurant."

Mindy didn't reply.

I craned my neck to try to get a glimpse of their exchange. "What's happening? I can't see."

"A catfight," Lance said. "Or maybe a cougar fight." He clapped and turned to me. "Oh, this is going to be fun!"

Rosalind continued. "As I was saying, thank you for being here. Many of you have expressed concern with the direction that *some* businesses downtown have taken." Her eyes lingered on the front row.

Alan Matterson, the owner of the Jester, sat three rows in front of us. I was surprised to see him here; he'd withdrawn from anything public since the restaurant closed. He jumped to his feet. "Just say it, Rosalind. Say it, man. We all know that you're talking about ShakesBurgers and that thief, Mindy. She's just in it for the bread. It bums me out."

Lance put his fingers over his mouth and grinned like the Joker. "I couldn't script this."

I elbowed him again. "You are terrible."

"I know." He smirked.

Rosalind nodded at Alan and motioned for him to sit. "Yes, Alan, I know you have firsthand experience and I want you to share that with everyone in a moment. Take a seat and let me finish, though."

Alan remained standing. Mom was right, he wasn't wearing one of his typical jester costumes. He looked like a different person. His long, graying hair had been tied into two braids. I couldn't remember the last time I'd seen him in street clothes.

"Our town jester and resident hippie is all cleaned up. Did he shave his beard?" Lance asked.

"It's weird, isn't it? I don't know if I've ever seen him out of costume."

"A tragedy." Lance straightened his ascot and gave me a somber stare. "A depressed jester. That doesn't work at all."

Rosalind continued. "It has been my honor to serve as the president of the Downtown Association for the past three years. As most of you know, I've lived in Ashland my entire life. There's no place I'd rather live. We have a thriving downtown business association, thanks to all of your hard work and effort, but the core of our plaza—the heart and soul of Ashland—is being threatened by businesses like ShakesBurgers that have no regard for Ashland's history or charm."

Heads began to nod around us.

"We are known around the world for the festival. When tourists arrive in town they want to feel like they've stepped back into the time of the Tudors. They come for the charm of downtown. They come for shops that serve meat pies and our bookstores that sell worn copies of Shakespeare's works."

Lance cleared his throat. "They come for my award-winning plays," he muttered under his breath.

But Rosalind had found her groove. "They don't come to Ashland to feel like they're in any other American town with strip malls and disgusting fast food. They come, they shop, and they spend their hard-earned dollars in all of your businesses because when they're here with us they feel like they could be on the pages of one of Shakespeare's plays."

She was right. Ashland has often been called the Disneyland for theater lovers.

Murmurs spread through the stuffy room.

"Our town has gone through a rough stretch," Rosalind continued. "Many of you in this very room have lost businesses or struggled to make ends meet. We've rallied around each other and supported each other through the tough times. As the economy continues to rebound, this is a time of great opportunity for our town." She paused for effect. "I know you all care as deeply for our downtown community as I do, and that's why I've called you here tonight. We need to preserve Ashland's charm. We cannot let businesses like ShakesBurgers come in and destroy what we've worked so hard for."

"Destroy?" Mindy got to her feet. "Are you kidding me? How has ShakesBurgers destroyed anything?" She turned her back on Rosalind and addressed the crowd. "I've modernized the building and given it a much-needed face-lift. That old, crumbling façade was going to come crashing down and kill a pedestrian."

Alan who was still standing, shouted, "That was façade was historic! You destroyed a piece of history, man. A piece of history."

Mindy studied her nails. She rolled her eyes. "About as historic as your idea of a restaurant. Maybe you should have spent more time on your wacky menu. You're complaining about burgers and shakes. Should we talk about cotton candy? How authentic was that? And if you want to get into it here, let's talk about how many health codes you were violating. This town should be grateful that ShakesBurgers has cleaned up that eyesore inside and out."

Alan lunged forward.

"This is taking an ugly turn," I said to Lance.

"I know, isn't it divine?" He grinned and took another

sip from his flask. He noticed my frown. "Kidding, of course. You know I'm on Alan's side."

Rosalind tapped on the mic, trying to gain control of the room. "Alan, I know you're angry, but please take your seat. I'm going to open the meeting to questions and comments from business owners in a minute."

"Too bad he doesn't own a business downtown anymore," Mindy said, staring Alan down.

The guy sitting next to Alan put his arm around his shoulder, trying to hold him back. Alan yanked him away. "You're going to regret what you've done," he said to Mindy. I'd never seen Alan so aggressive. He was usually one of the most laid-back people in town.

Rosalind motioned to the side of the stage. A teenager brought her a clipboard and a stack of pens. "I've made a formal petition and I'm asking for all of your signatures tonight. We need to protect our town and businesses from developers like Mindy who don't understand—or don't care—about preserving our Shakespearean old-world charm."

Mindy shook her head. "What? Protection from a multimillion-dollar chain that is going to bring much-needed revenue to a disorganized and outdated downtown. Is this a joke?"

Rosalind ignored her. She held up the clipboard. "This petition will tighten and redefine the specific guidelines for businesses in the downtown plaza. As most of you already know, Ashland has an established set of regulations when it comes to businesses. These include design esthetics and shop names that keep in the spirit of Shakespeare. I've pulled some examples of other towns that have created similar rules for businesses in a particular corridor. One example is our neighbor to the north—Leavenworth, Washington. The town banded together in the 1970s and transformed from an old run-down mill town into a Bavarian village. They have very clear rules about what storefronts can look like. We need to make sure that our design standards reflect this same level of preservation for all things Shakespeare." With trembling fingers she pointed to her shirt. "We must save our Shakespeare. And if businesses aren't willing to comply then they'll have to go elsewhere."

"You can't do that," Mindy protested. "There's no way that's legal. You can't ban a business from town. I read the design standards. We've adhered to every standard. Hell, our name is ShakesBurgers. It has the word 'shake' in it. Like, *Shake*speare. What else do you want from me? I can throw a pair of tights on our dancing milkshake."

"Oh snap." Lance snapped his fingers and gave his head a little shake.

Rosalind ignored Mindy and took the petition off the clipboard. Then she addressed the crowd. "I'll send this around now. Please take the sheets I have attached, which will spell out exactly how legal this is. Assuming the city council votes to adopt this new language you'll have thirty days to remodel." She ran her hand across her chest. "Oh, and I should mention that we have these shirts available for purchase tonight. You can all show your support by wearing them around town for the next few days."

She handed the petition to a woman in the front row and then turned her attention back to Mindy. "Let me assure you that we're not being unwelcoming. We're always welcoming of new businesses here in Ashland. If you want ShakesBurgers to keep its . . ." She paused as if trying to find the right word. "Uh, look, then there are plenty of re-tail spaces farther up from downtown. In fact, there's a beautiful space across the street from the college that would be a perfect match for you. What we are saying is that if you want to be on the plaza then you're going to have to remodel, and change the name." Her words might have held a welcoming sentiment, but her tone was clear. She wanted Mindy out of Ashland.

Mindy pulled one of the men she'd come in with to his feet. "Can you believe this, Mathew? This is ridiculous. It's like a witch hunt or something. We are a multimillion-dollar chain. We're not rebranding or remodeling any-thing. Period. You can take that to your city council while I call my legal team."

The man wore a gray suit with a ShakesBurgers T-shirt underneath. He gave Mindy a look to say, *I've got this* and then turned to face the audience. "I'm Mathew, Mindy's business partner and I assure you that we've done hundreds of renovations like the one at ShakesBurgers and we al-ways try to take input and feedback from local owners into account. It sounds like maybe we missed that step this time." He looked at Mindy.

Lance leaned toward my ear. "First rule of fashion. Never pair a cheap T-shirt with an ever cheaper suit. He looks like a walking pickle."

"Maybe that's what he's going for. He owns a fast-food joint, right?" I whispered.

"This is why I love you, darling."

"How can you tell that it's a cheap suit?"

Without a word Lance gave me a hard look.

Mindy threw her hands in the air. "What are you talk-ing about, Mathew?"

He slicked his gelled brown hair back. "Please accept our deepest apology for any misunderstanding we may have caused. We are always committed to being team players and bringing new business to the communities we place our restaurants in. ShakesBurgers is a recognized brand and I guarantee that name recognition alone is going to draw new customers to downtown that hadn't previously come. That means more shoppers for all of your stores."

"Mindy looks like she's going to explode," Lance said. "He's throwing her under the bus."

He was. Mathew walked up to the stage and took the mic from Rosalind's hands. "Do you mind if I speak directly to the business owners?"

Rosalind hesitated for a moment then stepped aside.

"Thank you." Mathew smiled at Rosalind. "I understand your concerns, I really do, but we have plenty of data that supports my argument. ShakesBurgers is going to bring new clientele to downtown. Unfortunately, this particular property got pushed through quickly." He paused and gave Mindy a knowing look. "We didn't have the kind of time we normally do to connect with each of you and share some data about what we offer to communities like yours here in Or-ee-gone."

"It's *Orygun*," Lance said aloud. Everyone around us chuckled.

Alan yelled, "That's because you stole it from me, man!"

Mathew made eye contact with Mindy again. I wished I could see her face. "We try to keep personal issues separate from business."

"Ooh, he's smooth." Lance leaned close to my ear. "Do you think there's going to be a fight?"

"I hope not." But I wasn't sure. The man sitting next to Alan had gotten to his feet as well. He had his arm around Alan's shoulder again.

Rosalind took the mic from Mathew. "Alan, I think it might be best if you stepped outside and cooled off for a moment. I know that we're all attached to our community and everyone is on your side, but let's try to stay level-headed. The best approach to deal with this situation is to work through legal channels, and for starters that means signing the petition that's coming around."

Alan threw his friend's arm off of him and stormed toward the door. "This isn't over." He pointed to Mindy.

"Darling, pinch me," Lance whispered. "It just keeps getting better and better."

"Lance, you're terrible. Can you imagine losing your business? Especially to a giant chain like ShakesBurgers?"

"You're always so serious. Have a little fun." He turned his head as Alan slammed the door behind him. "But of course, you're right. Poor Alan. Maybe I can workshop that anger and rage into something fit for the stage."

Mathew said something to Rosalind and then stepped off the stage. "I think maybe we could all use a little fresh air," she said. "If you can stay, please sign the petition tonight. We have to band together as a community of business owners. If for some reason you can't sign the petition tonight, I'll be coming by each of your businesses tomorrow. We have our next meeting scheduled for Wednesday evening at Puck's Pub. If you have any other comments or suggestions, please come see me. I know we are all committed to making Ashland the best place to live, and I'm confident that we're going to be able to find a resolution to this situation." She placed the mic in the stand. "Oh, and don't forget to buy your shirt. Let's Save our Shakespeare!"

Lance chuckled. "Well, this has been fun, hasn't it?"

"I'm going to take off. I have an early shift."

He screwed the flask lid on. "What? Without a shirt? And what will they say? Juliet Montague Capshaw isn't going to sign the petition to preserve our Shakespearean town? That's going to make front-page news."

"I'll sign it tomorrow. I agree with Rosalind. I don't want to see chain stores downtown, but I have to work bright and early. Actually just early. It'll still be dark when I get up."

Lance blew me kisses. "Ta-ta, darling. I'll keep you posted. I have a feeling the best action of the night is still to come." He nodded to the front where Mathew and Mindy were having a heated discussion.

I left before I got sucked into any more drama. In hindsight, maybe I should have hung around longer. Drama quickly found me.

Chapter Three

My alarm rang early the next morning. I dressed in the moonlight. Usually my morning routine involved a coffee ritual. I decided to forgo it in favor of getting a head start on the day. We stock eight different local coffee blends at Torte. Postponing my first cup by ten minutes wouldn't kill me. Well, probably not.

I tugged on a pair of jeans, a thin black sweater, and a red vest. Lance's comments about my appearance last night made me stop in front of the mirror. I hated to admit it but I did look like I could use more sleep. The skin underneath my eyes was puffy and my cheeks lacked color. I applied extra moisturizing lotion, a thin layer of under-eye concealer, and blush. My face brightened with the makeup.

Stars danced in the dark sky as I stepped out into the cold. Ashland might be experiencing a warm spell, but temps were near freezing in the predawn. My breath fogged in front of me. I tucked my hands into my vest pockets and hurried down the empty sidewalk to the bakeshop.

My apartment is above Elevation, the outdoor store, just

a few shops away from Torte. It makes for an easy commute, which I appreciate after years of working on a cruise ship. In fact, my commute in Ashland might actually be shorter than my walk from my room to the galley on the ship. My apartment is definitely bigger. It's not fancy, but it works for me. It's a small one-bedroom apartment with a kitchen, living room, and bathroom. Compared to the tiny room that Carlos and I shared on the ship, it's practically luxurious. I've learned to live lean. All of my possessions fit in two suitcases. I'm still not sure what to do with the extra space in my apartment. Mom says that it looks barren. I've been trying to remedy that by putting up watercolor artwork that I bought in Tuscany and the Greek Isles and unpacking my collection of vintage cookbooks.

It's not much, but it's a start.

Torte sat in a sleepy slumber when I arrived. A single light in the dining room had been left on. Mom and I had decided it was best to leave a light on at night after a recent break-in. I unlocked the front door, flipped on the overhead lights, and cranked up the heat.

White Stargazer lilies in red vases dotted the tables and the booths along the front window. They had been delivered yesterday and made the space smell almost tropical.

I hung my vest on a hook by the office and tied on an apron. My first task was getting the yeast rising. Coffee would be next, but first—the yeast. I mixed yeast and warm water in a glass measuring cup and left it on the butcher block counter to rise.

A latte sounded divine, but I didn't have time. That would have to wait until Andy arrived later. I settled for a dark French roast. The smell of the mild, citrusy beans pulsing in the grinder gave me an immediate jolt. I returned to my yeast, which had risen to the top of the measuring glass. Time to get to work.

Some restaurants and even a few coffee shops outside of the downtown plaza stocked our pastries, but the vast majority of our wholesale accounts were for our bread products. I attached the dough hook to the industrial mixer and preheated our one functional oven. The broken oven was a constant reminder of how much potential income we were losing. I had been impressed with the amount of product we'd been able to produce as a small staff and with one oven, but we couldn't keep operating like this.

While the coffee percolated, I mixed the yeast with sugar, flour, and salt. We offered wholesale clients five daily bread options—sourdough, marble rye, French, whole wheat, and sweet bread. The sourdough was our bestseller. It paired perfectly with soup, especially on a cool day.

Mom has been using the same sourdough starter for as long as I could remember. Starters improve with age, and ours has been passed down from generation to generation. Sourdough tends to intimidate home bakers. It shouldn't. Sourdough is simply fermented yeast, flour, and water. We store ours in a glass container in the walk-in. When we use the starter to bake we replace it with equal amounts of flour and water and a pinch of sugar. It's one of the easiest things to maintain and gives breads and pancakes a beautiful sour tang.

I poured myself a cup of coffee with a splash of heavy cream and grabbed the starter out of the fridge.

Stephanie arrived as I began kneading the first batch of dough.

"Morning," she mumbled, pulling off a knit cap. Her hair was dyed a brilliant shade of violet. It wouldn't work on many people but somehow it did on Stephanie. Without saying a word she poured herself a cup of coffee and walked like a zombie to the kitchen.

"You're loving this early morning shift, aren't you?" I teased, dusting my hands with flour.

Her head limped forward in what I assumed was a yes.

"This is early even for me." I gave her a reassuring nod.

She cradled the coffee in her hands and took a drink: "It's Saturday. No one is up this early."

"You're right." I coated the butcher block with flour and worked the large ball of dough with my hands. "It's crazy. I'm working on it, I promise. I have the order form for new ovens filled out and ready to go in the office. I just need to crunch the numbers one more time before I put the order in."

Stephanie rolled her eyes. "Jules, I'm here. Okay? I'm going to complain, but I'll be here as long as you need me."

I smiled at her. "Thanks."

She shook her head and drank more coffee. "But I am going to complain."

"Noted." I pointed to the whiteboard with the list of wholesale accounts. "Can you start on the marble rye and whole wheat?"

Stephanie gulped her coffee and poured herself a refill. She held up the half-empty pot. "You ready for another?"

"Please," I said, thrusting my cup in her direction.

We baked in a comfortable silence for the next hour. Stephanie didn't need much direction, and she wasn't much for morning conversation. She had our new routine memorized, and I appreciated that she wasn't overly chatty.

When I first met her, she seemed perpetually withdrawn and sullen, but I've learned that Stephanie's an introvert at heart. By the time everyone else arrived and we opened the door for business, the bakeshop would hum with lively banter and dialogue for the rest of the day. Having uninterrupted time was a godsend. So was the coffee.

Soon the kitchen smelled of baking bread. There's nothing like the smell of fresh bread to calm the mind. My thoughts drifted to Carlos. Since he had shown up at Lake of the Woods, I had felt unsettled. When I left him and the ship last summer I wasn't sure if I would ever see him again, but Carlos had other plans. He wrote me letters every single week during our time apart. I hadn't read them. At least I hadn't yet.

I had made a rash decision to leave him. It wasn't my proudest moment, but it was the only thing I could do at the time. Having him here was a reminder of how good things could be between us. It wasn't that easy though—there were still too many things left unsettled. Like why he had lied to me about having a son. Carlos and I had had a stage-worthy romance. I never imagined that he would keep something so important from me.

He tried to offer an explanation while we were at Lake of the Woods. It was only recently that Carlos had even learned that he had a son. Ramiro's mother had tried to raise their child alone. She realized that Ramiro deserved to know who his father was, but made Carlos promise that he would keep her secret. He agreed out of duty and protection. I believed him, I really did, and I wanted to forgive him and let it go, but I still couldn't understand why he would need to keep that secret from *me*. I was his wife. Wasn't marriage supposed to be about sharing each other's secrets, burdens, and joys? If Carlos couldn't tell me about Ramiro, what else could he be keeping from me?

Then there was the issue of what was next for us. It wasn't until I set foot in Ashland again that I realized how much I had missed being home and on solid ground. Working on the ship had been an almost mythical experience when I was younger. I was different now. I loved being home and as much as Ashland had welcomed Carlos in, I couldn't quite imagine him here permanently.

"Jules. Jules!" The sound of Stephanie's voice startled me.

I shook myself free from my thoughts. "What?"

"The oven's beeping."

"Oh, right," I said as I pulled on an oven mitt and turned off the beeping timer.

"You want me to do the deliveries?" Stephanie tucked her hair behind her ears, revealing a row of stud earrings lining her lobes.

"No, I'll do it. It looks like you've already started on the muffins. Just keep working on those and I'll be back in a few." I boxed the warm bread. It smelled so good that it was all I could do not to rip a hunk off the end of a loaf of sourdough.

"Do you have any specific flavors you want me to do?" Stephanie asked.

To simplify things Mom and I use the same batter recipe for our cookies and muffins. Each batter begins with the basic building blocks—butter, sugar, eggs, and flour. From there we can enhance the flavor by adding chocolate, sour cream, citrus, vanilla, berries, nuts, and so much more.

"Why don't you do chocolate sour cream and a berry streusel?" I had taught Stephanie the art of creating a balanced flavor profile. The key is in proportions. Since the cocoa would dry out the batter we incorporated sour cream to ensure that the muffins came out moist. The sour cream would also offer a hint of tang to cut the bitterness of the chocolate. The berries would have the opposite effect. As the muffins baked, the juices from the fresh berries would saturate the batter. Adding streusel would give the muffins some density and a nice crunch to balance the juicy berries.

"You remember the proportions?" I asked.

Stephanie nodded. "Yep. Two parts chocolate to one part sour cream, right?"

"Exactly." I untied my apron and placed it on the counter. "I'll be back in twenty or thirty minutes. Mom and Andy should be here soon. If you finish the muffins before I'm back go ahead and start on the cookie dough."

I picked up the large cardboard box. The sky had turned a light shade of purple as I opened the front door. While the sun might be making a slow and steady rise, nighttime temperatures in Southern Oregon were still bitterly cold. I placed the box on the front counter and ran to grab my vest. The deliveries wouldn't take me long, but there was no reason to freeze in the process.

My first stop was the Green Goblin, a bar at the far end of the plaza across from Lithia Park. The Green Goblin is known for its strong and unique cocktails. Their signature cocktail, the green goblin, was an avocado daiquiri blended with lime and mint. Food wasn't their forte, but they did serve meat and cheese plates to help customers soak up the rum in their daiquiris. They'd been using our bread for a couple of months now and had received rave reviews from customers.

After a short walk I arrived at the bar and tapped on the front window. I could see Craig, the owner and bartender, inside. He waved and came to unlock the front door. It's no surprise that tourists flock to the Green Goblin since the design inside is like stepping into a wooded forest. Ten-foot fake trees guard each wall, their branches stretching to the ceiling where they weave together, creating a green canopy overhead. Figurines of goblins, fairies, and elves hang from the branches. An iron candelabra is the main source of light for the dark, romantic bar. The tables and bar that runs the length of the narrow room are all carved to look like tree stumps with ivy snaking up the sides.

"Morning, Jules." Craig greeted me by taking the box from my arms and placing it on an empty table.

"You're here early, Craig. I was surprised to see you on the morning delivery list."

"I'm hosting a mimosa party for the art council this morning."

"That would explain the sweet bread." I pointed to the box of warm bread. It smelled so good my stomach rumbled in response. Maybe I should have grabbed something to eat.

"Yeah. You know me—my talent is behind the bar. I got some fresh fruit and cheese to go with your bread. Hopefully they'll drink enough mimosas not to notice my appalling lack of talent with food." He flicked a bright green bottle opener in one hand.

"That sounds perfect."

"You're too nice, Jules."

I smiled. "Not according to my kitchen staff. I don't think Stephanie appreciates the early morning shift."

"Tell her I feel her pain. I didn't get out of here until after midnight last night. I don't know how you do these kinds of hours. If it wasn't the off season I would have sent the mimosa party somewhere else, but you know how it is right now—I take business anywhere I can get it."

"It's so true. Hey, speaking of business, were you at the meeting that Rosalind called last night?"

He shook his head. "No. Friday is our busy night. I was behind the bar doing my thing. I hear I missed a good one. Everyone was talking about the showdown between Rosalind and Mindy."

"I snuck out early to go to bed," I confessed. "It was starting to get pretty heated before I left. Rosalind made it clear that chains are not welcome downtown."

"Can you blame her? ShakesBurgers is so out of place. I had to run off a couple of young actors wearing ridiculous ShakesBurgers costumes. They kept accosting my customers with free burger coupons yesterday." He pulled a rag from his belt loop and dusted the table.

"That rumor is true?"

"What do you mean?"

"Rosalind said something about Mindy hiring actors to advertise around town."

"Yep. She did. They were loitering around the front door. No one could come in or leave without having a coupon thrust at them. I finally had enough and told them to go find some other place to hang out." Craig took the paper bag labeled Green Goblin from the box and walked it over to the bar. "It sounds like you should have stayed. I heard that there was a fight. I didn't get the details but everyone was buzzing about it."

"What?" I followed him. The aroma of the bread wafted

toward my nose as Craig opened the bag and removed the golden loaves.

Craig placed the sweet bread on a cutting board. "That's the word."

"You mean like a physical fight?"

"That's what it sounded like to me. I wasn't there and you know once people get a drink or two in them their stories tend to become a little more far-fetched."

"With who?"

"Not sure. Someone mentioned Alan. Can you image?" He lined up six bottles of champagne on the bar. "You in the mood for a morning mimosa?"

I declined. "Too early for me. I should get going anyway. People get kind of crazy for their bread." I tried to wink, but I've never been able to master the move. It ends up looking like I'm contorting my face in a funky way.

Craig laughed. "I'm one of them. Torte's stuff is so good. I can see why demand is high. I'm glad we got in when we did. You're probably going to have to start turning orders down."

"Now that would be a great problem to have. Although you're half right. I'd love to do even more wholesale work but we just don't have the space right now."

"Space in the plaza is always an issue. There isn't much of it." He poured orange juice into one of the champagne flutes. "Hey, before you go I have a proposition for you."

"Okay." I waited for him to continue.

"Would you be up for creating a dessert-and-drink pairing? I'd love to add a dessert to the menu. I think it would be an easy sell to the late-night crowd. A nightcap and a hit of sugar before last call when I have to send them packing."

"Sure. That's a great idea. Let me sketch out a few ideas that will hold up well, especially if we deliver them late in the morning with your regular bread order. If you want I can bring over some samples for you to taste later."

Craig gave me a thumbs-up. "Bring over *anything* you want me to taste. I'm your guy."

I picked up the delivery box and walked to the door. "See you later today," I called as I went back outside into the cold. My mind was already creating flavor combinations for Craig. It was relationships like this that make Ashland an ideal place to live and work.

The next few deliveries were nearby. I dropped off each one with a quick chat with the business owners. Everyone was talking about last night's meeting. Rosalind was not alone in her quest. Every store owner I delivered to had already signed her petition. And in an act of solidarity everyone was wearing black SOS T-shirts.

I felt torn as I finished my last delivery and started back to Torte. I didn't want our downtown community to turn into a hub for big-box stores and retail chains, but running Mindy out of town didn't seem like the solution either. There had to be some kind of compromise.

ShakesBurgers does look completely out of place with its glaring neon signs and posters plastering its front windows, I thought as I neared the green building. It sat between the Merry Windsor, Richard Lord's Shakespearean-themed hotel, and Prospero, a magic and costume shop named after the magician from *The Tempest*. Both businesses met Rosalind's standards for downtown. If it weren't for a satellite dish on the Merry Windsor's roof, it would have been easy to believe that Shakespeare could have been a guest in the hotel, with its historic white plaster walls and ornate stained-glass windows. Prospero had a similar Old-English vibe, with a brick face and intricate ironwork.

ShakesBurgers, on the other hand, looked as if it belong on the party deck of the cruise line. An assault of flashing neon bombarded me as I neared the fast-food chain. Posters of greasy cheeseburgers and fries with pricing were strategically placed in the front windows. To my surprise the front door was propped open. Maybe Mindy was up early to plan her counterattack, I thought as I stepped closer and peered inside.

"Hello?" I called.

No one responded.

I knocked again and stepped inside. The interior was equally as gaudy as the exterior of the building. The neon green-and-orange color scheme extended from the floor to the ceiling. There were cardboard cutouts of the Shakes-Burgers mascots near the counter, plastic tables, and neon signage on every wall. My eyes couldn't focus.

"Hello, Mindy?" I called again.

Something crashed to my left. I spun my head in the direction of the sound. I knew immediately why there was no response. Mindy was lying on the floor. Blood pooled in dark circles around both of her wrists.

I dropped the box and screamed.

Mathew, her business partner, ducked behind the counter. His hands were covered in blood. He flinched and caught my eye.

"What are you doing?" My voice sounded distant, like it wasn't coming from my body.

"Trying to find something to stop the bleeding." Mathew wiped a bloody hand on his green ShakesBurgers T-shirt.

"Is she . . ." I couldn't bring myself to say the word *dead*. My feet moved like lead as I backed out the door one step at a time.

Mathew jumped over the counter. "Where are you going? Call 911!"

Chapter Four

I clutched the door frame. My heartbeat pounded in my head. I thought I might be sick. There was so much blood.

I grabbed the side of the building to steady myself. Was my mind playing tricks on me?

Mathew ran toward me. "Call 911!" Blood dripped from his hands.

I froze.

He clapped twice. Blood splattered onto the sidewalk. "CALL 911!"

I fumbled in my vest pocket and found my phone. I kept my eyes focused on Mathew while I punched the buttons for an emergency call. The operator picked up on the first ring. He asked me questions that I couldn't answer. I tried to hand the phone to Mathew.

Mathew held out his hands. "I can't talk like this."

I hit the speaker button. The operator asked Mathew how long he'd been on the scene and the status of the victim. Mathew kept looking down at his hands as he paced back and forth in front of ShakesBurgers. "I don't know, maybe five minutes. I tried CPR. Then I went to find something to stop the bleeding. I can't believe Mindy would do something like this to herself."

I paced with him, stepping carefully to avoid the drops of blood that splattered on the sidewalk as he paced.

The operator tried to keep him calm. "Did you check for a pulse? Is the victim breathing?"

Mathew pounded his fist against the window. It left a red splotch. "She's dead. She doesn't have a pulse. And she's definitely not breathing. She was dead when I got here."

I continued to hold the phone, trying to keep my hands steady while the operator walked Mathew through a series of questions. In the distance the sound of a siren wailed.

The police would be here soon. I wondered if Thomas, my friend and old high school boyfriend, was on duty this morning. I hadn't seen him since Lake of the Woods. Thomas was Ashland's deputy in training. He had been working as the Professor's assistant and taking on more responsibilities around town. The Professor was Ashland's lead detective and Mom's boyfriend. Things had been strained between us when Thomas accused Carlos of murder at the high alpine lodge. I knew that he was trying to do his job, but I also had a feeling that part of his focus on Carlos had to do with our past.

Red-and-blue police lights cut through the purplish sky. An ambulance sped to a stop in front of us. Before I could even process what was happening, two EMS workers hopped out and raced inside. The operator told us we could hang up now. I clicked off my phone and shoved it back in my pocket.

Mathew dropped to his knees. "I can't believe she would

do this. How could she do this to me? To herself? I know that she was stressed, but I never thought that she would do something like this."

"You think she killed herself?" I asked.

He glanced at the window behind him. "You think someone else slashed her wrists? Yeah. She killed herself." He looked at his bloody hands.

I couldn't believe it. Mindy had seemed so confident and focused last night. What had changed?

A police car zoomed up to the curb. Thomas got out of the passenger side. The Professor stepped out of the driver's side. I released the oxygen trapped in my lungs. I hadn't even realized that I'd been holding my breath.

"Juliet?" The Professor strolled over to me. He looked nothing like a detective in his jeans, tweed jacket, and wool scarf. "Pray tell, what are you doing here?" In addition to his duties as Ashland's only detective, the Professor was our resident Shakespeare enthusiast. He dabbled in community theater and lectured on the Bard's work. Mom and the Professor had been friends for years. Since I'd been home their friendship had blossomed into a full-fledged romance. I was thrilled to see Mom happy again.

"Delivering bread." I pointed to the box that I had dropped by the door. My hands started to shake.

"I see." He ran his fingers along his patchy reddish beard that had begun to streak with gray. His kind eyes met mine. Without saying a word he gave me a comforting look. I exhaled and placed my hand on my stomach.

"And might I assume that you found the victim?" he asked Mathew.

Mathew stood. "I did." He raised his hand. His arms, shirt, and jeans were stained red. "I found her."

A sick feeling rose in my stomach. My body swayed. Thomas gave me a concerned look. "Jules, you okay?"

I swallowed, trying to keep my coffee down. "I'm fine."

The Professor placed a firm hand on my shoulder. "Rest assured everything is indeed going to be fine. As the Bard says, 'Be just and fear not.'" He motioned to Thomas. Thomas looked the part of an all-American police officer in his blue uniform with a silver badge on his chest and a holster on his hip. He hadn't changed much since high school. His face had aged a bit, but he could still pass as a football player at Southern Oregon University.

Thomas grabbed a kit from the back of the police car. He and the Professor exchanged a look. The Professor continued inside while Thomas opened the kit and walked over to Mathew. "Jules, you're sure you're okay?"

I nodded. I wasn't sure I trusted myself to speak.

"Can you give us a little space? I'll have some questions for you in a minute, but first I need to talk to the witness." His tone turned professional.

"Of course," I said. "I'll wait over there." I pointed to a bench across the street by the bubblers.

I hadn't even noticed that a group of people had begun to gather, mainly early risers out for a morning jog or a cup of Joe. Police activity was rare in downtown Ashland, especially on the plaza. A few business owners who were preparing for the day had come out of their shops to see what the commotion and flashing lights were all about.

"Jules, what's up?" Sterling was standing in the front of the small crowd holding a paper coffee cup in his hands. He offered it to me.

"You brought me coffee? I could kiss you."

"Uh, that would be weird." He made a face. Sterling is

like a younger brother. He and I are kindred spirits. I just wished I could convince him to wear something other than a hoodie. He hides his soul-piercing blue eyes under a hoodie every day, and this morning was no exception. His face was shrouded by the black hood of his sweatshirt.

"How did you know where I was?" I took the coffee. It was hot to the touch and warmed my hands. I wasn't sure if it was from stress or the fact that the sun still hadn't risen, but my hands shook even harder. Coffee probably wasn't the best fix for this, but I didn't care.

Sterling nodded behind us. Torte was completely lit up. Inside Mom's, Stephanie's, and Andy's faces were pressed up to the window.

"Right. I guess it's kind of hard to miss the flashing lights."

"What's going on over there?" Sterling stuffed his hands into his hoodie. "It's freezing out here."

"Good. I thought it was just me." I took a drink of the coffee. It was dark with chocolate and a hint of something fruity. "This is amazing. What is it?"

Sterling shrugged. "I don't know. Andy made it for you."

I cradled the cup in my hands. "Mindy died."

"Mindy?"

"The owner of ShakesBurgers. She's dead."

"That sucks. Do they know what happened?"

"It looks like she killed herself."

Sterling's eyes widened. "Whoa. That's terrible."

I shuddered. "I know. It was pretty gruesome."

Thomas walked toward us. He held his hands out in front of him, motioning everyone to step back. "Hey, guys, I know you all want to help but we need you to go back to your businesses. That's the best thing you can do at the moment. The Professor has asked that everyone clear the plaza and go back to your normal routines."

A couple of business owners asked what was going on. Thomas cleared his throat. "There's been a death at ShakesBurgers. That's all I can tell you at the moment. I'm sure that once we have finished our initial investigation we'll come around and give everyone an update. In the meantime, we'd really appreciate it if you could head back to your shops. We'll take it from here."

One owner pressed Thomas for more information. Thomas held his ground, and the crowd began to disperse. There were murmurs as people moved toward their shops, but the tone was solemn. Thomas returned to ShakesBurgers.

The glare from the flashing emergency lights and the movement of so many people made me dizzy. I tried to focus on one spot. My eyes landed on the Merry Windsor. To my surprise Alan Matterson stood on the front porch. He was talking to Richard Lord and neither of them looked particularly happy. What was Alan doing here this morning? I was about to walk over and check in with him when I noticed the bald guy—or as Lance called him, Brutus—who was at the meeting with Mindy last night. He hung back near the bubblers. His bulky body was hard to hide. I watched as Alan left the Merry Windsor and headed to the center of the square. The bald guy saw him coming and ducked across the street and disappeared down the alleyway. Who was he? What was his connection to Mindy? And why were both he and Alan here in the plaza? Nothing was making sense.

Sterling tapped my shoulder. I startled. Coffee sloshed in the paper cup.

"Sorry. I was just going to tell you that it looks like you're wanted." He pointed to Thomas who was heading straight for us. "I'm going to head back to Torte and give everyone the rundown. Do you need anything else?"

I held up my coffee cup. "No. Please tell Andy I owe him. This is the best coffee that I've ever tasted."

Sterling's face turned solemn. "I will. Take it easy, Jules. I know it must have been tough."

I sighed as he left. Seeing Mindy like that had been tough, but having a team like the one I did at Torte made any situation manageable. How had I even thought for a moment about leaving them and Ashland?

Chapter Five

Thomas urged the few remaining stragglers to return to their shops, and then came over to me. "How are you holding up?" he asked, studying me, presumably for any sign that I was about to crack.

"I'm okay." I clutched the paper cup so tightly that it dented in the middle.

"Look, I know it's bad in there. You don't have to put on a brave face for me."

I attempted to smile. "Thanks."

"Let's sit." He led me toward the bench.

We both sat. The bench was slightly damp with morning dew. I didn't care. My head continued to spin. I clutched the cold slats in the bench to try and steady myself.

"Leave it to you to have coffee at a crime scene." Thomas chuckled and looked envious of my mangled cup.

"Sterling brought it over for me. They thought caffeine might help."

"And? Is it?"

I turned the cup upside down to show him that it was empty. "I'm not sure. Ask me when the caffeine kicks in."

Thomas placed his arm on the back of the bench and turned his body toward me. His voice sounded thick with emotion. "Jules, before we get into what you witnessed this morning, I owe you an apology."

"It's okay, Thomas." I waved him off.

"Let me finish. I'm sorry. I really value our friendship and I don't want to do anything to jeopardize that. I know that you don't believe me, but I was trying to do my job at Lake of the Woods."

I wanted to interject that his job didn't involve focusing solely on my husband as his prime suspect, but I could hear the regret in his voice.

"It's okay. I know. We're fine." The cup fell from my hands.

Thomas bent down to pick it up. He started to hand it to me, but instead lined up his forearm and made a perfect shot into a garbage can three feet away.

"Nice shot."

"I've still got a few moves in me." A dimple carved into his cheek as he smiled. "But seriously, Jules."

I cut him off. "Thomas, drop it. I'm not mad."

"You seemed pretty mad at Lake of the Woods."

I grinned. "Well, I was mad, but I'm not anymore."

"I knew it! You were mad."

"But I'm not anymore."

"But you were."

"Thomas, don't you have an investigation going on?"

"Fine, but you admit that you were mad."

"Thomas." I gave him a hard look.

"All right." He removed his arm and pulled out his iPad. "Walk me through what happened this morning."

I explained how I had finished my morning deliveries

and noticed the door at ShakesBurgers was propped open. "I don't know what made me go in. I guess it just seemed off. When I stepped inside I saw that Mindy was on the floor and Mathew was behind the counter."

"What was he doing?" Thomas looked up from his iPad.

"He said that he was trying to stop the bleeding. He was covered in blood." I closed my eyes hoping to rid myself of the memory of Mindy's lifeless body.

"Did you see him near her body?"

"What do you mean?"

"He said that he was looking for something to stop the bleeding. Anything else?"

I thought back to what I'd seen. "I don't know. Uh, I think he said he tried to give CPR. Honestly, all I wanted to do was get out of there. There was so much blood."

"Okay. Don't stress yourself out. This is helpful."

Thomas rested his iPad on his lap. I knew that despite the caffeine my brain cells weren't firing as fast as they usually do. Why did Thomas want to know about Mathew performing CPR?

"Is there something you're not telling me? Why does it matter what Mathew was doing if Mindy's death was a suicide?"

Thomas glanced over both shoulders. "It doesn't." He gave me a knowing look.

"Are you saying that Mindy's death isn't a suicide?"

"I didn't *say* anything."

"Thomas, stop speaking in code. You're the one dropping subtle clues. Not me."

He looked across the street. I followed his gaze. Richard Lord and Mathew were standing on the front porch of the Merry Windsor. Mathew had a foil emergency blanket draped around him like a cape. From their rigid body posture it didn't look like Richard was consoling Mathew. Why was Richard talking to everyone this morning?

"I don't understand. What's going on?"

"It's too early to know for sure, but the Professor says that he can already tell there are some things in the crime scene that don't add up."

"Add up how?"

Thomas lowered his voice. "It appears that the victim had some kind of struggle."

"Struggle?"

He nodded. "There is bruising and other evidence that leads us to believe that the victim put up a fight."

"Really?"

"Like I said, it's too soon to tell. She may have been involved in a fight and then took her own life. Either way, it changes our investigation."

"Wait! She did get in a fight." I twisted my back. My body felt tight. "At least according to the Ashland rumor mill. Craig told me this morning that everyone at the bar was talking about a fight after the meeting last night."

Thomas made a note and stood. He offered me his hand. "Looks like my next stop is the Green Goblin." His voice changed. "Listen, I know you've been through a lot. Take it easy, okay, Jules?"

Easier said than done, I thought to myself as I gave one last glance toward the crime scene and walked back to Torte.

Chapter Six

Mindy might have been murdered. I was surprised that Thomas was sharing information about the investigation. He'd made it clear that he'd wanted me to stay out of his cases in the past. Maybe it was his way of trying to make amends.

Who could have killed Mindy? If last night's meeting was any indication, practically everyone in town could be on the suspect list. My first thought flashed to seeing Alan Matterson on the plaza this morning. Why would he be downtown before any shops were even open? He had a serious grudge against Mindy and ShakesBurgers. Could he have killed Mindy?

Stop it, Jules, I told myself as I opened the front door to Torte. You don't even know for sure it was murder.

"Juliet, we were so worried about you!" Mom was waiting at the front counter. She wrapped me in a tight hug. "Sterling told us what happened. Are you okay?"

I squeezed her back. "I'm okay, Mom. Shaken, but fine."

She released me, but kept hold of my hands. "You need to eat. We made you a plate. Come sit."

"Mom, I'm fine."

Before I could protest she pulled me to one of the tables in the front. Stephanie brought a cheddar and bacon omelet, a biscuit with whipped honey and macadamia nut butter, and a cup of fresh fruit. Andy delivered another mug of steaming coffee. Sterling joined them as they surrounded me.

"You guys, I'm fine."

"You're not getting off that easy, young lady." Mom sat down across from me. The years had been kind to her. Subtle smile lines were etched on her cheeks and forehead. Her brown eyes still held the twinkle of youth and sparkled with golden flecks.

She studied me as I took a sip of coffee. Sharpening her eyes in her best mom-stare, she rested her chin in her hands and asked, "What happened to Mindy?"

I dug into the omelet. It was comfort on a plate. The egg had been cooked so that the sharp cheddar and salty bacon practically melted in my mouth. I had to admit that Mom knew exactly what I needed. I guess I was hungry.

"This is great. Sterling, did you make this?"

Sterling gave me a sly smile.

Mom tapped both of her hands on the table. "Don't change the subject, young lady."

I knew there was no way I was getting off without telling them the gory details. While I nibbled on the omelet and biscuit, I told them everything. Almost. There was no point in getting everyone worked up about a murder when we didn't know whether or not Mindy had actually been murdered yet. Plus, Thomas had asked me to keep that quiet. I wouldn't break my promise.

When I finished my breakfast and giving my recap,

Mom rubbed her temples and sighed. "How terrible." She put her hand over her heart. "Mindy didn't strike me as depressed." She looked thoughtful. "People only reveal what they want to reveal, don't they?"

The mood was somber. We all paused in a quiet reflection.

Andy finally broke the silence. "Hey, Mrs. C, there's a line outside. What do you want to do?"

Mom looked up. Andy was right. A line of people trailed down the sidewalk. "You don't suppose they're all here for our pastries, do you?"

Andy smiled. "Torte's pastries are the best, Mrs. C."

"Well said, Andy." Mom stood and pressed her hands against her apron. "Jules, you head back to the kitchen. We'll try to shield you from the mob. Everyone else to your stations. I have a feeling it is going to be a busy morning."

I hurried to the kitchen, happy that Mom was willing to take the brunt of the gossip. I didn't think I could handle telling the story over and over again. What I needed was to bake.

I washed my hands and found my apron where I'd left it earlier. Stephanie and Mom stocked the pastry case and Andy took his position behind the espresso machine. With full pastry cases and coffee ready to pour, Sterling unlocked the front door.

The bell on the door jingled repeatedly for the next two hours. I watched Mom circle the room with a coffee carafe. She stopped and chatted with locals between delivering chocolate–sour cream muffins and lattes. I knew that she was getting an earful at each table. This was big news. Everyone wanted to be a part of it.

Stephanie worked on refilling the pastry trays and baking sweets for the afternoon rush. I focused on the lunch menu. Torte is a popular lunch spot. We offer premade sandwiches and hearty soups that people can grab and go, or stay and linger.

I'd been craving a soup I had years ago when in port in Greece—tomato orange. Tomato soup and grilled cheese had been one of my favorite childhood meals and the version I planned to make for lunch would elevate the soup but still offer the same warm comfort.

I started by chopping onions and dicing fresh tomatoes. I sautéed them in butter, allowing the juices to mingle and the onions to turn translucent. The soup recipe was simple, but packed with a savory and slightly sweet flavor. In order to cut down on the acid from the tomatoes and orange juice, I would use a couple teaspoons of baking soda. Cooking and baking are science, and I always enjoy playing the part of a chemist in the kitchen.

Once the tomatoes and onions had simmered in the butter, I added them along with fresh-squeezed orange juice, chicken stock, and chopped thyme to a stock pot and turned it on medium low. It smelled like everything had been hand-picked from a garden. With the soup starting to bubble, I added in the baking soda and called Stephanie over to watch it foam.

"Baking soda in soup? That's weird." She didn't look convinced.

"Trust me. You're going to love it."

She shrugged and returned to scooping cookie dough onto baking sheets lined with parchment paper.

I would let the soup cook down for a while, and then use an immersion blender to create a thick texture. Right before I served it, I would mix in some heavy cream to balance the citrus.

While I whisked more orange juice into the stock pot I heard Carlos's voice behind me. "Julieta, what are you making? The smell is like heaven." He leaned over my right shoulder to get a look in the pot. His lips brushed the base of my neck.

I stood rigid, afraid that if I moved Carlos would too. We might have stayed that way indefinitely with the heat from the burning flame on the stove and the heat between us if it weren't for Sterling.

He broke the moment. "Hey, Carlos, I'm ready for you." He must have realized that he had interrupted something because he stopped at the island and pretended to be interested in the tray of breadsticks that Stephanie was buttering.

Carlos kissed my neck, patted my hip, and stepped away from the stove. "*Sí*, we will meet with the wine maker. Julieta, you have arranged this, yes?"

I smoothed the front of my apron in an attempt to regain control over my emotions. Placing the whisk next to the stove, I turned the heat to low and covered the soup with a lid. "Yep. It's all set. Jose should be here by early afternoon. He's going to bring some samples for you to taste, and he mentioned that you're both welcome to go out to the winery with him this afternoon if you're interested."

Jose Ortega owned a winery, Uva, about ten minutes outside of town. He has been our primary supplier of red and white blends for nearly thirty years. Mom contracted with Jose when he first moved to Ashland from California to work at one of the big vineyards. His story is so inspiring. He had made a deal with the owner to take lower pay in exchange for working a small section of the land. Initially Jose's plot was only a quarter of an acre, but he had a golden touch with the vines and a strong work ethic.

He and Mom and Dad grew their businesses together. Word spread, as it always does in Ashland, about Jose's bountiful grapes. Not many famers were using organic methods thirty years ago. Jose started the trend here, and over the years his plot continued to expand until he eventually bought the original owner out. Nearly every restaurant, hotel, and pub source their wine with Jose now.

Last year Mom had hit a rough stretch, thanks in part to her giant heart, since she fed half of the town for free when the economy tanked. It was a kind gesture, but it put her behind in her vendor payments. Jose had told her not to worry. He knew that she would pay him when her cash flow improved. I couldn't fathom the vendors I used to work with on the ship having the same kind of flexibility. If we didn't pay our bill on time, they would have stopped delivering goods. Not Jose. He brought Mom's order every week without fail.

Once Mom and I got the books sorted out, we paid off our balance with Jose and a few other vendors in town. For a while it looked as if Torte might close. If it weren't for friends like Jose, Mom probably would have had to shut down the bakeshop, or worse—sell to someone like Richard Lord. The thought gave me new appreciation for how Alan Matterson must feel watching ShakesBurgers take over his beloved business.

Thank goodness that didn't happen to us, I thought as I grabbed a spiral-bound notebook and pencil and joined Carlos and Sterling at the island.

They quickly hid something under the island as I approached. "What's going on?"

Carlos stifled a laugh. "It is nothing." He held out his phone. "I was showing a new picture of Ramiro. You must see. He is taking surfing lessons."

Sterling tugged on the strings of his hoodie. He wouldn't make eye contact with me. They were up to something. Carlos was notorious for pulling kitchen pranks, and I had a feeling that he was training his young prodigy in the art.

I took the phone. Ramiro stood in waist-high aquamarine water. A yellow surfboard on his left hip towered over him. His other hand was raised in a peace sign. He looked like a miniature version of Carlos with his olive skin and wavy dark hair. His smile was wide and his eyes danced with the same carefree spirit as Carlos's. My throat tightened. I'd never met Ramiro, but I knew that I already loved him.

"He looks good, no?" Carlos took his phone and gazed lovingly at his son.

"He looks great. A natural." I tried to glance under the island. Carlos nudged Sterling, who stepped to the side and blocked my view. They were definitely up to something.

"How did the meat curing go?"

"Hmm?" Carlos pretended he didn't hear me.

"The meat? Isn't that what you guys were doing last night?"

"*Sí, sí*. It was good. Easy, no, Sterling?"

Sterling coughed. "Yeah, good. Really good."

I was going to have to keep my eyes on them. "You guys are on Sunday supper duty, right? You take the appetizers and main course and I'll stick with dessert. Does that work?"

Carlos rolled up the sleeves of his white dress shirt. His forearms, which were naturally darker than my fair complexion, had been toasted from months spent under the Caribbean sun. The contrast of his crisp white shirt and tanned skin made my heart flutter. Carlos caught me looking at him. He grinned.

I ignored him and flipped open the notebook. Hopefully Sterling hadn't noticed. I wanted to keep my professional and personal life separate, but Carlos was making that very difficult. "You made antipasto and cured meat last night, right? Any other ideas? We're already sold out. Word has spread that there's a Spanish chef in town."

If Sterling had picked up on the tension between Carlos and me, he didn't show it. He pushed up the sleeves of his hoodie, revealing his tattoos and following Carlos's lead. "Last weekend we did pasta."

"Right. That was a hit."

"Everything's a hit here, Jules," Sterling said as he grabbed a cookie cooling on a wire rack.

"True. Good point, but let's do something totally different this week."

Carlos brushed a strand of dark hair from his forehead. His hair has a slight wave to it, and when it's longer it curls in the front. "Have you served tapas?"

"Ooh, tapas. I love tapas."

"*Sí,* everyone knows you love tapas, *mi querida.*" Carlos grinned. "She cannot resist the tapas," he said to Sterling. "I used to make them for the kitchen staff late in the night and everyone would joke that they must get to the tapas before Julieta. Otherwise she would eat them all."

Sterling looked surprised. "Really. I've never seen you put food away like that, Jules."

I punched Carlos in the arm. "That's not true. I shared. Okay maybe not the bacon-wrapped dates, but everything else."

Carlos threw his head back and laughed. "Do not believe this, Sterling. She is—how do you say—a tapas freak."

"Freaky for tapas. Good to know."

"Enough, you two," I said, tapping the pencil on the notebook. "Let's get a menu sketched out before Jose gets here."

We decided on a Spanish wine-tasting flight. We would start with mixed olives, cheese, and cured meats. For the main course Sterling and Carlos would make empanadillas, turnovers filled with vegetables and meat, skewered prawns, and carne mechada, a tender, slow-cooked beef. Sticking with the theme, I would make a lemon and olive oil cake.

My mouth was watering by the time we finished the supply list. Carlos had won me over with his tapas. I'd already been attracted to him from the first moment we met on the ship and when he made me tapas, I was a goner. I've had tapas all over the world. None compared to Carlos's.

Carlos didn't make you love food. He made you fall in love with it, and I had it bad for his tapas. There's something so refreshingly simple about Spanish cuisine. Maybe it's because the dirt is older in Spain, but from his salted almonds poached in olive oil to his Moorish meatballs with fresh sage and English peas, everything Carlos put on a plate tasted vibrant and alive. When he orchestrated tapas production on the ship he and his team did everything by hand, whether that meant breaking down a whole chicken or releasing the natural oils and intoxicating scent of Spanish saffron with a mortar and pestle. Dish after dish after dish would be sent out. Tapas nights were like one continual party. Torte's customers were going to be in for a sensory experience tomorrow.

Andy came into the kitchen balancing a tray of coffee drinks. "Anyone up for a taste test?" He placed the tray on the island.

I took a mug of the creamy, hot coffee. "What's your latest creation?"

"I'm calling this the chunky monkey."

Carlos scrunched his forehead. "Chunky monkey. I do not understand."

Andy passed a cup to Sterling and Stephanie. "It doesn't mean anything. It's just a funny name." His blue eyes perked up as he waited for us to taste his new drink.

Mom came into the kitchen with an armful of empty plates. "Hey, is there a party going on back here? Why didn't anyone invite me?" She winked.

"It's a new drink, Mrs. C. I have one for you too," Andy said.

Mom put the dishes in the sink and joined us at the island. "It smells great. Almost fruity."

Andy smiled. His freckled cheeks stretched toward his ears. "Try it."

I took a sip of the chunky monkey. It was sweet with a hint of nuts and something else.

"It is sweet," Carlos said. Carlos, like most chefs, tends to turn his nose up at anything sugary, but I knew from one taste that our customers were going to be lining up for Andy's drink. Torte was a bakery, after all, and sometimes dessert can come in a mug.

"What am I tasting?" I asked, inhaling the scent. "Banana?"

Andy nodded. "Yep. Banana, chocolate, and macadamia nut. Chunky monkey, get it?"

We all laughed. I noticed that Carlos returned his practically full mug to the tray. Stephanie sipped hers. Sterling took a big drink. "It's really good, man."

Mom walked over to Andy and squeezed him around the shoulder. "You've done it again. This is so good." She looked at Carlos. "Andy is more sweet than salty."

"Super sweet," I agreed, taking another drink. Most of Andy's coffee drinks feature the roast as the star of the show. The chunky monkey was a tad sweeter than our normal offerings, but he had obviously used a nutty roast, which mingled well with the fruity banana and dark chocolate.

"Let's get it up on the specials board," Mom said. "It can be our weekend drink special. Which reminds me, I need a new quote to go up there. Anyone feeling poetic this afternoon?"

On the far wall near the espresso machine we have a chalkboard menu that we update with specials and a rotating Shakespearean quote. The bottom quarter of the chalkboard is reserved for Torte's youngest customers. Mom keeps a basket with colorful chalk for kids to doodle on the board while their parents savor a morning coffee and crumpet.

I looked at Sterling. He was staring at his feet. I knew that he had been writing his own poetry. I'd asked him to share it on the board before but he hadn't been ready. I caught his eye. He gave me a quick head shake. I didn't push him. He would share it when he was ready, or he wouldn't.

Andy shrugged. "Unless you want a quote about football, I'm out."

Mom chuckled as Andy returned to the espresso bar.

Stephanie shook her head. "Don't look at me. I'm still asleep." She walked away with her head hanging down. I'd have to tell her she could have tomorrow morning off. I could handle the Sunday wholesale orders alone.

Mom clapped her hands together. "Come on, someone must have a quote for me. Sterling?"

"I'll have to think on that." He ran his finger along his hummingbird tattoo. "And Carlos wants me to check stock in the fridge with him, right, Carlos?"

Carlos nodded. "*Sí,* I need my young chef to help, is this okay?"

Mom pretended to be hurt. "Go ahead, go work. I'll have to come up with something myself."

Carlos looked at me to confirm that she was kidding.

"She's kidding, go." I motioned them to the walk-in.

He paused and reached into his jeans pocket for his phone. "Helen, I thought you would want to see the new photo of Ramiro. He is beautiful, no?"

Mom held the phone a foot from her face. "I need my reading glasses." She keeps multiple pairs of reading glasses in a vase on the front counter near the menus. "Just you wait until you hit forty," she said to me when I asked about the glasses. "Our older customers appreciate being able to read the menu if they forget their glasses."

"Hand me that pink pair, would you, Andy?" She pointed to the vase.

Andy tossed her a pair of glasses. Mom zoomed in on the photo of Ramiro. She pressed the glasses to the tip of her nose and looked up at Carlos and then back at the phone. "He is the spitting image of you."

Carlos wrinkled his forehead. "Spitting image. I do not know this phrase."

Mom handed him his phone. "He glows. I can't wait to meet him someday."

"*Sí*. Someday."

The sound of someone clearing their throat made us all turn. The Professor was standing behind her. He waved when she turned and caught his eye. "Did I hear correctly, you're in need of a new quote?"

A slight blush rose in Mom's cheeks. "You did, indeed."

"Indeed." He tilted his head. "Might I join you?"

Mom nodded.

The Professor looked at the tray of coffees. "Am I interrupting something?"

"Not at all," Mom said, touching the sleeve of his tweed jacket. "We were just finishing a tasting of one of Andy's newest coffees before the lunch rush hits."

"Ah. Of course." The Professor removed a pair of black reading glasses from his breast pocket. He put them on and then turned to read the board. "That's one of my favorites. It's a shame you have to take it down."

"We don't have to, but it's been up there for a week. I think it's time," Mom replied.

The Professor looked at each of us—Carlos, me, then Sterling and Mom. He tapped his fingers to his chin. His eyes sparkled. "I believe I have the perfect quote for you."

"Yes?" Mom waited for his response.

He removed his reading glasses and motioned with his hands as if he was on a theater stage. " 'All the world is a birthday cake, so take a piece, but not too much.' "

"Shakespeare?" I asked.

"Nope. George Harrison."

I looked at Mom. "The Beatle?"

"One and the same," the Professor said. "He's another favorite of mine, and I'd say he has a knack for the Bard's style, don't you think?"

Mom rolled her eyes. "You're too much."

"Maybe we should put it up there and see if people know the difference," I suggested.

"Let's do it." Mom assembled our coffee cups on the tray. "In fact we can make it into a contest. The first customer to guess correctly gets a coffee on the house."

"I'm sure Andy will love that," I said.

"Did you need something, Doug, or is this just a nice surprise?"

The Professor placed his hand over hers. "Seeing you is always lovely, Helen." There was a heaviness to his tone.

Mom's walnut eyes sparkled. "Doug, stop. You're going to embarrass me in front of the kids."

The Professor removed his hand and cleared his throat again. "Many apologies."

"Don't worry about me. I have to get back to work anyway," I said.

"Might I beg a moment of your time before you go?" the Professor asked.

I pointed to my chest. "Me?"

"Yes. I have a few questions about the murder this morning that I need to discuss with you." He massaged his temples.

"Murder?" Mom's eyes shot to the Professor and then back to me. "Juliet Montague Capshaw, you didn't say anything about a murder."

"I didn't . . ."

The Professor spoke before I could spit out a lie. "She did not know that the victim had been murdered. The coroner confirmed that fact mere minutes ago. Mindy Nolan did not take her own life. She was killed."

Chapter Seven

Mom squeezed the Professor's arm. "Oh, Doug, I'm so sorry."

The Professor rested his hand on top of hers. "King Richard III said it best, 'What ugly sights of death within mine eyes.'"

"I can't imagine." Mom's voice choked a bit. "Can I make you something?"

"That would be lovely." The Professor smiled, but there was a sadness behind his kind eyes.

Mom saw it too. She caught my eye and frowned. Then she started slicing whole-grain bread. "You two go talk up front. I'll bring you some lunch."

The Professor stepped aside. "Juliet, after you."

I walked to the dining room. The lunch rush would be in full swing within the hour, but for the moment there was a lull. I pointed to a two-person table near the pastry case. "Is this okay?"

"Yes, please sit." The Professor removed his scarf and placed his tweed jacket on the back of the chair.

I sat and waited for him to open a well-used moleskin

notebook. He flipped to a blank page and looked up at me. "I'm sorry to disturb your work. I have a few questions that I need to ask you and then I'll be out of your way."

"It's not a problem," I said. "Mindy was murdered?"

He sighed and glanced outside at ShakesBurgers. "Yes. I'm afraid that she was."

"How do you know? I mean, I don't need the details, but how can you tell?"

"That's the coroner's job. We suspected that whoever killed Mindy tried to make it look like a suicide. There were bruising patterns, among other things, that led us to believe someone else had a hand in her death." His voice sounded weary as he spoke. The Professor, despite being serious about Shakespeare, usually had a lightness about him. That was missing today. I wondered if the investigation was disturbing him.

I tried to keep my face neutral. Thomas had hinted about the same thing. Now it had been confirmed by the medical examiner.

"Establishing time of death is going to be critical in this investigation, which is why I'm here." The Professor flipped back a page in his notebook. "You said you thought you arrived at ShakesBurgers at six-twenty this morning, is that correct?"

"I think so but I'm not entirely sure. I wasn't really paying attention to the clock."

"Can you take a minute and walk me through what you did, leading up to finding Mindy?"

I told the Professor how I'd stopped at the Green Goblin, delivered the rest of the orders, and walked across the street to the plaza.

"And you think you crossed the street at six-twenty?"

he asked as he removed his reading glasses from his pocket and placed them on the tip of his nose.

"I wish I had paid better attention. That's just a guess. I left Torte at six and I was probably at the Green Goblin for ten minutes. You could check with Craig, maybe he was paying attention to the clock."

"Thomas is there right now."

"Can I ask you something?"

The Professor placed his pencil on top of his notebook. "Of course."

At that moment Mom arrived with a bowl of tomato orange soup and a grilled cheese sandwich. She set it in front of the Professor and patted him on the shoulder. "Eat."

I stared at his bowl. The soup was a beautiful coral color. "Did you add cream to that, Mom?"

Mom pursed her lips together and shook her head. "Oh ye of little faith." She pointed to the bowl. "What do you think?"

The soup was thick and a creamy color of blood orange. "It looks perfect. You blended it too?"

"I saw your notes back there." Mom winked.

"Thanks for finishing it."

The Professor ladled soup onto his spoon. Steam rose from the bowl. He blew on the spoon and had a taste. "It's excellent. Thank you."

"Eat the sandwich too. It's Havarti with just a hint of dill."

"You're too good to me, Helen."

Mom grinned and motioned for him to eat. "I'll leave you two to talk."

Her solution to every problem is food. Whenever a customer is feeling down or in need of a friendly ear, Mom will bring them a plate of pastries or a warm bowl of soup. It works like a charm. People open up to her. Fortunately, it doesn't show on her waistline. I watched as she danced back into the kitchen. She could pass for my older sister with her trim figure and shoulder-length bob.

"You wanted to ask me something, I believe?" The Professor bit into the gooey grilled cheese.

"Is there a reason why it's so important that you know the exact time I got to ShakesBurgers this morning?"

The Professor wiped his chin with a cloth napkin. "We're trying to establish time of death. The coroner thinks that Mindy was killed sometime between five and six-thirty A.M."

"I know I was there before six-thirty. I wasn't gone that long, and I always try to be back to Torte before the morning rush starts."

"That's very helpful. We want to make the time-of-death window as tight as possible." The Professor made a note. His fingers were stained with butter from the grilled cheese. They left a thumbprint mark on the page.

"Are you saying that Mindy might have been killed right before I got there?"

"It's highly possible."

"What about Mathew? He was there too."

"I'm aware of that fact." The Professor met my eyes across the table.

"Do you think Mathew could have killed her? He said he was trying to find something to stop the bleeding, but maybe . . ." I trailed off.

"Perhaps. Do not let your eyes deceive you though." The Professor finished his lunch. He asked me a few more questions and then stood. "Thank you for your time, Juliet, you've been most helpful. Most helpful indeed."

I didn't feel helpful. What did the Professor mean by letting my eyes deceive me? He had a way of speaking in code that I'd never been able to decipher. I had more questions now than I had before. A gust of cold came over me and it wasn't only from the fact that I was sitting next to the front door. What if I had walked in on Mathew killing Mindy?

Chapter Eight

The Professor left and I returned to the kitchen. It was a good thing. The lunch crowd was double the normal size. Word had spread. Everyone wanted a side of gossip with their soup. Stacks of handwritten order tickets backed up on the front counter. Sterling scrambled to jot down each order, collect payments, and box lunches to go.

The tomato orange soup was a hit. Mom and I kept an assembly line of grilled cheese sandwiches rotating in the Panini press. She sliced thick cuts of Gouda, Havarti, white cheddar, and swiss cheese. I buttered bread and managed the Panini maker. The combination of the rich soup and cheesy sandwiches had created a line out the front door.

I suspected that customers were looking for comfort food as an escape from the darkness of Mindy's murder. The winter sun had warmed the temperature outside. Usually soup and grilled cheese is a bestseller on cold and rainy days. Today was an exception.

When the line finally thinned, Mom wiped her brow. "Wow, that was something."

"You're telling me."

"How many soup-and-sandwich combos do you think we sold?"

I walked over to the stove and titled the empty stock pot for her to see. "By the looks of it, a lot. I think Stephanie scraped this clean with a spatula for the last bowl."

"Whew. I need a nap." She brushed bread crumbs from her hands. "How are you holding up?"

"I'm okay."

"Juliet?" She raised one eyebrow.

"Really, Mom. I'm fine. Like everyone else who came in for lunch today, I'm shaken up, but I'm still standing."

"I can't believe that Mindy was murdered." Mom ran a sponge under hot water in the sink and then began wiping down the counter. "What did Doug want to talk to you about?"

"He wanted to know when I got to ShakesBurgers. They think Mindy was killed right before I got there."

Mom dropped the sponge. "Oh, Juliet."

"I know." I scooped chunks of bread heels into a plastic bag. They don't work well for grilled cheese, but they make great croutons or can be used in bread pudding. "Hey, Mom, is something wrong with the Professor?"

She returned to wiping the butcher block. "You noticed?"

"He didn't seem like himself. He's usually so—I don't know how to explain it—steady, I guess."

"I know." She frowned. "I thought so too. It has to be tough on him—another murder investigation, here in our beloved city."

"Yeah." I thought about seeing Mindy's lifeless body on the floor. At least I didn't get a closeup look. The Professor and Thomas had to examine every piece of evidence.

"I wish he would talk about it with me."

"He will. He loves you, Mom. Give him some time."

She didn't look convinced, but forced a smile and tossed the sponge into the sink. "I hope so."

Stephanie stomped into the kitchen with a tray full of dirty soup bowls and plates. "People are crazy today."

"Thanks for helping out front. It looked like a mob scene up there."

She submerged the dishes in the soapy water in the sink and positioned the empty tray on her forearms to go back for another round. "You don't even want to know. Don't come out there. You'll both freak."

Mom's eyes widened. "Why will we freak?"

Sterling jogged into the kitchen and headed straight for the closet where we keep the cleaning supplies. He grabbed a broom, mop, and dustpan. "We got this. Don't worry."

"What's going on?" I asked.

Sterling ducked out of the kitchen with his cleaning gear. Stephanie shook her head. "It's fine. It's just a mess. It looks like a tornado hit. A soupy tornado."

Mom and I looked at each other and without a word raced to the front.

Stephanie hadn't exaggerated. There were splotches of tomato orange soup on the floor and the tabletops. Pieces of crust and bites of cookies were littered all over the floor. Discarded receipts and order tickets were scattered on the front counter like confetti.

"What happened?" I asked, holding up a vase with a white lily. It looked like it had been dipped in tomato orange soup.

Andy stood behind the espresso machine. His face matched the soup. Sweat dripped from his forehead.

Sterling pushed up the sleeves of his hoodie and started sweeping while Stephanie loaded up the empty tray with more dishes. Carlos was nowhere in sight.

"We couldn't keep up. So many people wanted orders to go, but then they stayed to talk while they were waiting. Soup got sloshed everywhere. We couldn't get the tables cleaned in time. No one seemed to mind. They loved the food, and all they wanted to do was talk about the murder." Sterling pointed out the window.

A makeshift shrine had been constructed in front of ShakesBurgers. People had left flowers, balloons, votive candles, and cards. I put my hand over my heart. This is why I loved Ashland. Mindy hadn't been loved, and yet our community rallied to pay their respects to her.

Mom put her arm around my waist and leaned her head onto my shoulder. She sighed. "How nice. We'll have to bring something over to add to the tribute."

"We will," I agreed.

She inhaled through her nose and glanced around the dining room. "But first we need to get this place back in order."

Sterling tapped the broom to the floor. "We got this."

We sped around the dining room picking up used plates and coffee cups. Sterling swept while Mom followed after him with a wet mop. Stephanie rinsed the dishes and filled the dishwasher. Andy restacked paper coffee cups and tidied up the sugar, honey, cinnamon, and cream station. I wiped down the front counter and restocked the pastry case with an assortment of afternoon sweets. Within twenty minutes Torte was in tip-top shape and ready for business again.

What teamwork, I thought as I washed my hands. I

would have been thrilled to have such a hardworking and enthusiastic staff on the ship.

The bell on the front door jingled just as Mom positioned the last flower vase on the tables. Alan Matterson walked inside. Strands of stray hairs fell from his braids. He wore a tie-dyed sweatshirt and a pair of jeans.

Mom greeted him with a hug. "Alan, how nice to see you."

He returned her hug. "Man, am I too late for lunch?"

"Never. What can I get you?" Mom asked.

"Surprise me." Alan headed for a window booth.

Stephanie dried the last mixing bowl and stacked it on the counter. "Do you need me to do anything else?"

I shook my head. "No. You've been great. Go."

She untied her apron and tossed it in the laundry bin. "I'll walk you home," Sterling said, as he returned the broom and dustpan to the closet. "As long as that's okay with you, Jules? Carlos said he'd be back around two. Apparently Jose is running late."

"Of course. Take a break," I said. Sterling gave me the namaste pose. I watched him place his hand on Stephanie's back and escort her to the door. Maybe things were progressing with them.

Mom sent Andy home too. "We've got it from here."

"Are you sure, Mrs. C?" Andy handed her his notebook. "You think you can handle the chunky monkey?"

"I'll give it my best shot." She grinned.

"Good one, Mrs. C. Your best shot. Get it? Like espresso shot?" Andy tossed his apron in the bin too. "I'll see you tomorrow."

That left Mom and me. On Saturdays during the off season we usually close around three or four. Sometimes we get a few late-afternoon customers who come in for a coffee or a box of sweets for the evening, but otherwise Saturdays are usually pretty slow after lunch. We've been using the time to prep for Sunday suppers and map out the menu for the following week.

Mom sliced sourdough bread. "I'm going to make Alan a sandwich. Do you want to see if he wants a coffee or tea to go with it?"

"Sure." I was secretly glad that she sent me to check on Alan. I wanted to ask him about Mindy. I stopped at the coffee bar on my way to the front and grabbed a carafe of coffee and a clean mug.

Alan was staring out the window watching the crowd milling around ShakesBurgers. The neon signs on the fast-food chain's window continued to flash in a steady rhythm.

"Hey, Alan," I said, setting the mug and coffeepot on the table and sliding onto the bench across from him. "How's it going?"

He sucked in his chest. "Whoa, Juliet, you snuck up on me."

"Sorry. I didn't mean to." I pointed to the coffee. "Mom thought you might want something to drink while you wait for your lunch."

"Your mom knows me too well." Alan poured himself a cup of the dark brew.

"Do you take cream with that?"

"Nah. I take mine black." He raised the mug in the air. "Thanks for this. It's been a day. Heavy, huh?" He looked out the window again.

"I know. It's terrible."

Alan sipped his coffee and considered my words. "True.

It is, but maybe this means I have a shot of getting the Jester back."

I swallowed twice to try to maintain a passive face. What did Alan mean by that?

"You're trying to get the Jester back?"

He took another drink and then placed his mug on the table. He didn't answer right away. "I don't know. It could happen."

"Won't Mathew take over ShakesBurgers?" From what I'd been told, Mindy and Mathew owned the franchise rights to ShakesBurgers' Ashland location.

Alan frowned. He picked a piece of lint from his sweatshirt. "Is that what you heard?"

"I haven't heard anything. It's probably too soon to know what will happen to ShakesBurgers. The most likely scenario is that Mathew will assume ownership, right?"

Alan's jaw tightened. "You think so? That's not what Mindy said."

"Mindy?"

"Nah, it's nothing. I swear to Buddha, I can't catch a break."

I had known Alan for years. His handmade corn dogs at the farmers' market were a weekend tradition when I was growing up. Unlike the standard white tents that most of the vendors at the farmers' market erected, Alan's tent was tie-dyed, with colorful streamers hanging from each corner. It was hard to miss, and even harder not to be drawn in by the delicious smells from his booth. In addition to his corn dogs, he served strawberry shortcake piled with organic strawberries and mounds of whipped cream and batches of fresh raspberry, mango, and mint lemonade. Mom, Dad, and I often stopped for corn dogs and glasses of lemonade that Alan served with red-and-white-stripped straws. His booth was ahead of its time. He was one of the first vendors in Ashland to fuse organic products with carnival food.

The rumor around town was that Alan had taken on too much with opening the Jester. Running a food booth with a small selection of items versus a fifty-seat restaurant with a full menu were two very different undertakings.

"You're still upset about losing the Jester, aren't you?" I asked.

Alan rested his chin on his hands. "You know, man, it was the worst. I'd been saving up and dreaming about owning a real place for years. I thought I really had something going. People liked the food, you know."

"I heard they did. I'm sorry I never had a chance to try it. Your corn dogs are one of my favorite food memories. Have you considered opening the market booth up again?"

He stretched and leaned back against the booth. "I don't know. Maybe. I've got a lot to figure out."

"Alan, can I ask you something?" I decided to try the direct approach.

"Go for it."

"It's about the meeting last night. You seemed pretty upset at Mindy."

"Yeah." He nodded. "I was wigging out. I guess I was venting my frustration, like everyone else in town."

I begged to differ, but I thought it was best to keep that to myself. "Did you know Mindy well?"

He shifted in his seat. "Why would you ask that?"

"I just wondered how the buyout process went. You must have worked with her, right?"

"Not really." He picked up his coffee mug but didn't take a drink.

I got the sense that he was holding something back. "It's sad that she's dead."

He gave a small nod in agreement. "Yeah. Bummer. It's a drag, but I guess some people probably won't share that sentiment."

"What do you mean?"

Mom arrived with Alan's lunch. "Here you go," she said, offering a plate with a deli sandwich, bag of potato chips, and two of our signature oatmeal-raisin cookies to Alan.

"Looks great, Helen." Alan picked up half of the sandwich and studied it.

"It's our chicken salad. I hope you like it." Mom caught my eye. I could tell that she sensed that she'd interrupted something. "I'm going to scoot back to the kitchen. I have some cleaning to do. Enjoy your lunch."

Alan took a bite of the chicken sandwich. Mom's chicken salad is legendary. The secret is in her homemade dill mayonnaise. She combines that with diced green onions, yellow onions, almonds, fresh dill, salt and pepper, and just a dash of sour cream. "Good stuff," Alan said with a mouth full of sandwich.

I prompted him to continue. "You were saying that you don't think everyone is upset that Mindy's dead."

He looked across the street. "Yeah. You missed it last night. You thought I was wigging out? You should have seen Rosalind, man."

"Really?"

"She and Mindy got into a huge fight at the end of the meeting. Rosalind grabbed Mindy's arm and almost yanked her to the ground. I think she might have thrown a punch."

"Rosalind?"

Alan nodded, buying himself time as he swallowed another bite of the chicken salad. "Yeah. She's ruthless when it comes to protecting Ashland."

"Wait. I thought you and Mindy got into a fight."

"Me? No. Mindy and I were fine. I was bummed about losing the Jester, but fighting isn't my style. Rosalind looked like she was about to murder Mindy last night."

Alan finished his lunch and left. Some of what he'd said didn't add up. He claimed that he wasn't angry with Mindy, yet he'd been vocal at the meeting last night that he didn't approve of how ShakesBurgers had taken over his restaurant. I couldn't picture the mellow food vendor murdering Mindy, but he could be lying. If it was true that Rosalind and Mindy had almost had a physical altercation, could she have returned early this morning to finish their fight?

Chapter Nine

Mom was organizing the spice rack when I returned to the kitchen with Alan's empty plate. "I think he liked it," I said.

"You two looked like you were having a serious conversation."

"I know. We were. I was asking him about Mindy and he said that Rosalind went after Mindy last night. That she knocked her off her feet and tried to punch her."

"Rosalind?" Mom looked as dumbfounded as I'm sure I had when Alan told me. "Sweet Rosalind?"

"That's what he said."

Mom twisted the cap on a container of cloves. "Did he tell Doug?"

"I don't know. I didn't even think to ask. I was so surprised that I think I just sat there, repeating, 'Rosalind, Rosalind?'"

"Doug and I are going to dinner tonight. I'll mention it to him. He probably already knows."

"Where are you going to dinner?"

Mom smiled. "His place. He's making me dinner."

"Ooh. Very romantic."

"Juliet, stop." Mom tossed an almond at me.

"Are you throwing food?"

"I am. Are you going to stop me?"

"No, but I might join you." I reached for a canister of flour.

"You wouldn't." Mom threw her hands out to protect her.

"I might." She knew that I was bluffing. The kitchen was practically spotless with the exception of the spices she was organizing and a bag of almonds waiting to be placed back in the cupboard.

"Truce." She picked up a bottle of cinnamon sticks. "I have important work to finish here."

"I see that."

Mom kept her gaze on the spices. "So how are things going with Carlos here?"

I wasn't prepared for that question. "Uh. Fine. I think." I picked up the bag of almonds and walked to the far side of the kitchen.

"He seems very committed to making things work. Do you think he's going to stay?"

"No." I clutched the bag. "I mean he can't. He has to be back on the ship on Tuesday."

"I know. I wondered if maybe he was reconsidering." Mom placed the last jar of spice on the rack.

I returned to the island. "What does that mean?"

"Nothing." She picked up the rack and slid it back into place on the counter. "I had the impression that maybe he was hoping for something more permanent."

"He is." I sighed.

Mom joined me at the island. She reached out and

touched my arm. "We don't have to talk about this now if you don't want to. I didn't mean to push."

"No, it's okay. I'm so confused. Having Carlos here is amazing. Everyone loves him—the staff, customers—everyone."

"And you?" Mom's voice was soft.

"And me, but it's complicated. He's going back to the ship. I'm here."

"Juliet, you know that I love having you here, more than anything in the world, but I want you to know that it's okay to go. If that's what you want or what you need for your marriage, I understand and I fully support you in whatever choice you make."

"You're trying to get rid of me, aren't you?" I hoped that making a joke would lighten the mood a little.

She smiled. "Guilty as charged. Can you blame me? I can't compete with my daughter's world-class culinary talent. It's not fair."

"Everything I know I learned from you."

"Ha!" She threw her head back and laughed. "Hardly. I've seen how you wield your pastry knife."

I laughed with her. It felt good. "Mom, can I ask you something?"

"Honey, you know that you can ask me anything."

I sighed. "Sometimes I feel like everything is spinning around me and I'm just trying to hold on."

"Technically speaking the world is spinning around you." She stepped closer and squeezed my arm. "A piece of advice, Juliet, stand in the center and let it spin."

Before we could continue, the door swung open and Carlos came in. Speak of the devil.

Mom brushed her hands together and took off her apron.

"We can talk later," she whispered. On her way out the door she greeted Carlos with a hug and waved good-bye to both of us. "See you bright and early tomorrow!"

Carlos strolled into the kitchen. "Julieta, I have heard the news. Everyone at the terrible Merry Windsor is talking about it. They are saying that you were at the murder. Why did you not tell me this earlier?"

"I meant to, but we were so busy I didn't have a chance."

He came closer. I could smell his cologne and the scent of herbs on his skin. "I do not understand why you did not tell me. I was so worried about you when I heard this news." He wrapped me in an embrace.

I breathed him in. His arms felt solid around my waist. We swayed together in the kitchen, lost in the moment.

The next thing I knew, he was lifting my chin and his lips were on mine. His kiss was slow and steady yet intense with yearning. I felt it too. His hands massaged my back and hips. I pressed my body closer to his.

A wave of heat and need rose in my body. I ran my hands through his thick hair, as he kissed me deeper.

"Carlos," I said, coming up for air. "We have to stop."

His eyes searched mine. "Why?" He pulled me to him again and kissed my cheeks, my forehead, and eyes. I let out a low moan.

We were both so caught up in the moment, that neither of us heard the door open.

"Hey, hey!" I heard a voice call from the front.

I jumped back from Carlos's embrace to see Thomas staring at us with his mouth hanging open.

Chapter Ten

"Thomas." I could hear how breathless my voice sounded. I didn't sound like me. "Come on in."

Carlos stiffened.

"Uh, it's okay." Thomas stayed by the front door. "I was looking for the Professor."

"He's not here," I said, walking toward the counter.

"I see that." Thomas glanced at Carlos and then back to me. "If he comes by, let him know that I'm looking for him, would you?"

"Of course, but I think he and my mom have a hot date."

"That's right. I forgot. He mentioned that. All right, well, catch you later." He turned to leave.

"Wait," I called.

He paused. "Yeah?"

"How's the case going? Any updates?"

Thomas shook his head and looked beyond me. I was pretty sure he was looking at Carlos. "I'm not at liberty to divulge that kind of information."

"Right."

"I've got to go. See you later, Jules."

Carlos muttered something that I couldn't make out.

"What did you say?" I asked as I returned to the kitchen.

"Nothing, *mi querida*." He smiled. "Your friend, he has the worst timing, no?"

"Maybe." Or maybe Thomas had arrived at the perfect moment. Given how intense that kiss had been, the next thing I knew we might have been removing articles of clothing, which would have been problematic on many levels. For starters Torte's kitchen windows look out onto the plaza. I wouldn't have wanted to give anyone a show. And also I wasn't sure that I was ready to take things to the next level with Carlos yet. It was silly, but things were different now. I didn't know if I could handle being that close to him again and watching him leave. It would hurt too much.

Sterling arrived a minute later. I wondered if Thomas had seen him outside and sent him in.

"I'm not late, am I?" he asked.

Carlos rolled up his sleeves. "No, you are right on time. Come, come, let's get started."

Sterling pointed to the rack of aprons. "Do I need an apron?"

"No. Jose will be here soon. We will do a tasting and go see the vineyard." Carlos waved him closer. "I want to show you the meats we have, and I want to hear how it went with your special lady."

Carlos and Sterling went into the walk-in fridge. Special lady? Did Carlos mean Stephanie? What were the two of them up to? I would have to keep my ears open.

I went through tomorrow's orders for our wholesale accounts. Sunday was a light day for wholesale orders. I was glad that I'd told Stephanie to stay home. I could do some quick prep this afternoon while I waited for any customers to come in.

Jose arrived right on time. Despite the fact that he and Mom were about the same age, his face was lined with deep wrinkles and had begun to leather. It was evident that he had spent many years in the sun. His jeans and work boots were dusty and smudged with grape juice. "Juliet, how nice to see you!" He gave me a hug with one arm. The other arm held a wooden case of wine.

"Come sit," I said, showing him to a table. "It's so great to see you."

Jose had always been like an uncle to me. "It is wonderful to see you too. Your mother has not stopped talking for months about how happy she is to have you here."

"I feel the same way." I smiled. "Can I get you a coffee or a pastry?"

Jose set the box on the table and walked to the pastry case. He rubbed his belly. "I shouldn't, but I have to."

"You do," I agreed. "It's a requirement when you come into the bakeshop. Imagine if I came to the winery and refused to taste your Pinot. You would be offended."

Jose laughed. "I do not want to offend my favorite blond chef. Do you remember when you were young and your parents would bring you to the farm, and everyone would call you blondie?"

I tapped my head. "I do. It fits. I was the only blonde around. I used to love coming out to the vineyard. You'd let me eat all of the grapes I could pick off the vine."

"Yes. That's what they are for. You should come see it now. You won't believe how much it's grown."

"I'll have to take you up on your offer." I tapped the case. "Now, back to business. What can I get you?"

Jose pointed to a double-chocolate brownie. I went to plate it and pour Jose a fresh cup of coffee. On my way, I opened the walk-in and told Carlos and Sterling that Jose was waiting for them.

While I dusted the brownie with cocoa and powdered sugar and added a sliced strawberry for garnish, I eavesdropped on their conversation. Jose cradled each bottle of wine. He clearly felt very proud of his product. Sterling kept reminding Jose and Carlos to speak English. They both quickly slipped into their native tongue. It didn't seem to matter that their dialects were different. Their hands flew in the air as the spoke in rapid Spanish. I could tell that they were going to be fast friends.

When I brought the brownie and coffee to the table, Jose insisted that I sit. "Stay, Jules. I am showing them my new hybrid kale. I've been experimenting with growing some vegetables. It is beautiful, no?" He handed me a bunch. "Try it."

The kale leaf was a deep shade of green with variegated purple veins.

"Taste it, everyone," Jose encouraged us by ripping off a piece and eating it. "This is my winter crop. Can you believe it? I think you will love it."

I tore a piece of the earthy leaf. Kale is extremely versatile. We use it in salads and sandwiches. It can be cooked and even added to smoothies for extra greens. Kale grows well in Southern Oregon all year long, even more so with the mild winter we were currently experiencing. Jose's kale tasted like it had been harvested minutes ago. It probably had. There was no bitter aftertaste, and the texture was nice. Some varieties of kale can be stringy, but Jose's wasn't.

"This is wonderful," Carlos said, as he held the kale up to the light. "See these veins," he said to Sterling. "This is the sign of a good and hearty plant."

Jose beamed as Carlos raved about the kale.

A customer came in, so I left them to admire the red blend that Jose was uncorking and baskets of different varieties of grapes. They spent an hour talking and tasting. I chuckled to myself as I worked in the back. Three men all geeking out over organic produce and wine—it reminded me of being in culinary school. I watched Sterling's face. He was taking it all in, but wasn't tasting the wine. Sterling had made a new start in Ashland. When his mom died he turned to drugs to numb the pain. His late teen years had been spent on the streets. Coming to Ashland had been the first step in turning his life around. I hoped that learning about wines wasn't going to put him in an awkward position.

When they finished, they called me to the dining room.

"Julieta, we are taking Sterling on a field trip—is that how you say?"

I nodded.

"A field trip to Jose's winery."

"But Sterling doesn't drink." I watched his reaction.

"It's cool, Jules," Sterling said. "I've been tasting the grapes. Not the wine. If I want to be a chef I've got to know wine, but that doesn't mean I have to drink it."

Carlos put his arm around Sterling's shoulder. "*Sí, sí.* It is good. There is nothing to worry about."

"You must come. You will not believe how different things are now." Jose offered me another armful of kale. "And take this. You must try some recipes with kale."

"Gladly," I said, taking the kale. I glanced at the clock

on the wall. It was almost three. I could have closed for the day and tagged along with them, but I was exhausted. Plus, I was happy that Carlos had a distraction for the moment. "Thanks. But I'll take a rain check. I have a bunch of work to get caught up on. You guys have fun!"

On their way out, I heard them discussing Jose's new greenhouse. I knew that would keep Carlos busy all afternoon.

Carlos and I had dreamed about opening our own restaurant one day. In his vision we would buy a property that had enough space for a small greenhouse, garden, and vineyard. "There is nothing like the taste of handpicked vegetables, Julieta. The food, it knows fresh."

I had been on board with the idea until things fell apart. Now I didn't know what was next for Carlos and me.

Chapter Eleven

Torte was quiet for the remainder of the afternoon. A handful of customers came in for orders to go, but otherwise I was happy to have some time alone. Had it really only been this morning that I'd discovered Mindy? It felt like I'd been awake for days.

I immersed myself in baking and barely noticed when the front door jingled. The beefy guy who I'd seen with Mindy last night and in the plaza this morning came inside.

"Can I help you with something?" I asked, coming up to the front counter. "I don't think we've met. I'm Jules."

His beady eyes gave me the shivers. "Reggie."

"Did I see you with Mindy at the meeting last night?" I was glad to have the pastry case between us. A barbed-wire tattoo crisscrossed his forearm. Thick muscles bulged underneath his T-shirt.

"Yep." He didn't offer more. Lance was right—he would make a perfect Brutus.

"I guess you've probably heard the news, then?"

"Huh?"

"About Mindy. Do you know that she's dead?"

"I'll take a couple of those pink things." He tapped on the pastry case.

"The petit fours?"

"Whatever."

I folded a small box together and placed the petit fours in it. "So you heard about Mindy?"

"Yeah. She was my boss. I kinda figured it out when I showed up for my shift."

"Your boss?"

"Yeah. I'm the cook."

"Oh. Is this good?" I showed him the box.

"Gimme a few more."

I placed three more petit fours into the box. "How long have you worked for Mindy?"

"Three days."

"Did you work at another ShakesBurgers location?"

"Nope."

I closed the box and handed it to him.

He gave me a crumpled ten-dollar bill. I tried to ask him more questions while getting his change, but he grabbed the box and left without another word. I wondered what his story was. What did Mindy know about him before she hired him? Fast-food cooks didn't need culinary degrees, but I wondered how and if she had vetted him.

As soon as he left, I locked the front door and switched the OPEN sign to CLOSED. Then I popped a classical CD into the stereo and blasted the music. Sometimes classical music helps me clear my head. It was a good thing that I had the kitchen to myself. Andy and Sterling were both into indie music. They'd probably tease me forever about jamming to a string orchestra.

I wanted to go over our accounts and spend some time roughing out a plan for the upcoming Chocolate Fest. Ashland hosts one of the biggest foodie events in the state every March, just after Valentine's Day when everyone's heart belongs to chocolate. This year Torte was going be one of the featured vendors. It was a fantastic opportunity to showcase our pastry art and chocolate offerings, but we had lots of work to do to get ready to serve tastes to the thousands of chocolate lovers who would be attending.

With the relaxing sound of the orchestra reverberating through the room, I poured myself a glass of Jose's red wine, cut some cheese and bread, and cocooned myself in the office for the next hour. The books were in good shape. I'd been trying to stay on top of them and make sure we were still on track for upgrading our kitchen equipment. Thanks to our Sunday suppers and some recent catering jobs it looked like we would be about ready to purchase the equipment just in time for the opening of the season.

The Chocolate Fest was a great marketing opportunity, but it meant spending some cash. I worked out a budget for supplies, food, staff, and promotional materials. Mom and I wanted to expand our occasion and wedding cake business. The Chocolate Fest would allow us to showcase a variety of cakes. When I was in culinary school the head chef drilled in us that the profit and salary of any successful bakery is in occasion cakes. Even in tough times people always order specialty cakes for birthdays and baby showers. Once we had new ovens we could expand our cake business.

I like to think of myself as an artist when it comes to cake and pastry. Customers commission us for our unique designs and flavors. I was looking forward to training Stephanie on some new techniques. She has a natural talent and an eye for design.

Mom and I had discussed printing colored brochures of some of our sample cakes and café menus to hand out. It wouldn't be cheap to have professional materials printed, but hopefully the cost would be worth the return.

Tomorrow Mom and I could go over the budget and start ordering supplies. Preparing for the festival, especially during the height of Valentine's Day orders was going to take time and careful planning. I sipped my wine and nibbled on the cheese and bread. The afternoon rush had made me hungry. My stomach rumbled as if to thank me for feeding it.

Once I finished the budget and printed out tomorrow's orders, I washed my wineglass and plate and decided to call it a night. There were two extra loaves of sourdough bread in the kitchen. I placed them in a paper bag and brought them with me.

The plaza was busier than usual when I stepped outside. People continued to mill around the sidewalk in front of the crime scene. One woman stopped to place a bunch of wildflowers and card at the growing shrine. I averted my gaze and headed for A Rose by Any Other Name. Mom has made it a habit to share leftover product with our fellow business owners, especially when we only have a few of something left.

Thomas's family had owned the flower shop for years. I knew that his mom was a fan of our sourdough bread so I decided to swing some by. Black pots with an assortment of winter flowers sat on the sidewalk. The display window at the busy shop was under construction. Thomas's mom stood on a short stool and was stringing up pink, red, and white tulle.

"Juliet, what a lovely surprise," she said as she climbed off the stool.

"I brought you some sourdough. We had a couple of extra loaves."

"My favorite. How did you remember?" She had the same youthful face as Thomas.

"We have a secret notebook," I joked. "It's very red and pink in here." The refrigerated cases housed a variety of bouquets all designed by hand.

She took the bag of bread and placed it on her workspace. "I know. Can you believe it, I'm already changing the shop over for Valentine's Day. Soon love is going to be in the air. It's our busiest day of the year, so I like to get a jump on the design. As soon as February hits we'll be up to our ears in roses."

"It's hard to believe it's almost Valentine's Day. I feel like it was just New Year's. Mom and I are in the same mood with preparing for the Chocolate Fest."

"And I hear love is in the air for you." She cut strips of pale pink ribbon. "I haven't met your husband, but I've seen him pass by and everyone in town seems absolutely captivated by him."

I wasn't sure how to respond. Thomas's mom had hinted that there was something left unsaid between us, but she'd never said anything more.

"Yeah. He's enjoying being in town."

"Is he staying for long?"

"Uh, no. He has to get back to work on the ship."

She wrapped the strips of ribbon around the base of a

fragrant bundle of pink roses. "Of course. I hear he's a famous chef."

"I don't know about famous, but a chef, yes."

"Famous for our part of the world. Everyone is talking about him. I tried to get a ticket for your Sunday supper, but it's sold out. Rumor has it that he's cooking."

"He is." I glanced out the window. "I should go. It looks like you have lots of decorating ahead and I have an early morning date with butter."

"Thanks so much for the bread. I'll have your flowers for the Sunday supper ready to go for tomorrow. Either send someone to pick them up or I'll have Thomas drop them by."

"Will do," I said. I turned and hurried out of the shop. Talking to Thomas's mom about Carlos was just weird.

"Juliet!" I heard someone call the second I stepped outside.

It was Richard Lord. He bellowed from the porch of the Merry Windsor across the street. "Juliet, come here!"

Richard Lord was the last person I wanted to see right now. I considered pretending not to hear him, but half the people in the square stopped and turned at the sound of his booming voice. There was no ignoring Richard Lord.

I sighed and crossed the street.

"Juliet!" He puffed out his beefy chest and waved me toward him with both hands. He could see that I was coming, there was no need to continue to shout at me.

"I'm coming," I said, trying to get him to stop calling attention to me.

Richard Lord's name fit him. He and I hadn't exactly been best friends since I came home. He'd made a play to take over Torte, and his methods hadn't been exactly ethical in my opinion.

He liked to lord over Ashland in his ridiculous golf outfits. Today he wore a pair of orange-and-white plaid pants, a matching orange shirt, and a green vest that highlighted his rotund waist.

"I want a word with you, Juliet," he said as he stuffed a handful of sunflower seeds into his mouth.

"What's going on, Richard?" I asked.

He chomped on the seeds and studied me. "You know what's going on."

I stood on the top porch step, trying to stay out of range of his spit spray. "I do?"

"Don't play dumb with me."

"Richard, I promise, I never play dumb. I'm exhausted. I just want to go home, so tell me what you need or I'm out of here." I rarely had patience for Richard Lord. This evening was no exception.

He folded his arms across his chest and glared at me. I was about to back down the stairs when he finally said, "What's going on with Jose? I saw him at Torte earlier with your husband."

"Jose Ortega?"

"Do you know anyone else named Jose?"

I did, in fact. I had met a number of men named Jose during my time on the ship. Most cruise lines have an international staff. I didn't bother to tell Richard that though. In addition to trying to micromanage everyone in town, Richard was a worse gossip than any little old lady. I was convinced that he had the front porch built at the Merry Windsor just so that he could stand out there and keep an eye on everything and everyone in town.

He continued without waiting for my response. "What was he doing? I saw him leave with your husband and that tattooed thug you have working for you."

I sighed. Sterling might have tattoos but he was the furthest thing from a thug of anyone I knew. Reggie, Mindy's chef, who I'd officially met earlier, he could be mistaken as a thug, but Sterling—no way. I debated whether I should defend Sterling, but decided that would only lengthen our conversation. "I have no idea what you're talking about. Jose delivered our wine, like he always does. Why do you care?"

Richard leaned over the porch and spit sunflower seeds into the small patch of grass below the porch. "If he was delivering your order then why did your staff leave with him?"

"How is this any of your business?"

"You're up to something, Juliet, I know it. I tried talking to your husband, but he wouldn't stop. He's been too busy trying to weasel his way into everyone's good graces around here."

"Richard, I'm leaving. I don't know what your problem is, but there's nothing going on at Torte. It's business as usual."

"What did Jose tell you?"

"Tell me? Nothing. We talked about his kale."

Richard scowled. "And . . ."

"And, nothing. We talked about kale and the wine he delivered. I don't understand why you're so concerned about Jose. Doesn't he deliver wine to you too? What's the big deal?"

He spit again, and then stared at me. I could tell that he was trying to decide whether or not he believed me. "I'm going to be watching you, Juliet."

"Glad to hear it, Richard." I waved with one finger and turned to walk down the stairs. I could feel Richard's eyes on my back as I crossed the plaza and headed for Elevation. Keep your eyes focused ahead of you, Jules, I told myself. I refused to glance in Richard's direction. I didn't want to give him the satisfaction of thinking that he'd rattled me.

Richard was prone to crazy outbursts, but this was an entirely new level. Why did he care what Jose was doing at Torte? The only thing I could imagine was that he was trying to convince Jose to only work with the Merry Windsor. That would be a classic Richard move. Jose and Mom had been friends and business partners for way too long. There was no way Jose would ditch us for Richard. At least I hoped not.

Chapter Twelve

I don't remember falling asleep, but I must have. My alarm beeped in my ear at four the next morning. It took me a minute to figure out where I was. I had fallen asleep in my jeans and T-shirt. I needed coffee and a shower, in that order.

Waiting for coffee to brew is agony. I stumbled into the kitchen, found a bag of whole coffee beans, ground them, and shook them into the coffeepot. The robust scent permeated my small kitchen.

Much better, I thought, breathing in the scent as I walked to the bathroom. While my coffee brewed, I would shower. I turned the water to its hottest setting. The bathroom quickly filled with steam. I let the stream of water run over my shoulders and down my back. It felt so refreshing. Long showers were a luxury on the ship. As staff we were reminded to limit our water usage. Amenities were for the passengers, but I didn't mind. I was usually too busy baking anyway. Since returning to dry land, I had enjoyed indulging in a long hot shower every once in a while.

I scrubbed my skin with a eucalyptus and mint body wash that I'd purchased at Sensory, a natural skin-care shop downtown. The smell brightened my mood and made my skin tingle. After my skin had been buffed and turned a shade of pink, I shut off the water and toweled myself dry. My morning beauty routine is fairly simple. There's no need for heavy makeup or jewelry at the bakeshop.

I massaged my hair with a towel, applied a thin layer of eucalyptus and mint lotion, and pulled on a pair of black skinny jeans and a thin camel tunic sweater. Before I blew my hair dry, I needed coffee. I wrapped the towel around my head and flipped on the overhead fan.

The coffee had brewed to a deep ebony. I poured myself a cup and added a splash of heavy cream. There's something so indulgent about the first cup of coffee in the morning. It's almost a spiritual experience for me. I follow a steadfast ritual of warming my mug in the microwave, pouring in the rich liquid from the gods, and allowing the cream to turn it a lovely shade of caramel. Then there's the smell. I cradled the mug in my hands and drank in the scent of the Italian roast. I could almost feel my eyes brighten and my synapses start to fire. Finally, I took the first sip. Magic. Pure magic.

With my coffee in hand, I danced back through the living room and into the bathroom. Now I could concentrate on my appearance. I gave my hair a quick blow-dry and twisted it into a high ponytail. Thanks to the invigorating body wash and a full night of sleep, my skin looked bright. I was worried I would have deep bags under my eyes from the stress of yesterday, but thankfully I didn't. I dusted my cheeks with a light pink blush, applied some mascara and lip gloss, and studied my appearance in the mirror. The camel sweater brought out the natural honey highlights in my hair and the blush gave my face a bit of color. My skin is so fair that a hint of pink on my cheeks always helps accent my strong jawline.

Satisfied that I wouldn't scare off any customers, I finished my coffee, grabbed a jacket, and headed for the front door. An eerie fog had settled over the sleepy town last night. Old-fashioned streetlights glowed behind the mist. I quickened my pace as I made my way to Torte. It wasn't far, but with a killer on the loose I didn't want to take any chances.

The dense air weighed heavy on our little village, like the cloud of worry and fear that hung over all of us. Ashland was a friendly, welcoming city. We'd only recently recovered from a murder in our idyllic community. No one had expected it to happen again.

I rubbed my hands together and sucked in the frosty fog. It reminded me of a time on the ship when we'd sailed through a bank of clouds so thick that they looked like they could be molded together like pastry dough. I remember taking a break on the top deck. Gray mist enveloped the ship in every direction and stretched seemingly forever out into the vast sea. It was a creepy feeling. Fortunately it didn't happen very often. We usually sailed in calm and warm waters. Not that day. That day everyone from the staff to the passengers, even the captain, seemed on edge. Whatever direction we sailed the fog loomed over us. Our cruise director tried to distract everyone with movies and a scavenger hunt through the hidden corridors of the bowels of the ship. It didn't work. I heard the passengers voice concerns about slamming into another ship. Staff assured them that the modern technology on board wouldn't allow it, but in the kitchen there were whispers and rumors that the computer system had gone down. We were sailing blind.

Carlos noticed that I was worried, probably because I kept wrapping my ponytail around my finger.

"Julieta, do not worry. It is only fog. We will be okay. We will weather through and soon you will see the sun." He kissed my head. "You must bake. It will take your mind off of these clouds."

I followed his advice. He was right. Baking helped relieve my fear, and we did sail into the sun.

Could we find our way out of the fog we were in now? Could we sail back into the sun? I wished it was as simple as navigating a ship out of the clouds.

I made it to Torte through the gravy-like fog. Time to focus on baking, Jules, I told myself as I unlocked the front door and quickly locked it again once I was inside. The fog was so thick I couldn't see across the plaza. Maybe that was a good thing.

I turned on the heat and the kitchen lights. It was just going to be me for the next hour or so. Stephanie had the day off, and Mom and Andy wouldn't arrive until sometime after five.

Thanks to having some time to myself yesterday afternoon, all the prep work was done for the morning's wholesale accounts. The order sheets were exactly where I'd left them on the island in tidy stacks. I preheated the oven, and started my yeast rising. Like my morning coffee ritual at home, my morning routine in the bakeshop rarely changes. With yeast rising, I got another pot of coffee started and assembled flour, sugar, salt, and sourdough starter.

It felt like déjà vu. At this time yesterday, I'd been following the exact same steps, only I never imagined that I'd find a dead body on my morning delivery routine. While I kneaded bread dough and formed it into soft balls to rise, I thought about everyone who might have wanted Mindy dead.

There was Mathew. He was the most obvious suspect, but what was his motive? I couldn't think of a reason that he would want Mindy dead. He and Richard Lord had been arguing about something yesterday. Could their fight be connected somehow? I wasn't sure. I was never sure when it came to Richard. And I certainly didn't want to have another conversation with him.

Alan Matterson definitely had motive, but he was such a laid-back and fun-loving guy. I couldn't imagine him hurting Mindy, even if he was upset about losing his restaurant. Could that be it? Could Mindy have killed his fun, so he killed her?

Then there was Rosalind. I would have to ask around today and see who else had witnessed her and Mindy fighting. Was it possible that she loved our town so much, she would kill to preserve it? I loved Ashland too, but not enough to kill for it.

The only other person I could think of who had a relationship with Mindy was Reggie, the cook who I'd met yesterday. He had been hanging around the plaza when Mindy was killed. His demeanor was less than friendly, but that didn't make him a killer.

I sighed and brushed flour from my hands. Perfectly round balls of bread dough lined the island. I placed them in greased bread pans, covered them with thin dish towels, and placed them on the industrial steel rack near the oven to rise. The heat emanating from the oven would give the yeast a boost.

Sundays tend to be a later start for our regular customers. Unlike the early morning weekday rush, our busiest hours on Sunday are around brunch. Locals come in for a late-morning coffee and pastry with the Sunday paper. I wanted to make something hearty and comforting to serve this morning, and I knew just the thing.

On cold winter mornings, my dad would bake a creamy potato casserole. With the bread rising, I gathered all the items I needed to recreate his casserole, with my own spin. I started by scrubbing russet potatoes. Once they were cleaned I pricked holes in them with a fork and dropped them into a pot of boiling water. They would boil until tender.

Next I chopped yellow onions and sautéed them in butter. I heated cans of cream of chicken soup with our homemade chicken stock, and added the onions and butter to the milky mixture. I let that simmer for a few minutes while I checked on my rising bread dough.

The round balls had stretched in the bread pans. I poked each one with my finger. The dough sprang back with every touch. My bread was ready to bake. I slid the pans into the oven, set the timer, and returned to my casserole.

Steam funneled from the pot of boiling potatoes. It reminded me of the fog outside. I turned the heat off and drained the potatoes. Once they had cooled I would peel and grate them. The kitchen windows began to drip with sweat and the smell of bread baking made me smile. This is how Sunday mornings should start.

I grabbed a cup of coffee and a block of sharp cheddar cheese and two pints of sour cream from the refrigerator.

This casserole was not low in fat or milk products, but if it turned out the way I remembered, it would be a savory and creamy accompaniment to our sweeter offerings.

The coffee wasn't quite as strong as the pot I brewed at home. I'd used a breakfast blend. It's a customer favorite— a light roast with a bright finish.

I sipped it as I began peeling the potato skins. I shredded them into a large plastic bowl in the sink. Mom uses most of our fruit and vegetable waste for her garden at home. She takes home a container every night and dumps it into her composting bin. As Torte's menu continues to expand, her garden might have to as well.

After the potatoes had been skinned, I grated them and the cheddar cheese into another bowl. Then I poured the soup mixture over the top. I incorporated the cheese, soup, and potatoes and added both pints of sour cream, a handful of chopped fresh chives, and sprinkled in pepper and salt. The dish smelled exactly like I remembered it.

I poured the potatoes into two ceramic casserole pans and slid them into the oven with the bread. When Sterling arrived, I would have him fry some thick-cut bacon and breakfast sausage links to serve with the casserole.

My mouth watered as the cheesy potatoes began to bubble in the oven. The timer beeped to alert me that the bread was done. I pulled on oven mitts and removed the loaves of bread. They had nice golden crusts and had risen a few inches over the top of each pan.

As I was placing the bread on cooling racks, the front doorbell jingled. Sterling and Mom arrived together.

Mom flipped on the dining room lights. "Good morning, honey. It smells amazing in here." She shook of her puffy white coat.

Sterling, not surprisingly, wasn't wearing a coat, just a gray hoodie with a skateboard design on the front. "Hey, Jules," he said as he tugged an apron from the rack. "What do you want me to do?"

I pointed to the coffeepot. "There's coffee if either of you need a cup."

Mom tucked her hair behind her ears and greeted me with a kiss on the cheek. "Have I told you lately how much I love having you home?"

I grinned. "You'd say that to anyone who offered you coffee. You should check it though. It's been sitting for about half an hour." Coffee is the one thing that I admit I'm a snob about. I prefer my coffee scalding hot and freshly brewed. That's how we serve it at Torte. If a pot has sat for more than thirty minutes we'll refrigerate it to use in our dark chocolate cakes and coffee muffins but we won't offer it to our customers. Coffee turns to sludge, loses its flavor potency, and develops an acidic taste when it sits for more than thirty minutes. We pour all of our coffee into preheated carafes at the bakeshop to preserve its taste a little longer. If kept on the heating element, the oils that give coffee its rich taste will continue to burn off, making it bitter.

She elbowed me and winked. "I'm sure it's fine." She grabbed a mug from the cupboard and turned to Sterling. "Do you want one too?"

"That would be awesome." He watched me place the last loaf of bread on the cooling rack. "When did you get here, Jules?"

"Not that early."

Mom shook her head. "Don't believe her, Sterling. She's a terrible liar. Have I ever told you the story of when she tried to convince her dad and me that she hadn't been swimming when she was soaking wet?"

"Mom, stop. You'll ruin my professional reputation."

Sterling's bright blue eyes looked even lighter. "No way, I have to hear this now."

Mom handed Sterling a cup of coffee. "It's true. Juliet was maybe seven or eight at the time. It was summer break and she was spending the night at a friend's house. They went swimming in the lake."

"Ooh, busted," Sterling teased.

"No, that was the funny thing," Mom continued. "Her friend's mom took them swimming, but for some reason Juliet was worried that her dad and I would be upset, so when she arrived at the bakeshop with dripping wet hair she told us they got caught in a rainstorm. It was ninety degrees and sunny outside."

Sterling laughed. "I can't imagine you doing that, Jules."

"Me neither." I frowned. "I remember that. I felt so bad because Dad wanted to take me to the lake. The city had installed a waterslide and he was so excited about it. I didn't want him to know that I had gone without you guys."

Mom caught my eye and smiled. Her eyes looked misty. "You had to miss out on a lot of things. That's the drawback of owning a business. Your dad and I talked about it all the time."

"No, Mom, I loved being part of Torte as a kid. I didn't feel like I was missing out."

She sighed and smiled again. "But you did. Your dad and I felt bad about that."

I walked over to her and put my arm around her shoulder. "Don't feel bad, I promise that Torte has always been the place for me."

She smiled again, but there was a real sadness in her eyes. How had a funny conversation turned so heavy? I started to say more, but she clapped her hands together and pointed to the dry-erase board. "Okay, put us to work. What's next?"

We would have to revisit this conversation later. Maybe Mom didn't want to talk about our past in front of Sterling, but I wondered why she was so upset about my childhood. I had had an ideal lifestyle as a kid. Sure, I hung around Torte a lot, but it wasn't as if they forced me into slave labor. I loved sitting on a bar stool at the counter and watching my parents work. They would always offer me tastes of new recipes and seemed genuinely interested in my feedback.

Sterling pushed up his hoodie sleeves. "Yeah, what do you want me to do first?"

"Actually I was kind of hoping that you might be willing to do the deliveries this morning. Are you okay with that?"

"Not a problem." He and Mom exchanged a look. I knew they both probably suspected that I didn't want to do the morning deliveries due to what happened yesterday. They were right.

"Will you tell Craig at the Green Goblin that I'll be over later with some tasting samples for him? I meant to stop by yesterday, but the day—well, you know."

Sterling loaded bread into the delivery box. "No prob. I'll let him know."

"Thanks, I really appreciate it."

"I know." Sterling hoisted the box into his arms and headed toward the front. "See you in a few."

Mom took the cap off a dry-erase pen. She made a

checkmark through the bread orders. "Wholesale orders are out the door. What's cooking? Something smells amazing, but I don't see anything up here."

"I made Dad's potato casserole. I thought we could serve it with bacon and sausage for brunch."

"I haven't had that in years. Yum." Mom walked over to the oven and flipped on the light. She bent over to take a peek inside. "Oh, it's oozing with cheese and goodness. I can't believe you remember how to make it."

"I don't—at least not exactly. I kind of pulled it together from memory and put my own spin on it."

"You always were watching us, weren't you?"

"I was, and that's what I was trying to say a few minutes ago. I loved being a part of Torte, Mom."

She turned the light off. "I know you did, honey. I feel bad sometimes that you didn't have a real childhood. I wonder how that affected you."

"Mom, what's going on?"

"Nothing." She walked back to the whiteboard and tapped on the list of baked goods we needed to fill the pastry case. "How about if I start on the scones and muffins?"

I could tell that she didn't want to talk about whatever was bothering her. I decided to drop it for the moment, but she and I weren't finished with this conversation. Growing up in Ashland and Torte had ignited my passion for food and travel. I didn't understand why Mom was suddenly nostalgic and blaming herself for ruining my childhood. Something else had to be going on with her, and I had a feeling it had something to do with the Professor.

Chapter Thirteen

Mom cubed butter for scones. I started on cookie dough. One of my favorite things to do with cookies is to combine unexpected flavors. I decide to make my chocolate-molasses crinkles.

The cookie dough I use for this recipe is a basic molasses base. I creamed butter, sugar, vanilla, molasses, ginger, and cinnamon together in a mixing bowl. I cracked in eggs, and then I sifted in flour, salt, and baking soda. The dough was a dark brown color. I tasted it with my pinky. It had a nice bite from the ginger, and the cinnamon and molasses gave it a spicy-sweet finish.

I shook a bag of dark-chocolate chips into the dough and mixed them in by hand. Molasses cookie dough does best if it's chilled. It's easier to work with and will make the cookies bake flat with a nice crisp on the outside and a chewy center. I chilled the dough and checked on my potato casserole. The potatoes had baked with golden brown edges. The cheese and soup mixture had melted together, creating a rich, thick, and creamy glaze.

It smelled divine. I removed the casserole dishes from the oven as Andy walked in the front door.

"Whoa. What smells so good, boss?" he asked, taking off his ski hat. His shaggy hair was naturally messy. The look worked for him. It matched his laid-back and easy-going style.

"It's a potato casserole," I replied.

Andy came into the kitchen and stuck his head over the piping hot casseroles. "I could eat one of these myself."

Sterling arrived with an empty delivery box. "I'll take the other one," he said, standing on his toes to push the delivery box onto a high shelf out of the way.

"Dude, right?" Andy waved his hands above the casserole so that scent could waft up to his nose. "What do you say, boss? Can Sterling and I each have a tray?"

I laughed. "Sorry. I'm afraid these are for our paying customers."

They both protested. Sterling pulled a five-dollar bill from the front pocket of his ripped jeans. "I've got cash. I'll pay."

"I'll make you a deal," I said, pushing Andy toward the espresso bar. "You can be my taste testers as soon as it cools, but right now back to work."

Andy looked at Sterling and shrugged. "I can live with that. You?"

Sterling nodded.

"I can tell you right now, boss, I don't need to taste that stuff. It's awesomeness on a plate. I know it."

"Awesomeness on a plate," I repeated. "Maybe that's what we should call it. Potato casserole sounds pretty lame in comparison. Maybe you should actually taste it first though."

"Nah," Andy said as he went to start up the espresso machine. "It's awesomeness."

Mom ladled muffin batter into paper-lined tins. "That's what we get for hiring twenty-year-old help. They're not kidding, you know. If we gave them the green light they'd devour both of those casseroles before we could blink."

"Locusts," I agreed. I grabbed the chilled cookie dough from the fridge and used an ice-cream scoop to spoon round balls onto parchment-lined baking sheets. As soon as I took the cookies out of the oven I would dip them in granulated sugar.

"Hey, I heard that. Who are you calling locusts?" Andy spun around from the coffee machine and made his eyes bug out. "Can you blame me? Everything you both make is so good, plus with football and helping on the farm at home, I'm always hungry."

Mom's tone turned serious. "We're kidding, Andy. We'll always feed you and Sterling. You two are the hardest workers in town."

"Thanks, Mrs. C." Andy returned his focus to the coffee. I could tell by the way his shoulders arched back that he appreciated the praise.

"Yeah, thanks." Sterling dried his hands. "Lay it on me, what do you want me to do now?"

"How did deliveries go?" I asked, sliding the trays into the oven.

"Fine." He made eye contact with me. "No major crimes. Everyone was happy to get their bread."

"Good." I sighed. Maybe things were back to normal. "I'm going to put you on grilling duty this morning. You can fry bacon and sausage links to serve with the casserole."

Sterling gave me a half salute. "On it."

"Yeah, thanks."

My stomach growled as I scooped two heaps of my potato casserole onto plates and handed one to Sterling and the other to Andy. They both scarfed the casserole down. "Any chance we can get seconds?" Andy asked.

"Let's see how it goes over with customers. The leftovers are all yours."

Mom held up her index finger. "Uh, don't hold out on me. I need a taste too."

I dished up a serving for Mom and one for me. The casserole was even better than I remembered it. It was comfort on a plate for sure. Baking the potatoes in the cheese and soup made them soft and supple.

"Maybe you should make more, Juliet," Mom said, holding up her empty plate. "I have a feeling this is going to go fast."

"Yeah, make more," Andy said. "I was just thinking about licking my plate clean."

"Okay, okay." I held out my hand to stop him. "I'll make more. No need to start licking the plates."

By the time we opened the door I had more casseroles in the oven and dozens of my chocolate-molasses crinkles dusted with sugar. The bakeshop was alive with the smell of Andy's coffee, muffins cooling on the counter, and frying bacon. It was a good thing that Mom had suggested I make a second batch of the "Awesomeness on a plate," which Andy added to the specials section on the chalkboard. We went through the casseroles within an hour.

"Should you make another?" Mom asked, placing a cranberry-orange muffin on a plate.

"I don't think I have enough potatoes. I thought today was going to be slow."

Mom motioned to the crowded dining room. "Not with a murder investigation going on across the street."

I hadn't looked up from my work. The fog had lifted outside. Mom was right. People continued to gather at the sidewalk shrine in front of ShakesBurgers. A TV satellite van had arrived on the scene, probably from nearby Medford. I noticed a pretty young reporter interviewing none other than Richard Lord in front of the police caution tape. Of course Richard had found a way to put himself in the spotlight.

"Look at that," I said to Mom.

She rolled her eyes. "Richard loves to hear himself talk. I wonder what he's telling her."

"He's probably finding a way to get free publicity for the Merry Windsor." I did my best Richard Lord impression in a deep, booming voice. "Come to the best restaurant in Ashland where we serve everything processed and nothing fresh."

Mom chuckled. "Maybe we should give him the benefit of the doubt. Maybe Mindy's death touched him, and he's sharing that on camera."

I gave her a hard look. She held my gaze for a minute and then stuck out her tongue and wrinkled her nose. "Or maybe not."

At that moment Carlos walked past the front window. My breath caught in my chest. Mom noticed. She caught my eye and winked, then she waved at Carlos. He returned her greeting with genuine enthusiasm. His dark eyes sparkled with delight at seeing us. He gestured with his hands, pointing at himself, then us, then nodding, as if to let us know he was coming inside. That was obvious.

I watched as two women chatting in front of the bubbling fountains in the center of the plaza elbowed each other and stared at Carlos as he strolled inside, completely oblivious of their lusty gaze. I couldn't blame them. Carlos looked good. Really good. His tight jeans emphasized his firm derrière and muscular legs. He wore a baby-blue button-down shirt and casual loafers. The look was very European. Definitely not Ashland.

"Good morning, beautiful ladies," Carlos said, kissing Mom and then me on both cheeks. "It is busy today, no?"

"This is slow. You should have seen it an hour ago." Mom scooted past Carlos and stood on her tiptoes to try to reach the top shelf of a cupboard. Even in her clogs she could barely reach the bottom shelf.

Carlos stepped in to help. "Helen, what do you need? I will get it for you."

She touched his sleeve. "Thanks, you're such a dear. Can you get that box of lights down for me?"

He obliged and stretched his arm out with ease to pull the box from the high shelf. I inherited my height from my dad. When I met Carlos I was attracted to his good looks and witty charm, and also to the fact he stood a few inches taller than me. Being tall had been a pain when it came to meeting guys. Aside from dating Thomas in high school, I hadn't dated much in culinary school because most guys were too intimidated to ask me out.

"I'll leave the kitchen to the two of you." Mom took out a string of twinkle lights from the box. "I'm going to work on getting everything set up in the dining room for our Sunday supper now that the rush should be done."

Carlos scooped the box from the counter. "I will take this for you, Helen."

Mom protested. "It's not heavy."

Carlos insisted. "Where do you want it?"

He followed Mom to the front with the box in his arms. I wiped down the counter and island. It was time to shift gears. We had forty guests coming for a three-course meal in just a few hours.

Sterling and Carlos began assembling the tapas. After much deliberation I decided to make two desserts. The lemon olive oil cake and a simple almond cake. Spanish desserts tend to be much less sweet than American desserts. The almond crumb cake would be an understated yet delicious finish to the elaborate tapas that Sterling and Carlos had planned, and the lemon olive oil cake would offer a tangy citrus to cleanse everyone's palate at the end of the feast.

I started with the bag of almonds. I shook them into the food processor and ground them into a fine powder. That way we could offer a gluten-free option to customers. Non-gluten-based cakes and pastries were all the rage these days. Next, I creamed butter and sugar together and added in a splash of almond extract and eggs. I beat everything on low in our industrial mixer and then sifted in almond flour, the ground nuts, and a little salt.

The cake baked in round pans and would be served in single-layer slices. I reserved a handful of almonds to use on the top of the cake. Since my theme was simplicity, I would dust the top of the cake with powdered sugar and arrange sliced almonds on the top once it cooled.

The batter smelled incredible as I spread it into cake pans. Carlos looked up from the shrimp he was deveining. "That is smelling very good, *mi querida*."

"Thanks." I slid the cakes into the oven and began gathering everything I needed to make the lemon olive oil cake.

Carlos taught me how to make the cake on the ship. It's made with an extra-virgin olive oil, giving it a more pronounced and fruitier olive flavor. It was a staple on the ship. We would serve it with fresh berries and mascarpone cream. I was excited to re-create that for our guests tonight, taking them on an excursion to the Spanish seaside all while being very landlocked at Torte.

I whipped egg yolks and sugar in the mixer until they became pale and thick. Carlos instructed Sterling, "No, not like that. Watch. Do it like this," he commanded while slicing tomatoes at lightning speed. In a flash the tomato was diced into perfect tiny squares.

Sterling's jaw hung open as he watched Carlos. There was no denying that Carlos had talent, and insane knife skills. "Man, Carlos, you're good. There's no way I can do that."

Carlos handed him the knife. "*Sí,* you will practice and you will improve."

I appreciated that, in spite of Carlos's innate ability in the kitchen, he was always willing to help mentor young talent. He'd done the same thing on the ship, staying late after his own shift was done to help a new line cook or sous chef improve their skills. I often wondered if Carlos would find his way into one of the top culinary institutes. He'd make an excellent teacher.

"Watch that thumb!" Carlos cautioned as Sterling

attempted to dice a tomato. "Wrap it under. We do not want any thumbs chopped off." Carlos placed his hand over Sterling's thumb and showed him how to tuck it safely under his hand while using the knife.

Educating young sous chefs and line cooks on safety procedures was imperative. Carlos didn't take the responsibility lightly. He stood over Sterling's shoulder and watched until he was satisfied that Sterling's technique would keep all his fingers intact.

I was surprised that Carlos didn't break out one of his usual kitchen pranks. When he trained new staff on the ship he would put on a thumb tip and fill it with fake blood. Then he would demonstrate the wrong cutting technique and pretend to chop off his thumb. It made for a messy and entertaining session. The trainees would scream as fake blood squirted out of Carlos's hand.

Carlos played it up. He would squeeze his thumb and keel over in pain. Fake blood would ooze on the spotless stainless steel countertops as the staff members rushed around in a mild panic trying to find towels to stop the bleeding. Once Carlos finally revealed his hand with a full set of fingers and intact thumb everyone would laugh and sigh with relief. The prank worked. It wasn't just for fun. No one ever lost a thumb—or any other body part—in Carlos's kitchen. The only person who ever cut himself in the kitchen was Carlos, but that was another story.

I smiled at the memory and glanced toward the front. The brunch crowd had thinned. A few customers lingered over their coffee in the front booths. While Mom topped off their cups I heard her say, "Stay as long as you like. I'm going to move some tables around for our Sunday supper tonight, but don't feel like you need to leave anytime soon."

She swayed to the beat of the Latin jazz playing overhead as she pushed the small two- and four-person tables together into one long table. It was draped with a white linen tablecloth. She placed vases with single red roses and votive candles in the center of the table.

"Have you seen the red napkins anywhere, Juliet?" she asked, returning to the kitchen for a stack of brilliant white plates.

My hands were covered in lemon juice. I nodded to the office. "Have you checked in there?" We keep a stack of fancy tablecloths and napkins on hand for special occasions. Like our food, we keep our designs simple and elegant. We have napkins, dish towels, and tablecloths in our Torte cherry red, teal blue, and white. Mom keeps a stack of chocolate-brown napkins and towels on hand too. It all blends together well and gives the space a bright and welcoming vibe.

Mom opted for white plates on a white tablecloth with red roses and red napkins as an accent. She found the napkins in the office and went back to work setting the table.

"Do you need any help up there?" I called as I folded the egg mixture with olive oil and lemon juice.

"Actually, if you have a sec I could use a hand with these lights."

I looked toward the dining room to see Mom standing on one of the dining room chairs. A string of twinkle lights was wrapped around one hand. Another strand was looped partway through the hanging chandelier.

"What are you doing, Mom?" I ran to help her.

"Nothing, honey." Her big brown eyes twinkled.

"Get off that chair." I used my most serious voice and pointed to the concrete floor. "I'll do that for you."

She climbed down.

I reached for the lights, but couldn't quite get them to twist through the chandelier. I guess I was going to have to give the chair a try too.

Mom folded her arms across her chest and tapped her foot on the floor. "It isn't as easy as you thought, is it?"

"Hand me that string," I said.

She tossed me the second string of lights. I plugged the strands together and snaked them through the chandelier. They wouldn't reach to the far wall without me having to lean my body out into a prone position. I decided it was best to climb down and move the chair versus falling and breaking an arm or something.

Mom handed me a metal hook. "Screw that into the picture rail."

I scooted the chair against the wall, climbed back on it, and screwed the hook into the wall. Then I looped the lights through the hook and repeated the process on the other side of the room.

"It's going to look great." Mom clapped when I finished. "Should I plug them in?"

"Definitely." I pushed the chair back in place.

Mom bent down to plug in the twinkle lights. "Drum roll, please." She pounded her knees and then stuck the plug into the outlet.

Little golden lights sparkled to life above us. The ceiling danced. Flecks of white and gold reflected off the windows and created a canopy of light overhead.

"It's perfect." Mom placed her hand over her heart. "Enchanting."

"It looks great."

"I have one more finishing touch to do. I'm going to run over to A Rose by Any Other Name and grab a few things. I'll be back in a minute. Do you need anything while I'm out?"

"Nope." I shook my head. "I think we're in good shape. It looks so festive in here we should take a picture and submit it to one of the foodie magazines."

Mom's beaming smiled matched the lights. "Honey, you're being too nice."

"I'm not, Mom. It's gorgeous." I turned and called Sterling and Carlos to the front. "What do you think, guys?"

Sterling gave Mom a thumbs-up. Carlos wiped his hands on his apron and lifted his hands in the air. "It is— how you say? *Magnifique*."

Mom shooed them back to the kitchen. "I'll finish arranging the chairs. You go ahead and get your own work done."

I watched her sway as she made her way to the front door. Mom has the best eye for design. It's one of the many reasons that our customers keep coming back to Torte. That, and her delicious pastry. I was glad to see her mood lighter. I wondered if she and the Professor had a chance to talk last night. If we had any time alone this afternoon I would have to ask her.

The kitchen smelled like a street fair in Spain. I breathed in the scent of roasting peppers and chopped cilantro. Sterling and Carlos had taken over every square inch of countertop and island with meats, cheeses, vegetables, and spices.

"You two aren't messing around," I said as I walked to the sink to wash my hands.

Sterling nodded at Carlos. "He says that it's customary to eat a lot in Spain."

"*Sí, sí*," Carlos said. "Julieta knows this. Yes?"

"I do." I massaged honey lotion into my hands. "You have to pace yourself when you have a meal with Carlos. The food just keeps coming and coming."

Carlos squinted and squared his jaw. "Do not say it like it is a bad thing. Food is an experience. You should savor and drink some wine. Then take a little siesta, and eat some more. This is the Spanish way."

"Sounds good to me." Sterling carefully sliced an olive.

"I'm kidding. It is a pretty fantastic experience to have a true tapas dinner in Spain. Carlos isn't exaggerating. People sit around the table for hours. They take breaks and just when you think there's no possible way you can fit another morsel into your mouth, out comes another round and the next thing you know you're eating again."

"This is how food should be." Carlos held his knife as he spoke. "This is the problem with American cuisine, no? It's all about fast. Like the ShakesBurgers. Food should not be fast. Food should be love."

The doorbell jingled. Mom had returned with an armful of evergreen boughs, more roses, and Thomas. Uh-oh. Speaking of love . . .

Chapter Fourteen

Mom shot me an apologetic look as she set the box of flowers on the front counter. "Look who I bumped into at the flower shop."

Thomas carried another box of evergreen boughs and twine. "Where do you want me to put these, Mrs. Capshaw?"

Mom made room for him on top of the pastry case. "Right here is great. Thanks for bringing those over, Thomas. They smell amazing." She held a flower to her nose.

Carlos stopped sautéing garlic and walked up to the opposite side of the counter. "Helen, let us help you." He motioned for Sterling to come to the front.

Thomas clutched the box.

"I can take that, Thomas," Mom offered.

"What?" Thomas stared at her.

"The flowers. I'll take them or you can put them right there."

"Sorry, Mrs. Capshaw. Of course. Here." Thomas set them on the pastry case.

Carlos immediately picked up an evergreen bough and took a whiff. "It is nice, Helen. Good choice." He didn't acknowledge Thomas and I could tell by the way he emphasized Mom's name that he was trying to make it clear he had a very different relationship with her than Thomas.

Mom tried to break the tension. "Carlos, don't let me keep you from your work."

"It is no problem." Carlos nudged Sterling. "We can help if you need it, yes?"

Sterling tugged on the strings of his hoodie. "Sure. Whatever."

"Really," Mom insisted. "I know you two have a ton going on back there. Get to it. Don't worry about me."

Carlos frowned. Then he recovered and blew Mom a kiss. "Okay. If you need some muscle you call us, yes?"

"I will call you, first, I promise." She made a cross over her heart.

Sterling and Carlos returned to the kitchen. Thomas stood near the front door. He picked needles from one of the evergreen branches. They collected in a pile on the countertop. Mom began taking the boughs from the box and wrapping them together with the twine. She swept the pile of needles into her hand and tossed it into the garbage.

Thomas cleared his throat. "Hey, Jules, do you have a second? I need to talk to you about the investigation."

"Sure." I could feel Carlos's eyes on me.

Thomas must have sensed it too. He glanced to the kitchen. "Can you step outside for a minute?"

"Yeah." I looked at Mom. "As long as you're okay for a few?"

She smacked my hip with an evergreen branch. "Please. I can do this with my eyes shut. You go. I'll take care of *everything* in here." Her meaning was clear. I knew that she wasn't just talking about decorating for Sunday supper.

I followed Thomas outside and pointed to a bench on the far side of the plaza, out of sight of Torte's windows. The fog had lifted. A few tourists milled around the plaza. One of them snapped a photo of the shrine in front of ShakesBurgers with her phone. Not exactly the kind of photograph I'd want of a vacation, I thought.

"What's up?" I asked, taking a seat on the bench.

Thomas sat too. He stretched his legs out and crossed his feet. He wore his standard blue police uniform and black running shoes. I wondered how often he'd had to run a criminal down on Ashland's quiet streets.

"I need to ask you a couple follow-up questions."

"Shoot."

He removed a sleek gray iPad mini from his breast pocket.

"New toy?"

"Yeah." He handed it to me. "I love it. I tested it for a month. The Professor gave me the green light to order my own. The department is updating all of our equipment. This is so much faster than my old one. I can fit it in my pocket and take it with me when we're on scene."

"Nice." I gave it back to him.

Thomas clicked the iPad on and scrolled through it to find what he needed. "I need to double-check a couple things." He read something on the screen. "You arrived at ShakesBurgers at approximately six-twenty, is that correct?"

I nodded. "Yeah. Why are you asking this again? I already went over this with you, and the Professor asked me about it too."

Thomas stared at ShakesBurgers. Crime-scene tape had been stretched in front of the door and some sort of official notice had been posted in the front window. "Sorry about that. Welcome to the world of police work. It's standard procedure and the Professor is pretty uptight about making sure we double- and triple check each suspect's statement."

"Am I a suspect?"

Thomas grinned. "Not the last time I checked." He shifted position on the bench as a group of women wearing cashmere coats and leather gloves walked past. "California tourists," he whispered under his breath.

"Totally," I agreed.

He readjusted his feet. "Is there something you want to tell me?"

"I don't think so." I paused. A breeze blew from the south. Hair flew in front of my face. I untied my ponytail and cinched it tighter. "You've talked to Alan Matterson, right?"

"Multiple times. Why?"

"What about Craig from the Green Goblin?" Shoot. Craig. I still needed to prepare Craig's tasting cake. As soon as I was finished talking with Thomas, Craig's order was going to the top of my list.

"I've talked to Craig too. Why, Jules?" He rested his iPad on his knees and narrowed his blue eyes at me. "I don't need to remind you that this is a murder investigation, do I?"

"No." I tried to avoid staring at Mindy's shrine. A card caught in the wind and rattled along the sidewalk. Did Mindy have a family? I wondered what would happen to the cards, candles, and flowers that people had left as a tribute to her. "I don't even know if it's true, but Alan told me that Mindy and Rosalind Gates got into a physical fight the night before the murder. When I dropped off Craig's delivery earlier he mentioned that customers were talking about a fight at the business association meeting. Everyone assumed it was Alan, but maybe it was Rosalind."

"Or maybe Alan is lying." He scanned his iPad for a minute. "A lot of people didn't like Mindy."

"What's that supposed to mean?"

"It means that I don't think the Professor and I have ever had a case like this where there are so many people in town who didn't like the victim. That's not even strong enough— who had a reason to want the victim dead."

"Really?"

Thomas nodded. "Really." His gaze traveled to the Merry Windsor. A teenager in a ridiculous green velvet bellboy costume was polishing the wooden deck.

What did Richard Lord have to do with Mindy's murder? My curiosity was piqued. I thought back to seeing Richard arguing with Mathew. Although Mathew was staying at the Merry Windsor too. It was just as likely that Mathew was complaining about the hotel's musty rooms or overpriced meals.

Then there was Richard's weirdness about Jose Ortega and what he was doing at Torte and why he was talking to Carlos. Could there be a connection I was missing?

Thomas asked me a few more questions, all of which were a repeat of things I had already answered. He tucked his iPad away and thanked me for my time. As we stood he leaned close. "One last thing, Jules. You haven't noticed anyone hanging around across the street, have you?"

"Hanging around?"

"Yeah. You have a prime viewing spot of the crime scene from Torte."

"I know. Everyone has been hanging around. Since it happened there's been a crowd, news vans, and of course Mindy's growing shrine." I pointed to the sidewalk. "Don't you find it interesting that Mindy wasn't well-liked, yet her shrine is spilling onto the street?"

Thomas considered this for a moment. "Murder and death have a way of putting things into perspective."

"You sound like the Professor."

"I've been taught by the best."

"What should I be looking for?"

"You shouldn't be looking for anything." Thomas gave me a disapproving look. "I only wondered if you'd seen any movement or anyone hanging around, that's all."

"I'll keep my eyes open."

Thomas shook his head. "Jules," he said with a warning tone. "I didn't say to keep your eyes open."

"What?" I tried to wink.

"Don't even try. I know your tricks and I also know that you can't wink to save your life. You better get back to the bakery. It looks like there's a party happening tonight."

I stood and twisted my ponytail tighter. "Will do. See you later, and I'll call you right away if I see any action across the street." I hurried off with Thomas shouting a warning for me to leave it alone.

If he wanted me to leave it alone he shouldn't have mentioned anything about keeping an eye on ShakesBurgers. I also wondered about his vague response when I asked him about Mindy and Rosalind's fight. I knew who I needed to ask—Craig, and I knew exactly how—with a delicious pastry delivery.

Chapter Fifteen

The dining room had been completely transformed when I returned to Torte. In addition to the red roses, votive candles, white linens, and twinkle lights, Mom had twisted evergreen branches together to form a long vine that she wrapped between the vases and candles on the table. She had tied vines to the chandelier and hung red roses from the branches. The space smelled incredible with the earthy flowers and boughs and the scent of tapas grilling in the kitchen.

"Wow! This looks amazing, Mom," I said.

She snipped the stem from a rose and tucked it into an evergreen branch on the table. "The final touch. What do you think?"

"Seriously, I wasn't kidding about submitting this to a magazine. Everything looks gorgeous."

"It's not half bad, is it?" She stopped and surveyed her work. "I'm going to give each guest their own rose and bough. After I finish that I think my work here is done."

"I'll say. Thanks for doing this."

She snipped another rose. "My pleasure. Are you sure you don't need me to stick around tonight?"

"Not unless you want to. We've got it covered."

"In that case I'll finish this up and be on my way, but I want a full report first thing tomorrow, got it?"

"Got it." I gave her a serious salute.

"Juliet, I'm serious."

"Me too. I'll give you the play-by-play over our morning coffee."

"Perfect."

"Are you going out with the Professor tonight?"

Her browed furrowed. "I think so."

I walked closer to her. "Mom, is everything okay with you and the Professor?"

She set her scissors on the counter and sighed. "I think so, but to be honest I'm not exactly sure."

"What's going on?"

"I don't know. At first I thought it was this new case. It rattles him, you know, to see something so brutal in our hometown. Doug loves Ashland more than anyone I know."

"I know. It shows."

She smiled. "It does, doesn't it?" She swept a handful of needles into her hand and tossed them. "I figured that he was distracted with the case. He's been a little more distant than normal. I tried to talk to him about it last night. He didn't seem to want to talk. I'm a little worried."

"Why?"

She wiped her hands on her apron. "It's hard to articulate. I'm not even sure what it is myself. There's something between us that isn't being said, but I don't know what it is. I've tried to ask him about it. He gets pensive and thoughtful. Whenever I try to push a little he says it's nothing—that he's distracted by the case."

I helped her gather the rose clippings. I had a feeling I knew why the Professor was being distant, but I couldn't tell her. The Professor had asked me what I thought about Mom getting remarried when we were at Lake of the Woods. He didn't officially say that he was planning to propose, but he definitely hinted. Since we'd been home he'd been unusually quiet. I didn't want to ruin his surprise if he proposed, but I felt bad keeping something from Mom.

Maybe he was having second thoughts. Or maybe he was trying to work up the courage to ask her.

I tossed a handful of stems into the garbage. "Mom, the Professor adores you. I'm sure there's nothing to worry about. Your first instinct is probably right. I'm sure he's wrapped up in the case."

"Probably." She sighed. "My gut is usually right about things like this, Juliet. There's something he's not telling me and I'm not going to be able to relax until I figure out what it is."

"Talk to him tonight."

"I plan to. It might require a special pastry." She winked and placed the last rose on the table. "What do you think?"

I walked over to the table and kissed her head. "I think it's perfect, and I think you are too. Don't worry about the Professor. It'll all work out."

She squeezed my hand. "Thanks, honey."

After she left I thought about what she'd said about not being able to relax until she figured out what the Professor was keeping from her. I knew the feeling, and suddenly I knew where I'd inherited the trait.

Carlos salsa danced his way around the kitchen island to the beat of Latin music. His hips swayed from side to side. He held a serrated bread knife in one hand and used the other to pull me toward his body.

"What are you doing?"

"We must dance, Julieta. The music it is wonderful, no?" He drew me closer and nuzzled my neck. "Sterling, you see, this is what I was telling you, you must show a woman how much you love her. Telling her is not enough."

"Got it," Sterling replied.

I freed myself from Carlos's grasp. "I don't have time to dance. We have so much to do."

"There is always time to dance, *mi querida*." Carlos looked to Sterling for support.

"Don't look at me. I'm not getting in the middle of this one." He tossed his apron in the laundry basket by the office. Being Carlos's understudy in the kitchen was not for the faint of heart, and Sterling's apron looked like it had taken a beating. He tied on a clean one. "And I'm not dancing. I'm not really the waltzing type. Maybe if there was a mosh pit or something."

"You don't have to dance, Sterling," I assured him as I walked to the far counter where we keep a notebook with all of our family's original recipes. "Don't pay any attention to him. The kitchen is no place for dancing. It's way too dangerous."

Carlos gasped. "How can you say this, Julieta? I'm trying to teach him the ways of love, and you tell him there is no dancing. Terrible. Terrible."

I picked up the notebook and flipped it open. "Should we talk about the time you sliced your finger open when you tried to convince the kitchen staff to do a conga line?"

A sly smile tugged at Carlos's cheeks. "Ah, but that was a very fun night, no?"

It was a fun night. Carlos served sangria and flatbread. We all drank way too much and ended up doing the conga through the kitchen and down the hallway. Carlos, who led the charge, had slipped and cut his hand on a paring knife. He handled it like a pro. Professional chefs are trained in first aid and CPR. On the ship we had mandatory safety protocol workshops and drills. Working in tight spaces with multiple chefs, line cooks, dishwashers, and waitstaff meant that everyone had to be acutely aware of their surroundings. From open flames to cast-iron skillets to razor-sharp knives and boiling water, the kitchen can be deadly.

Carlos had bandaged himself up and rejoined the impromptu dance party. His philosophy was simple—happy staff, happy food.

I caught his eye and we smiled at the memory. Those days felt like another life.

Sterling called Carlos over. "Is this a good size?" He pointed to a bowl with diced onions.

"*Sí, sí,* it is perfect." Carlos shifted back into chef mode.

I thumbed through the recipe book. My almond and lemon olive oil cakes were both baking. Now it was time to create something for Craig. Mom had preserved her mother's and grandmother's handwritten recipes by laminating them. They were splattered with batter and had notes in the margins where they had substituted a flavored extract or reduced the amount of flour. Since the Green Goblin was known for its cocktails I wanted to bake something slightly irreverent for Craig to serve to late-night revealers. I knew just the thing—red velvet cake.

My grandmother used to bake the layered cake for my birthday. I'd had many red velvet cakes over the years and none compared with hers. The secret was her frosting. Southern-style red velvet is served with cream cheese frosting and sometimes with traditional buttercream. My grandmother's red velvet frosting is boiled with a flour base. The frosting requires a bit more work and patience, but the end result is well worth any extra effort. It's so light and creamy that it's like tasting air. I like to pair it with layered cakes so that the cake can be the star of the show.

For the cake, I whipped butter and sugar in the mixer. Then I incorporated eggs, buttermilk, flour, a dash of vinegar, and cocoa powder. Once the batter was smooth, I added the red food coloring. The batter turned a deep shade of red as the drops of food coloring swirled in.

Carlos snuck up behind me and pinched my waist.

I jumped and let out a little scream.

"It is only me." His face lit up.

"What are you doing?" I asked. I knew that look. He was up to something.

"Nothing. I wanted to taste your cake. That is all."

"You don't even like cake."

He pretended to be injured. "How can you say this? I love your cake."

"Go ahead." I stepped aside.

Carlos didn't move. I noticed that one of his hands was hidden behind his back.

"What are you doing?"

"Nothing." He grinned.

"What's behind your back then?" I lunged toward him.

He was spry. In one quick move he ducked away from me and tossed something to Sterling. "Catch!" he yelled.

Sterling caught whatever Carlos had thrown at him with one hand. "Oh, no."

Carlos had tossed him a bottle of green food coloring, but in his haste to get rid of the evidence, he hadn't screwed on the lid. Green food coloring splattered on Sterling's red apron. He looked like a Christmas craft gone terribly wrong.

I couldn't help but laugh. "That's karma, you two."

Sterling's shoulders sagged. Carlos swept in with a dish towel and soapy water. He helped Sterling scrub green food coloring from his apron and the island.

"I warned you that he wasn't to be trusted," I said to Sterling. "Carlos can't go a day without playing a prank. That better not stain my island."

I will take care of it." Carlos wrung out the towel in the bowl of soapy water. "It is true, but you know the pranks they are for the food."

"The food?" Sterling looked confused.

"*Sí*. The food it tastes better when it is infused with fun."

"What were you planning anyway? To turn my cake green?"

Carlos's eyes twinkled.

"You know. That's not a bad idea actually." A green cake for the Green Goblin. Carlos wouldn't have been very successful in turning my chocolate cake batter green. He knew that. But I could make a vanilla cake and tint it green. That would give Craig a chocolate and vanilla option for his customers and a hint of whimsy. While Carlos and Sterling scrubbed green food coloring from their work surface, I quickly mixed together my vanilla cake batter. I found a new jar of food color paste and worked it into the batter until it was the color of summer grass. I slid both cakes into the oven and gathered the ingredients I needed for my grandmother's frosting.

Flour isn't usually associated with frosting. I remember my grandmother teaching me how to make it and being in awe of how the flour and water transformed from a thick paste into a light and airy frosting. It didn't seem possible. Flour in frosting? I don't know who the genius pastry chef was who created this masterpiece, but if I ever met them I knew I would be in the presence of greatness. This frosting is so unbelievably divine it should be illegal.

To begin I whisked flour and water on the stove until it turned into a translucent paste—almost like a béchamel. Then I set it aside to cool while I whipped butter, sugar, and vanilla in the mixer. Once the flour paste was completely cool I began whipping it together with the butter, sugar, and vanilla. It's imperative to make sure the flour isn't the least bit warm otherwise it will melt the butter. The stainless steel beater worked at full speed whipping the mixture until it turned ivory in color.

I stuck my pinky into the mixing bowl. The simple butter flavor was understated with a sweet creamy finish. It was by far the most delicious frosting I've ever had. Paired with my chocolatey red velvet cake the frosting would be nothing short of perfection.

After my cakes cooled I sliced them into four thin layers and spread generous amounts of my flour frosting between each layer. I piped the top layer with more frosting and dark chocolate shavings. On the whimsical green cake, I opted to decorate it with crystalized green sugar. I stood back to survey my work. The cakes looked beautiful and (fingers crossed) they should taste good too.

I boxed them up and waved to Sterling and Carlos. "I'm off on a delivery. Be back in a couple of minutes. Sterling, you're in charge while I'm away. Keep your eye on that guy. He's up to no good. I can see it. Oh, and change your apron. That one is a disaster."

Sterling looked down at his apron. "What, you don't like the tie-dye look?"

I curled my top lip.

He took off the apron. "Right. I'll watch him, Jules. Don't worry."

"Good." I stared at Carlos. "Set a good example for my staff."

His dark eyes gleamed. "Me? Always."

I carefully positioned the cake boxes in my arms and headed for the front door. The late-afternoon air outside was warm and refreshing. Puck's Pub had set their bistro tables on the sidewalk. Was it really January? An Irish band played on stage as I walked past the popular pub. I stopped to listen to for a minute before continuing on to the Green Goblin.

Craig was behind the bar when I came inside. "Come on back, Juliet," he said as he squeezed a fresh lime into a stainless steel cocktail shaker. I walked to the far end of the bar and waited for him to finish making the drink. Cocktails have never exactly been my thing. I enjoy a well-made drink, but mixology isn't my medium. Pastry is.

He shook vodka and fresh lime juice and poured it into a cocktail glass. He had rimmed the glass with crystalized sugar and finished it with a twist of lime. "You want one?" he asked, after he passed the light green drink to a customer waiting at the bar.

I licked my lips in response. "That looks so good."

"Let me make you one."

"It's tempting, but we're hosting a Sunday supper at Torte tonight. I have to get back to the bakeshop." I opened the cake boxes. Craig bent closer to get a better look in the dimly lit bar. "This one is a red velvet," I said, running my hand over the first cake.

"I love red velvet." Craig gave me a thumbs-up. "Good choice."

"This one is a little more fun. Do you have a plate and knife?" I asked, removing the second cake from the box.

"Sure. One sec." Craig walked to the other end of the bar and came back with two plates, two forks, and a knife.

"This is a simple vanilla on vanilla." I sliced the cake and handed a piece to Craig.

He studied it for a minute. "But it's green."

"That's just food dye." I cut a thin slice of the red velvet too. "Go ahead. Tell me what you think."

He started to taste the red velvet cake. I stopped him. "Start with the vanilla. When you're tasting you should always start with the lighter flavor and work your way darker."

"Like beer. That's funny. I had my distributor here earlier and he took me through a tasting flight and he said the same thing. We started with the pilsners and ended with a stout." Craig pointed behind him to a four-foot-long row of beer taps.

"Exactly—pastry, beer—it's the same concept."

Craig took a bite of the green vanilla cake. "Hey, that's an idea. What if you made a beer cake or booze cake?"

"I'd love to." I glanced around the bar while Craig took another bite. A group of hockey players were toasting with celebratory pints at the back of the bar. Closer to me, an older couple was sharing a bottle of champagne. My eyes rested on a high table at the very front. Reggie and Mathew were drinking beer from cans and talking intently. Neither noticed me. Mathew passed Reggie a sheet of paper. Reggie pushed it back to him. I wondered what was going on with them. Maybe Mathew was offering Reggie a new contract, but Reggie was refusing.

"Okay. A booze cake," Craig said as he polished off the vanilla cake.

I returned my attention to him. "Booze."

"Except I need this too. This is amazing, Jules. It's so light. What's that frosting?"

"It's a flour frosting."

"Flour? No way. It's the best frosting I've ever tasted. I don't even usually like frosting."

I smiled. "That's the idea."

Craig tasted the red velvet next. "Oh man, this is good."

"Glad you like it."

"Love it." He stabbed it with his fork and took another bite. "Yeah. We have to have these."

"Good. They both should hold up really well, especially with that frosting. It will help keep the cakes moist. You can cover them and serve them by the slice. They'll even do okay in the refrigerator. You'll just want to make sure to let them come up to room temperature before serving."

"Jules, you're making it sound like we're going to have a problem keeping them fresh. We are going to have a problem, but it won't be that."

"What is it?"

"Keeping them in stock. I'm telling you. I get asked for dessert all the time." He pointed to the open shelf behind us. "I bought two of those glass cake stands. I'm going to put your cakes on either end of the bar. That way customers can drool over them while they're waiting in line for drinks. It doesn't look like it now but come back when the band is on and you won't be able to get within an inch of this bar. Not without a fight anyway."

"I believe it." On any given night in Ashland there's music playing somewhere. Most of the bars and restaurants showcase Ashland's musical talent with free performances. From Irish funk to light jazz it's easy to find a new band or relax with a glass of wine to the sound of classical music over dinner.

"I want to start offering both of these right away. When can you start delivering them?"

"How's tomorrow?"

"Perfect. And what do you think about a beer or vodka cake or something? That could be really fun."

"I love it. I'll play around with some recipes and bring you another round of samples."

Craig walked to the cash register. "What do I owe you for these?"

"Nothing. They're yours. Keep them for yourself or give samples to your customers."

"You sure?" He held up a twenty-dollar bill. "Can I at least give you a tip for delivering?"

"Craig, put your money away. I'm not taking it." I scanned the bar. There were two women drinking their lime cocktails at the far end of the bar. A couple of the tables were taken, but otherwise it was pretty slow. I was sure that within the next hour or two there would be a line of customers jockeying for position at the bar. "Hey, before I go, I wanted to ask you one thing."

"Shoot." He pushed the cash drawer shut.

"It's about that fight you mentioned yesterday." I glanced over my shoulder to make sure Mathew and Reggie hadn't come up for another round.

"Oh, yeah. Get this. Word is that Rosalind is the one who hit Mindy. Can you believe that?"

"I know. That's what I heard. When you mentioned that Mindy was in a fight, I guess I assumed it was Alan. Did you hear anything else yesterday?"

Craig shook his head. "Not really. We were slammed though. Were you?"

I nodded.

"I guess murder is good for business."

I grimaced. "I guess so."

A customer approached the bar. "Be with you in a sec," Craig said.

"I'll let you go. I'll deliver your cakes with your bread tomorrow morning and start brainstorming some cakes with booze."

Craig gave me a thumbs-up and turned his attention to the customer. I passed by Reggie's table. Mathew had left. Reggie chugged the rest of his beer and gave me a strange look. I waved and continued out the door. On the way back to Torte, Craig's words replayed in my head: murder was good for business.

Chapter Sixteen

By the time I arrived back at Torte, Sterling and Carlos had begun plating the first course, a gorgeous charcutería board with chorizo, duck-liver mousse, chicken pâté, and foie gras. I dusted my almond cake with powdered sugar and decorated it with almonds. Then I whipped mascarpone cream with a little sugar and vanilla to accompany my lemon olive oil cake.

Right before we opened the doors, I lit the votive candles that Mom had placed on the table, dimmed the overhead lights, and plugged in the twinkle lights. The dining room looked like a scene from one of OSF's most romantic productions. Carlos arranged bottles of Spanish wines and sparkling wineglasses on the front counter, and Sterling turned up the volume on the Latin salsa music.

"Are we ready?" I asked.

They both nodded enthusiastically.

I unlocked the front door, and placed a chalkboard sign on the sidewalk. It read: SUNDAY SUPPER. A LATIN FEAST. TAPAS AND SPANISH WINE. ADVANCED TICKETS REQUIRED.

Sterling brought the tray of cheese, cured meats, and

olives to the front as the first guests arrived. I took tickets at the door. Lance was one of the first people in line.

He greeted me with a kiss on both cheeks. "Juliet, the place looks absolutely divine. It must be that Latin lover of yours. His romantic influence is rubbing off on our young starlet."

"Stop." I ushered him to his seat.

"I see a rosy blush rising in those gorgeous cheekbones of yours, darling. No need to blush. I would swoon too."

"Lance," I whispered. "I'm not swooning or blushing. It's hot in here."

He threw his head back and laughed. "Nice try." He removed his perfectly cut black jacket and rested it on the back of his chair. His crisp pink shirt was color-coordinated with a pink-and-silver-striped tie. Not many men could pull of the look, but Lance wore it well.

"Do tell, darling. What's the word on this murder business?"

"I don't know." I reached for a pitcher and filled his water glass.

"Don't play coy with me, Juliet. We've been here before. I know that you know something."

I glanced to the line of people waiting at the door. "I can't talk right now, Lance. I've got to get everyone else seated."

"Fair enough, fair lady, but mark my words, you are going to dish." He smiled like a Cheshire cat. "I might have some *clues* to share with you."

Drat. Lance knew that he had me. I hurried to seat the remaining diners. Each time I passed Lance's seat, he caught my eye and winked.

Carlos uncorked the first bottle of white wine and

circulated the table, filling glasses and explaining the vintage of the wine and the growing region for the grapes. Soon the dining room was full of happy chatter and the sound of wineglasses clinking.

I waited by the door. We were missing three guests. If they didn't show up in the next ten minutes we'd begin serving tapas without them. In the meantime everyone appeared merry and lively. Carlos's wine selections were a hit. I overheard a woman comment on the roses and greenery. "Such ambiance. It must be Helen's work. She has the touch."

I'd be sure to tell Mom that everyone was impressed with her décor. At that moment the last group of guests arrived, and I recognized one of them right away. "Rosalind," I said, extending my hand. "I didn't that know you were coming tonight. I didn't see your name on the guest list."

She wrapped her wrinkled hand over mine. A deep scratch ran the length of her arm and a red bruise marked her wrist. "I wasn't. A friend became ill at the last minute and offered me her ticket."

"I'm sorry that your friend isn't feeling well, but I'm glad that you could join us." My eyes lingered on her arm.

She tucked it close to her body. "I took a bit of a tumble."

"Are you all right?"

"Right as rain." She walked with a pronounced limp as I showed her to her seat.

"Have you been to a Sunday supper before?"

"No. This is my first time. It smells spicy."

"You're in for a treat." I took her and her friends to their seats. "We're serving authentic Spanish tapas tonight."

"I can't wait." Rosalind pulled out her chair, but hesitated before she sat. A look of pain washed over her face as she used her hands to steady herself.

"Are you sure you're okay?" I asked.

She grimaced for a minute and then lowered her body into the chair. "I'm fine. Creaky knees. That's all. It's no fun getting old, Juliet. Enjoy your youth while you still have it."

Carlos came up behind me to fill Rosalind's wineglass. I scooted out of the way and headed to the kitchen to help Sterling plate the next round of tapas. If Rosalind had trouble sitting, how could she have possibly knocked Mindy over? But where had she gotten that bruise and scratch?

I didn't have time to think it over. Smoke was rising from the grill in the kitchen. I hurried to the back. Sterling was grilling shrimp. I suspected that he had used too much olive oil.

"Hit the fan," I told him. I didn't want the kitchen and dining room to smell like smoke. Smell is a huge part of the tasting experience. If everything smelled like grilled shrimp it would overwhelm the other flavors that Sterling and Carlos had worked so hard on melding together.

He clicked on the fan and waved smoke from his face. "Why are they doing that?"

"It's probably the olive oil." The fan started sucking the smoke up immediately. "Try turning down the heat a little too. They smell great. We just don't want to smoke out the guests."

"Hey, that could be our next Sunday supper theme." Sterling's shoulders relaxed.

"Not a bad idea." I washed my hands. "How can I help?"

Sterling kept his eyes focused on the shrimp, and

pointed behind him with his thumb. "Can you assemble the empanadas on the platters?"

"For sure."

"This is weird," Sterling said as he turned a perfectly grilled shrimp with a pair of tongs.

"What?"

"You're asking me what to do. That's not how it's supposed to work."

I wiped the platter with a dish towel. "Come on, that's exactly how it works. We're a team around here. You know that."

"Yeah. I know. You and your mom have been incredible. I guess I just feel really honored that you trust me to do this." Sterling cleared his throat.

"You're the best." I dabbed a spot on the tray. "Plus the real reason that we keep you around is because all the teenage girls squeal when they see you. Mom thinks we've doubled our cookie sales thanks to the fact that half the girls in town are in love with you."

"Right. Great. Glad to know that I've got the fourteen-year-old-girl set covered."

I arranged the empanadas on the platter. It was hard not to break into one of them. They were a golden brown color and stuffed with meat and veggies. Aromas of peppers and garlic hit my nose. If the smell was any indication, I had a feeling that everyone was going to be talking about this supper for weeks.

Carlos was pouring the second wine—a Brazilian chardonnay. I listened as he explained the wine's origin.

"You see this lovely light green color?" Carlos asked as he held up the bottle of wine for the guests. "It is because the grapes reflect the tropical flavors of the region. You will smell some melon and peaches. Even some banana. You taste and tell me what you think."

That was my cue to bring out the empanadas. I picked up the tray and walked to the front. Carlos poured glasses of the chardonnay. "This is a very light and refreshing for your palate. It will go well with chicken and fish. I see that Julieta is bringing you some of our empanadas. These are very Spanish. We eat them all day long back home in Spain. Even for dessert with fruits and berries."

Carlos had the same effect on our guests as Sterling did on teenage girls. I watched as the women seated at the table hung on his every word. One of them raised her hand. "Am I tasting apricots in this?"

He nodded enthusiastically. "*Sí, sí.* Good job." He ran the bottle under his nose. "Just a hint of sweetness with the apricots, no?"

I thought the woman might faint at Carlos's praise. She batted her eyelashes at him and copied the way he swirled his wineglass. He gave her a nod of approval and continued on, completely oblivious to her advances.

Lance caught my wrist as I returned to the kitchen for the next platter of tapas. "Darling, your husband has done it again. This is absolutely charming."

"Thanks, Lance," I whispered.

"Wait, don't go. We haven't had a chance to talk yet. You know—*talk.*"

"Lance, I'm working."

"So am I, darling. So am I."

I knelt on the floor next to his chair. "Okay, two minutes. Go."

Lance strummed his fingers together. "I knew you couldn't resist talking murder for long."

"I'm serious. I have to work. If you want to dish, get started."

He gave a subtle nod to the end of the table where Rosalind was seated. "Let's start with Ashland's gran-dame. What have you heard?"

I checked to make sure that Rosalind wasn't looking our way. She wasn't. She too had fallen under Carlos's spell. "I heard that she and Mindy got into a fight. What do you know?"

"Nothing. Absolutely nothing."

"But you made it sound like you had inside info to share."

"I might."

"Lance, stop with the games. Do you know something or not?"

"Not, but I have a plan, darling." The light from the vo-tive candles reflected off of Lance's silver tie.

"A plan?"

"It involves you."

"Great." I couldn't keep the sarcasm from my voice.

"Come on, play along. It'll be fun."

"What are you thinking?"

"How are your acting chops? I know it's been a while since you've graced the stage."

"Wait. I'm not getting on any stage and you're not rop-ing me into any show."

Lance made an exasperated sound with his lips. "You're no fun tonight, Juliet. I'm not talking about *my stage*. I'm talking about a little performance right here, tonight."

My feet were starting to tingle. I shifted position. "Just tell me what you're thinking. I have to get back there and help Sterling."

He leaned closer and whispered, "I have a perfect plan to cozy up to our matronly suspect down there. When you come back out drop something in my lap. I'll play it up. You'll have to reseat me because—obviously—I can't ruin this look with food in my lap." He ran his hands over his pink shirt. "Then you can shift things around and put me next to Rosalind. If you get me next to her I guarantee I'll get her talking. Especially because she appeared to be absolutely charmed by your husband and his sexy Spanish wines. Keep the wine flowing and I'll work my magic."

I hated to admit it, but it was a pretty good plan. I agreed and returned to the kitchen.

"The shrimp are ready to go," Sterling said, handing me a platter of shrimp. "I'm working on the next course."

I couldn't dump a plate of shrimp on Lance's lap. That would be too obvious. Instead I placed the tray in the middle of the table and picked up the bottle of chardonnay. Carlos was uncorking the third round of wine. I circled the table and refilled people's glasses. When I got to Lance I pretended to trip and spilled the wine on his plate.

Lance jumped to his feet and immediately began brushing imaginary droplets of wine from his suit.

"I'm so sorry," I said, grabbing a napkin and dabbing the imaginary drops. I was pretty impressed with my performance and the fact that I'd been able to pour the wine on his plate without ruining his suit. "Let me get you a new plate, and chair," I said.

Lance took the napkin from my hand and patted his cheeks with it. "Don't give it a thought, darling, although I do believe your lovely table setting has been ruined."

"I'll move you," I replied.

The guests had turned their attention from Carlos and

were watching us. I pointed to the head of the table where Rosalind was seated. "Would you mind if I move Lance down by you?"

Rosalind scooted her chair and patted the tablecloth. "Not at all. We'd love to have him come sit with us. I'm eager to hear about the new season at OSF anyway."

Lance blew her a kiss. He picked up his wineglass and strolled to the far end of the table. As he passed me he whispered, "Well played. The game is afoot."

Chapter Seventeen

I tried to eavesdrop on their conversation, but each time I returned to the front with tapas someone would stop me to tell me how delicious everything tasted and how entertaining Carlos was. It warmed my heart to hear that our guests were enjoying the evening. They were definitely enjoying Carlos. He opened the fourth bottle of wine—a Tempranillo, my personal favorite—and caressed the cork. "This is from a high mountain region and is full of the scent of the earth. It will complement the beef."

He passed the cork around the table for everyone to smell. A woman reached out and grabbed my sleeve. "Can I get you something?" I asked.

"No, I have everything I need. I wanted to tell you that this is the most amazing evening. It's my first time here. I'll be telling all of my friends about this. The food is absolutely to die for and your chef is beyond delicious." She placed an ivory embossed business card in my hand. "Can you give him my number?"

I took the card and smiled. "Will do. Although rumor has it that he's married."

The woman scowled. "Lucky woman." She stared at Carlos and sighed. "Lucky, lucky woman."

Sterling was plating the last tray of tapas in the kitchen. "Everyone is going crazy for the food."

"And for Carlos." I tossed the business card on the counter.

"Can you blame them? Look at him. He knows how to work a crowd, that's for sure."

"Especially a crowd of single women." Did I sound jealous?

Sterling met my eyes. "Jules, you have to know that he's crazy in love with you. It's obvious."

"Crazy in love—that sounds like something from Beyoncé."

"Nope. That's mine. All mine."

"Are you speaking from personal experience?" I raised an eyebrow. Sterling and I were alike in many ways, but most alike when it came to being forlorn in love. He escaped with poetry. I baked. It worked for the most part.

"Nah. I'm good. Who needs love anyway? I'm swearing off women and falling madly for tapas." He handed me the tray. "Want to do the honors?"

"Gladly."

The guests were sipping Burgundy wine. I held up the platter of tender beef that Carlos had marinated for hours, before searing, served with a garlic, chili, and coriander paste. Everyone ooohed and ahhhed. "Last course. Be sure to save room for dessert."

I glanced to the far end of the table where Lance was practically sitting in Rosalind's lap. He gestured with his hands and used his napkin like a fan. Whatever he was saying to her was working. She was so captivated by his story that she didn't even flinch when Carlos refilled her wineglass.

"Julieta, let me take that." Carlos discarded the empty wine bottle and took the tray from my hands. "It is going well, no?"

"It's great."

"You like the tapas?"

"Honestly I haven't even had a chance to try them. We've been so busy."

He looked disappointed. "I made them for you. They are all your favorites. You remember how you loved the tapas I make for you on the ship?"

I remembered. "Yeah. I remember." My voice sounded wistful and far away, as if it weren't coming from me. "I have to get back to finish dessert."

Carlos took one hand from the platter and touched my wrist. "After the guests leave, we will stay and have some tapas and wine, *sí*?"

"Sure." I hurried away. His touch was unsettling.

"What's next?" Sterling asked. He had filled the sink with soapy water and was soaking the empty trays and platters. Carlos was going to be out of luck. It looked like every single nibble and bite had been devoured.

"I'm going to plate the lemon olive oil cake. Can you take the almond cake out in a minute?"

"You got it."

My mascarpone cream had whipped to a light and airy consistency. I sliced the moist lemon cake onto individual plates. Then I assembled fresh raspberries and finished each slice with a healthy dollop of the cream.

Sterling and I worked in unison. As soon as I had a slice plated he delivered it to the table. Carlos served a sweet dessert wine with the final course. I sliced thin pieces of my almond cake. It was moist and dense, almost like a pound cake. We served it with scoops of homemade raspberry sorbet. The buttery almond cake with the deep red berry sorbet was striking on the plate. I finished it with a drizzle of dark chocolate glaze.

Lance caught my eye as I made my way in his direction with a carafe of coffee. "Coffee, anyone?" I asked.

Rosalind held up her glass. "That would be lovely, my dear. I think I might need the entire pot. Somehow every time I looked my wineglass was full again. It must be that husband of yours." She fanned her face with her free hand. "I think I might be tipsy. It's a good thing I can walk home."

Lance winked at me and put his arm around the back of Rosalind's chair. "I'll escort you."

She swayed a little in her chair and caught herself on the table. For a second I thought she might yank the tablecloth and Mom's exquisite centerpieces off. Fortunately she steadied herself. "I can't remember the last time I felt this tipsy."

Lance scoffed. "I wish I had that problem."

Rosalind's eyes moved away from Lance and toward ShakesBurgers across the street. "I believe I got caught up in the celebration. There's so much to celebrate, isn't there?"

I watched her stare at the modern restaurant. Her jaw tightened as she repeated, "Yes, so many reasons to celebrate."

Lance gave me a warning look. I filled their coffee cups and left Lance to play the part of detective. A small shiver ran down my back. I had to get Lance alone and find out what—if anything—he'd learned.

That proved to be harder than I imagined. No one

wanted to leave. Guests lingered at the table, polishing off the last of the wine and sipping strong coffee. Sterling helped me clear the dishes and clean the kitchen. Carlos worked the room like a politician. He thanked each guest for coming and promised that the next time he was in town, he'd make tapas again.

I had blocked out the fact that he was leaving—and soon. In some ways it would be easier to have him gone. It was nearly impossible to concentrate with his seductive body and accent whispering in my ear, but the thought of him leaving for good made my chest tighten. I knew why people called it a heartache. My heart hurt at the thought of having to say good-bye to him.

Lance and Rosalind were the last guests out the door. Rosalind didn't look as unsteady as she had earlier, but I noticed that Lance had looped his arm through hers and had a firm grasp on her waist.

"Darling, don't forget that special order. I need it first thing," he said as he blew a kiss with one hand.

"Order?" I hadn't seen an order from OSF come in.

Lance squared his jaw. "Don't be silly, Juliet, you know, my *special* order. I need it first thing."

I realized Lance's meaning. He was speaking in code. He wanted to dish on what he'd learned from Rosalind. That was good news—it meant that he had actually learned something.

"Right, right. Sorry, it's been a long night. Yes, I'll have your special order bright and early. In fact, I'll deliver it myself."

"You are a gem."

Rosalind placed her frail hand in mine. "Thank you for a wonderful evening."

I watched Lance usher Rosalind out the door and down the sidewalk. I wished that I could follow after them. Had Rosalind revealed something important under the influence of too much wine and Carlos's irresistible tapas? I would have to wait until tomorrow to find out, but I knew for sure that a stop at Lance's office was going to be the first thing I did in the morning.

Chapter Eighteen

Sterling wrung out a dish towel in the sink. "That's the last of it, Jules. Anything else you want me to do?" He pushed the sleeves on his hoodie back down. "I wasn't sure what to do with the candles and flowers. They're all sitting on the counter up there, but everything else is back in place."

I leaned against the counter. My feet were sore. "You're the best. Thanks for everything. We could not have done it without you. Do you want some food to go? I bet you never had a chance to eat, did you?"

Sterling shook his head. "Nope, but we've got that covered." He motioned for me to wait and walked over to the fridge. Before I had a chance to push the start button on the dishwasher he returned with a to-go box and a small silver platter of tapas. "Carlos had me box up tapas for me and save some for you."

I pulled out a bar stool and sat. What time had I started this morning? I glanced at the clock. It was after nine. No wonder my feet hurt. "I was going to offer to make you a sandwich or something," I said to Sterling. "Tapas sound much more delicious."

"No need." Sterling held up the box. "I'll take my to-go tapas and see you tomorrow." He started toward the front, but stopped. "Hey, do you mind if I grab a few of the extra flowers?"

"Not at all. Are they for your special lady friend?" I couldn't help but tease.

I couldn't see Sterling's face, but I knew that I must have embarrassed him because he mumbled something I couldn't hear. "Thanks again for all of your help," I said with sincerity. "Get out of here, and say hi to Stephanie for me."

He gave me a two-finger wave and grabbed his skateboard from the office. Carlos saw him to the door. They spoke briefly in tones I couldn't hear. I wondered if Carlos was offering him parting advice on how to romance Stephanie.

Carlos locked up after Sterling left and turned off the main lights. He kept the twinkle lights plugged in and waved me to the front. "Julieta, come have a seat. I will open a new bottle of wine for us."

The tightness in my chest loosened. I picked up the plate of tapas that Carlos had set aside and grabbed napkins and forks.

Carlos held out my chair for me. "Sit, sit. You have been working too hard, *mi querida*."

"I'm fine," I said, but I was glad to be off my feet.

He handed me a glass of red wine. "Try this. I ordered it special for you."

The wine reminded me of a bottle we had shared in Costa Rica one summer. The ship we were working on had experienced some electrical issues while out at sea, so we ended up docked in Costa Rica for three extra days. We used the time to explore its rain forests and white sandy beaches. Carlos talked me into taking a scuba diving lesson with him. I'll never forget the feeling of gliding under the water. It was like being on another planet. Only we were the aliens. We swam with giant sea turtles and watched schools of neon-colored tropical fish dart through the current in geometric patterns. Carlos, always the jokester, pretended to moon walk on the sea floor. He held my hand and we watched in awe as a pod of dolphins played in the waves above our heads. It was like being in a trance. I never wanted it to end.

That night we ended up in a tiny restaurant with aquamarine walls and umbrellas made out of coconut husks. We ate grilled fish caught fresh that afternoon and laughed for hours over a bottle of the restaurant owner's homemade wine. The wine wasn't on the menu. Wherever our travels took us Carlos befriended chefs. They befriend him back with their personal wine and custom dishes made just for us.

We made it a point never to eat near tourist hubs. "Let's go explore," Carlos would say as he flagged down a taxi driver. "Take us to where you eat."

Our culinary tours took us to places far off the beaten path. My palate developed on those excursions. I tasted things that I never imagined, from sea urchin to Peruvian pisco, a strong amber-colored brandy. Carlos encouraged me to immerse myself in the food wherever we landed.

The Costa Rican wine held a special place in my tasting memory. It was scarlet in color with a brilliant fruity finish and robust flavor. The restaurant owner made it from wild grapes growing on his property. For years I've tried to find a similar wine. I've come close, but never been able to match its unique flavor and color.

I swirled the glass that Carlos handed me. It had the same scarlet color and with one whiff I was back on the beach in Costa Rica.

"What is this?"

Carlos grinned. "Do you like?"

I took a taste and inhaled the happy memory. "Is this it?"

He pointed to the unlabeled bottle.

I sat up in my chair. "This is it! How did you find it?"

His smile widened. "I have been making some calls."

"This is *the* wine from Costa Rica? Not just something that tastes like it? You found the actual wine. How?"

He poured himself a glass and sat down next to me. "I visited the restaurant when we docked in Costa Rica last month. The owner is no longer there, but they gave me his address. I took a bus out to a tiny village and knocked on his door."

"You did?"

"*Sí.* It was an adventure." He watched as I drank the wine. I closed my eyes and savored the moment. His voice turned husky. "I do this and more for you, Julieta, to see you smile like this. You like?"

"I love." I held up my glass.

"This is why I find the owner. He was very surprised to see me and to know that we remembered his wine. He makes it for his family. He wouldn't let me pay him for the bottle. He says it is a gift for you. You must come and see him in Costa Rica. He wants to see my beautiful American wife again. I show him your picture. He remembers you."

"That's so sweet." I shook my head in disbelief. "I can't believe you found him."

Carlos refilled our glasses and nudged the plate of tapas closer to me. "Eat, eat."

I chose an empanada to start. It was filled with savory meat and vegetables that had been sautéed so that they were still slightly crisp. The meat had a nice kick of spice and the dough was like a flaky, buttery pie crust. "This is really good." I took another sip of wine to wash down the empanada.

"You remember the first time I make you empanadas? You ate the entire plate and left nothing for the rest of the staff. I think that is the first time that I knew I was in love with you. A beautiful woman and pastry chef who loves to eat. *Sí,* that is the moment that I knew I must marry you."

My heart flopped in my chest. I remembered that night too. Carlos's tapas were hot and spicy. Just like him. I couldn't hold myself back from eating the entire plate, or wanting to be with him.

Things were different now.

Carlos swirled his wine. A thin film of the burgundy liquid clung to the sides of the glass. "May I ask you something?"

He leaned so close that I could hear his heartbeat. It was slow and steady. "Julieta, I have missed you so much."

"I've missed you too."

He caressed my hand. "I cannot live without you. This has been a wonderful week, being together in the kitchen again, *sí*?"

"It has."

"I do not want it to end. I cannot leave you again."

"What are you trying to say?" Was Carlos considering staying in Ashland? I'd daydreamed about him staying, but I never thought that he might actually consider it.

He scooted his chair even closer and wrapped his hand around the base of my neck. His touch was hot. "Come back with me. Come back to the ship."

I placed my head in my hands. "Carlos, I can't."

"Julieta, you are my wife. We belong together, no?"

"We do." I massaged my temples. Carlos moved his hand to my knee. Candlelight flickered in his eyes.

"Then you come back with me. Come back to the ship and I will show you every minute of every day how much I love and cherish you. I want you to meet Ramiro too. You will love him. He is pure light and joy. We will go to Spain and spend a week in the sea. We will surf and eat and drink wine."

I sighed. "I want to, I really do, but I can't. I can't leave Mom and Torte, not now."

He scooted away a little. "Or do you not want to? Are you still angry with me? I will find a way to prove my love to you, if you come home with me."

"Honestly, I don't know if I want to come back to the ship."

His face flinched as if I had wounded him.

I put my hand over his. "I'm not mad anymore. You don't have to do anything more to prove your feelings for me. I know. I do."

He started to respond, but I squeezed his hand. "Wait, let me finish. When I first came home it was about me being angry—and hurt. I had to get away. I needed distance and space. In some ways it was easy to just be mad at you for lying. If I was mad then I didn't have to think about how much it hurt to be away from you."

I paused to consider my words. Until this very moment I hadn't articulated my thoughts on my transformation since I'd returned home. "But things have changed, Carlos. I've changed. I love Ashland. I love Torte and I've realized that I don't miss the ship. I miss you, but I don't miss that life. I like being settled. I like that everyone in town knows my name and remembers me in pigtails with skinned knees. I like that I can't walk down the street without being stopped by one of the shop owners to talk about town gossip. I even like that people who knew me when I was young call me Juliet. I never thought I would say that, but I do."

He took in a breath and nodded. "I see."

I sat up and grabbed both of his hands. "It's not you. I miss you. I do, Carlos. I don't know what to do. I'm so torn. I want to be with you *and* I want to be here."

He leaned his forehead toward mine. We sat in silence with our heads touching. "I understand, *mi querida*."

I wanted to stay frozen in time. Why did it have to be so hard? Why couldn't I just hate him? He could have made it easy for me to stay angry and not forgive him, but I understood too. He hadn't told me about Ramiro because he made a promise to Ramiro's mother, and then it became too hard. He couldn't find a way to tell me.

Where did that leave us now?

Carlos kissed my head and pulled away. "You do not have to decide tonight. Why don't you sleep on it?"

"What about Ashland? Can you see yourself here?"

He spread his hands out. "Torte is beautiful, *sí*. It is you and your mother—the expression of both of you. It is wonderful, but is it for me? I do not know. I do not know if there is a space for me here."

"We would make space for you."

His lips moved in a smile. His eyes didn't. "Maybe. *Sí*.

I know you would try." He stood and grabbed my hand.
"Come, I will walk you home. You sleep tonight. Tomorrow
we will have a beautiful dinner together and then I must
go back to the ship. At least for now."

I took his hand. I didn't want to let go.

Chapter Nineteen

I don't think I slept much. Most of the night I spent questioning my decision. Should I go back to the ship? Was I making a huge mistake? And then there was Ramiro. I wanted to meet him, but was it fair to insert myself into his life when I didn't know what I was going to do with my own life?

I finally gave up after hours of running different scenarios through my head. I wasn't going to solve the problem by lying in bed and staring at the ceiling. And there was no way I was going back to sleep. There was only one solution: coffee. I got out of bed sometime after four and made myself a pot.

Even coffee tasted off, as I slugged it down and headed for Torte. It was a new week. I should have felt energized and ready to start brainstorming our chocolate extravaganza for the upcoming festival, but I couldn't stop thinking about Carlos. I felt like Shakespeare's lovesick Juliet.

When I made it to Torte and unlocked the front door, I made a promise to myself to stop the crazy loop I was on. It was time to focus on baking. I went through the motions of the morning routine—started the yeast rising, preheated the oven, and made a strong pot of coffee. The leftover evergreen boughs and red roses were all stacked on the front counter. They were still in great shape. We could use them as table decorations. I found Mom's garden shears and snipped the long evergreen garland into smaller half-foot pieces. While the coffee brewed, I adorned each of the tables and booths with a vase of roses and a sprig of evergreen.

With the dining space smelling like a winter forest I poured myself a large cup of coffee and started kneading the bread. Stephanie arrived a while later.

"Whoa, you must have been up early even for you. It looks like you've been here for a while." She tossed her coat on the counter and helped herself to a cup of coffee. "Guy troubles?"

"What?" I scrunched my brow. Was it that obvious?

She shrugged. "I can't sleep when I have guy issues."

"I didn't know that you had guy issues."

"Sometimes. It depends on the guy." She tucked her violet strands behind her ears and cradled her coffee mug. "Want me to start on muffins and cookies as usual?"

"That would be great." I pointed to the butter I had removed from the fridge. "That should be up to room temp."

Stephanie wrapped an apron around her waist. "I heard it went well last night."

"How did you hear that? The sun isn't even up yet. The Ashland rumor mill can't be that fast."

She cubed butter and added it to the stainless steel industrial mixing bowl. "Sterling stopped by on his way home. He brought me some tapas. They were really good."

"Oh, that's right. He mentioned that he might. How did

things go?" I tried to keep my tone casual. Getting information out of Stephanie is like trying to break into a bank vault.

"Fine. He knew that I was studying for midterms and thought I might need some food."

"That was nice of him."

Her nostrils flared slightly. "It's no big deal."

"Right." I kneaded the dough with my elbow. "But it is sweet." I couldn't help but want to be Sterling's cheerleader. I was pretty confident that Stephanie reciprocated his feelings. But I wasn't sure that she would ever tell him that.

I knew that I wasn't going to get anything else out of her. When Mom arrived I would have to put her on the case. Mom has a way of getting the toughest customers—Stephanie included—to open up.

Within an hour there were beautiful rows of cookies and muffins cooling on wire racks and loaves of bread waiting to be sliced and packaged. Stephanie and I had the morning routine nailed down. Yet another reason I couldn't imagine leaving Torte.

By the time Mom and Andy showed up, I had all of our wholesale orders waiting to go in delivery boxes and Stephanie was stocking the pastry case with the first round of morning treats. I blew Mom a quick kiss. "Have to run. I'll be back in a few. Stephanie is in the zone back there, but we haven't started on any specials yet."

Mom laughed and waved. "And to think that some people hate Mondays."

"Not around here," Andy said.

He held the door open for me and I hurried off before anyone else volunteered to do the morning delivery route.

I had tucked a box of mini muffins in for Lance. I was eager to hear what he'd learned from his chat with Rosalind last night.

I breezed through the deliveries. Mondays tended to be slower. Most business owners were focused on getting their shops in order for the new week. Even during OSF's season the theater took a hiatus on Monday. At the Green Goblin I dropped off Craig's bread and two cakes. He pointed to the empty cake plates. "Your samples went over well last night. We might have to double our order."

"That's great. Don't double it yet. I'm going to experiment with alcohol-infused cakes for you this afternoon."

"It's a deal, but these might be gone before noon if last night was any indication. Sunday isn't even my busy night."

"Just give us a call if you run out. Mom or I can always bring more over if you need them."

"You're the best, Jules." Craig thanked me and returned to a stack of paperwork on the bar.

This is why you love Ashland, I told myself as I crossed the plaza. You can't leave this. As if to prove my point I looked up and took in my surroundings. The plaza glowed under yellow streetlamps. A royal-purple Shakespearean banner waved in the wind. In the distance morning bells rang. I could almost smell the sulfur bubbling up from the Lithia Springs fountains. Each shop and storefront seemed to greet me with their royal exteriors and whimsical Old English signs.

My eyes stopped on ShakesBurgers. The lime-green building reminded me of a baking experiment gone completely wrong. I paused and blinked twice. Was that movement inside? A flashlight flicked. That's strange, I thought, crossing the street. Maybe Thomas and the Professor were working already. But why wouldn't they turn the lights on? And would they really be on the crime scene at this early hour?

I stopped and peered in the window. As I stared through the window I noticed something else—the front door was open. Not again. My stomach dropped and I started to back away. A flash of movement caught my eye. I looked up to see Alan Matterson behind the front counter. What was Alan doing here?

Before I could decide what to do next, Alan sprinted to the front door and caught my arm.

"Juliet! What are you doing, man? Trying to give me a heart attack?" He sounded breathless. Sweat dripped from his forehead. His fingers dug into my arm.

"Alan, you're hurting me." I yanked my arm free and almost dropped the delivery box.

Alan looked startled. "Sorry. I didn't mean to hurt you. You surprised me, that's all."

"You surprised me. What are you doing here? This is a crime scene." I pointed to the caution tape.

"No, no, you got this all wrong. This isn't what it looks like." Alan's eyes widened. He glanced to both sides as if we were being watched.

Why was he being so jumpy? Had he lied about Rosalind getting into a fight with Mindy? Maybe he was back at the scene of the crime because he'd left a piece of evidence behind.

A chill ran up my spine. I had learned my lesson and there was no way I was staying here with Alan. I started to back away. He reached for my arm again. I was about to scream when the sound of a screen door slamming banged nearby. Richard Lord stepped out onto the porch of the

Merry Windsor. He was talking on his cell phone and he didn't sound happy.

Richard Lord wasn't exactly my favorite person, but I knew that if I screamed he would do something.

"Stop trying to grab me," I said to Alan. "You're not making yourself look very innocent right now, and Richard Lord is right there. I'll scream for help if you try to touch me again."

Alan threw his hands in the air. He looked absolutely shocked. "Juliet, what you saying? I would never hurt you. I'm sorry. I didn't want you to book outta here without letting me explain, that's all, man, really."

I wasn't sure that I believed him. "Try me. What are you doing snooping through a crime scene?"

"I wasn't snooping."

"That's what it looked like to me. You're sneaking around in the dark."

"I know." Alan sighed. "It's not what you think, though. I didn't hurt Mindy and I'm not trying to hurt you."

"How about if you tell me what you were doing then?"

"I'm digging around for my contract."

"Contract?"

He nodded and looked around to make sure no one was nearby. Why was he so paranoid? "Mindy and I were going to hook up, partner together, you know."

"What?" I shifted the box in my arms. "But I thought you hated Mindy. You yelled at her at the meeting for taking over your dream."

"I know. She was one cool chick. That was her plan. I was supposed to wig out and make it look like I was totally pissed."

"She asked you to yell at her? Alan, none of this makes sense."

"Yeah. I know. It was part of her plan. She thought it would be cool if we kept things quiet—laid low, you know. At least at first."

"Quiet about partnering?"

"Yeah. Mindy wasn't getting along with Reggie, the cook she hired. He was supposed to be some hotshot cook from Portland, but he didn't know his way around the kitchen at all. And his sanitary practices were terrible. Mindy and I met last week. She offered me a job as head chef and a small piece of the business."

"But I thought you hated chain restaurants like Shakes-Burgers."

"I do, but I'm out of dough. I put everything I had into the Jester. I'm too old to start over again. Mindy told me that I could add some of my street food to the menu. She was going to let me create a daily Ashland special. They've done that in some of their other locations and I guess it's been a success. She was a smart businesswoman. She knew that the town was upset about them coming in and about me losing the restaurant. That wasn't her fault. It was mine. I was in over my head. I should have stayed with the food cart. Now I'm working for the man. Go figure."

"Running a restaurant and food booth are two very different things, aren't they?"

Alan nodded. "Yeah. Totally. I didn't realize what I was getting into. I wish I had never bothered, but anyway, Mindy thought that Ashland would embrace ShakesBurgers if she hired me as the new chef and if I was a partial owner she thought that would help lend some credibility."

"That is smart."

"I know, but we never had a chance to finalize the contracts. I was supposed to meet her here the morning that she was killed. We were going to sign the paperwork and she was going to cut Reggie loose."

My mind raced to keep up. Alan and Mindy were going to partner together and Alan was going to be her head chef. That changed everything. Why would Alan kill Mindy if she was helping to get him out of debt and giving him a job?

"What are you doing here then?"

"I have to find the paperwork. I'm not sure that the Professor believes me. I told him all of this, of course, but I don't have any proof. Mindy did. Without proof, it's just my word, man, that's all. For all the Professor knows, I'm making it up to protect myself. He said they looked for the contracts, but couldn't find them. I know it's stupid but I couldn't sleep this morning. Mindy gave me a key." Alan reached into his pocket and held up a silver key. "I thought I would come by before everyone was up and have a quick look myself. Maybe Mindy hid the paperwork. She was worried that Reggie was going to be upset—even violent—when she fired him. She wanted me here with her as backup when she did it. I figured she made sure to keep the contracts somewhere out of sight so that he didn't see them."

"Why did she think that Reggie might get violent?"

Alan shrugged. "She didn't say. She just asked me if I would be willing to be here when she let him go. I said I would, although I wasn't sure what help a potbellied old hippie would be to her. She didn't care. She just made me promise that I would be here."

"What about Mathew? Why don't you talk to him? He and Mindy were partners. I'm sure he has copies of all the contracts."

"Nah. Mindy said this was a deal just between her and me. I got the vibe that she and Mathew were on the outs."

"And you haven't seen Reggie since? Do you think there's any way that he could have known that Mindy was going to fire him?"

"He might have split. I haven't seen him." Alan frowned. "I don't think he knows, unless he found the contracts. Do you think he could have? Maybe that's why they're missing. If he found them he could have ripped them up and no one would have ever known what Mindy was planning."

"Maybe, but there must be digital versions somewhere even if he destroyed the paper copies," I said. My arms were getting tired. I shifted the box. "You've told the Professor and Thomas all of this, right?"

Alan nodded. "Everything. I told them everything."

"Even about Reggie?"

"Yeah."

"That's good." The sky was turning brighter. I needed to get to OSF, figure out what Lance had learned last night and get back to Torte. "Alan, I believe you but I don't think it's a good idea for you to be sneaking around inside whether you have a key or not. Hey, speaking of a key, did you tell the Professor that you have a key?"

"No. I didn't."

"I think you should call him and tell him that Mindy gave you a key. That might be the proof you're looking for, and make sure you explain that Mindy was scared about being alone with Reggie. That might be important."

"I will, and sorry again if I scared you. I really didn't mean to, man."

At that moment Richard Lord shouted, "I'm done" into his phone and slammed it on the porch railing. He caught me staring at him, glared, turned on his heels, and stormed back inside.

"It's okay," I said, returning my attention to Alan. Alan may have just cleared himself and given me a new suspect to focus on—Reggie. After I met with Lance I intended to find out everything I could about Mindy's cook.

Chapter Twenty

I repositioned the box and headed for OSF. The theater complex was a short walk up the hill from downtown. In the summer "the bricks," as locals call the courtyard in front of the Elizabethan and Bowmer theaters, would be packed with tourists milling around before a show. The green stage outside hosts a variety of musicians and artists who entertain theatergoers while they wait for the featured performance.

Not surprisingly the bricks were deserted this morning. I couldn't believe that Lance was in his office this early. He claimed that he used the off season to catch up on his beauty sleep, so he must have something particularly juicy to share if he was willing to drag himself out of bed before the sun.

I wondered if the theater would be locked. When I made it to the front door there was a note taped to the window. It was written in Lance's dramatic scroll: *Come around back.*

Lance's office is on the east side of the building. He has

a corner office with windows that look out onto the courtyard and down into Lithia Park. To reach the back entrance I passed the ivy-covered walls of the Elizabethan theater. The theater is modeled in Shakespearean fashion with balconies and open-air seating. It's truly one of the most spectacular places to watch a production. There's nothing like the scent of honeysuckle and the glimmer of stars above while taking in a world-class show.

The back door had been propped open with a rock. I let myself in and headed to Lance's office. I knew my way around the theater complex. When I was younger I had participated in a number of productions. The company often hires child actors from town as extras or background singers in some of the musicals. I loved getting to dress up as a kid. The props and costume department were like a playground. The other kid actors and I would fence with fake swords and dress up in ornate powdered wigs and billowing skirts.

As I entered my teenage years the lure of being on stage dissipated for me. I preferred to watch the action on stage from the comfort of the seats. Since I'd been home Lance had been trying to convince me to give it another go. I'd been successful thus far in holding him at bay, but he was persistent.

"Delivery!" I called from the hallway.

"It's open, come in," Lance replied from his office.

I walked inside. His office was a testament to OSF's world-renowned reputation. Playbills and awards lined the walls. Plaques and statues were displayed on shelves above his desk. Lance had a vision for OSF and had been successful in seeing it through to fruition.

"Darling, you're right on time." He sat behind a mahogany desk. Black reading glasses were pressed to the tip of his nose and he had a script in his hand. "Have a seat."

I sat in the chair in front of his desk and handed him the box of mini muffins. "Your special order, sir."

"Feisty this morning, aren't we? I like it, Juliet. I like it a lot. This is why you need to be on the stage. Harness that energy into something spicy."

"Lance, you know that is never going to happen."

He removed his reading glasses and opened the pastry box. "One can always dream."

I waited for him to peel off the wrapper from a bran muffin. He broke the tiny muffin in half and took a bite.

"Delicious, as always. But brining me healthy treats, darling. What is that all about? Are you trying to send me a not-so-subtle message?"

"I thought you might want something with a little fiber after last night's feast."

Lance rolled his eyes. "Healthy? Please."

"Noted. No bran in the future. Now, tell me what you learned from Rosalind last night. You two looked pretty chummy."

"Patience, darling. Patience. You're so eager."

"Lance." I pursed my lips.

He threw his head back. "Please." Then he ate the second half of the muffin piece by piece. He could have easily consumed the entire half in one bite. When he finished he brushed his hands in the air and looked at me expectantly. "No coffee?"

"Did you want coffee?"

"I believe that goes without saying. Of course I want coffee."

"Guess you'll have to make it yourself or have your

assistant do it. We're not in the coffee delivery business at Torte."

"Not even for your dearest pal?" He made a pathetic face.

"I know what you're trying to do, Lance. Get on with it. Do you have news from last night? Because if you don't I have to get back to the bakeshop."

"And to your dreamy husband. I can't blame you for that."

"To work, Lance. Some of us aren't on hiatus."

He gasped and tapped a pile of scripts on his desk. "Hiatus. Do you want to read all these dreadful scripts?"

"No, thanks." I smiled. "Are they all bad?"

"You do not even want to know. I'm considering poking my eyes out soon. I'm dying for an original script. Is that too much to ask?"

I shrugged.

"If I have to read one more fangs-in-the-neck horror script, I'm going to absolutely scream."

"Everyone is submitting vampire stories?"

"That or the most pretentious dialogue. I'm going to have to widen my reach. This year's submission pile is about to go straight into the recycling bin." He pointed to an overflowing basket of paper near his desk. "You don't want to write by chance, do you?"

"No, thanks. I'll stick with pastry."

Lance took a strawberry crumb muffin from the box and ate it in one bite this time. "A wise idea. You do know pastry. And I do like this sweet delight."

"Okay. We've covered pastry and that you have a stack of scripts to read. Can we get back to Mindy's murder? Did you learn anything from Rosalind last night?"

He ran his fingers over his goatee. "I did, indeed."

"And?"

Lance leaned his elbows on his desk and spoke in a conspiratorial tone. "Well, it seems that Rosalind has been successful in her quest to sway the town council. She got them to pass a new city ordinance that requires all businesses downtown to adhere to strict guidelines in terms of name, design, et cetera. She's creating quite the Old English village."

"But she just gave everyone the petition at the meeting on Friday night. How did she already get the council to pass the ordinance?"

"Your guess is as good as mine. She didn't say how she made it happen, but she was very pleased that she had done it."

"Pleased as in you think she could have killed Mindy?"

Lance strummed his fingers on the desk. "That's another question, isn't it? I got the impression that Rosalind would do anything—*anything*—to protect her precious town."

"Anything as in murder?"

"Who knows, but perhaps."

"How could she have killed Mindy though? Rosalind is in her seventies. Do you think she has the strength?"

"That depends on her motivation. As I tell my actors, everything comes down to motivation."

"Maybe." I wasn't convinced. Watching Rosalind struggle to sit down made me wonder how she could have managed to hold Mindy down. Something didn't add up. Although Rosalind was pretty banged up last night. I wondered how she got the scratches and bruises on her arm.

"Chin up, darling," Lance said. "That gloomy look isn't becoming on you."

I sat back in my chair. "Thanks." I sighed. "I just feel like we're missing something, you know?"

Lance gave me a devilish grin. "I do enjoy being on a case with you. Your beautiful brain just cannot quit, can it?"

I scowled at him, which had the opposite effect that I was hoping for. He laughed and then clapped his hands together. "This is too much fun."

"This isn't fun. Mindy is dead. Someone who we know may have done it." I started to get up. "Thanks for the info from Rosalind. I better go."

"Wait, wait." He pointed to the chair. "I haven't gotten to the best part."

"The best part?"

"Don't stand there with your mouth hanging open. Sit." He nodded to the chair.

I plopped back down. Lance grinned. He was enjoying this way too much.

"Well?"

"Well, I did learn one other tidbit of information from our Ashland ambassador, Rosalind."

"Which is?"

"Oh, Juliet, if only I had a mirror. It brings me such pleasure to watch you squirm."

"I'm not squirming."

He nodded to my foot, which was bouncing on the floor.

"Okay, fine." I stopped moving my foot. "Now I'm not."

I waited. Lance leaned back and savored the moment.

"It seems that in preparing her case for the city council that Rosalind did a bit of her own digging into Mindy's background and business practices."

"And?"

"And it seems that Mindy wasn't entirely truthful about her staff."

"What do you mean?"

"I'm sure that you heard that she hired a top-notch cook, Reggie—our Brutus—from Portland. The rumor around town was that she scooped him right up from one of the best restaurants."

"I did hear that."

"According to Rosalind, that's not true."

Lance paused and studied me. "Rosalind learned that Reggie didn't get his training at a world-class restaurant. It turns out his training was behind bars."

"What?"

He waited for me to make the connection and then nodded enthusiastically. "Reggie is a convicted felon. He was just released from prison. He hasn't been working at a swanky restaurant, he's been a cook for some nasty fellows in orange jumpsuits."

"Reggie was in prison?"

"It's true. Isn't that just a divine twist?" He thumbed through the stack of scripts. "In fact, I should write this myself. A prison cook. How dramatic. Do you think he served up a slice of murder with that greasy junk Mindy had on the menu?"

If Reggie had learned that Mindy was planning to hire Alan, could he have killed her? What had he done to land in jail?

Lance cleared his throat. "Darling, what are you thinking? I can almost see the brain cells firing in that pretty head of yours."

"Nothing." I stared at a glossy framed photograph of one of OSF's leading ladies on the wall.

"She's stunning, isn't she?" Lance said. "That was from a production of *The Merchant of Venice* two summers ago. She embodied Portia." He dropped the affectation from his speech. "Jules, all kidding aside, is everything okay? You don't seem like yourself."

"Why?"

"You've been different the past few weeks. That gorgeous face of yours gives away everything." He tossed a muffin wrapper in the garbage can. "You and I are so alike. Have you ever considered that you can only love one thing?"

"I'm not sure I know what you mean."

He waved his long, lean arm across the pile of scripts and then up the wall behind him. "This. This is what I love—the theater. You love pastry. Maybe like so many of Shakespeare's lovelorn characters we can't have both."

Lance rarely broke free of his OSF persona. He'd never mentioned his love life, or anything about his personal life, for that matter. Our friendship revolved around his quick-witted banter. This was an important moment in our friendship. I didn't want to lose this moment.

"Your love life is a mess too?" I leaned my elbows on his desk.

His face softened. "There was a time when I had it all. That doesn't make for good drama though. Life is conflict, darling."

A siren wailed outside. Our moment of authenticity was lost. Lance tapped his bony fingers on his goatee. "You don't think there's been another murder, do you?"

"I hope not." I stood and picked up the delivery box. "Listen, I have to get back to the shop. Thanks for the info from Rosalind."

"Are you holding out on me, Juliet?"

"Not at all," I lied. A clock chimed behind me as if on cue. "The coffee rush is going to hit soon. I have to get back. We'll chat later. I'm going to see what I can learn about Reggie. I wonder if Thomas knows."

Lance shrugged. "No idea. But you must keep me in the loop. Agreed?"

"Agreed."

He blew me a kiss. "Ta-ta. Run along. I'll stop by later for a coffee since you so rudely neglected to bring me one."

I turned and hurried out the door before he could stop me. Lance loved the drama of Ashland gossip. I couldn't exactly blame him. Even more than the gossip, I knew that our brief exchange had shifted something between us. Lance had had his heart broken. By who? I knew that mining emotional information was going to take some time. That was fine. I wasn't in a hurry.

Chapter Twenty-one

On the way back to Torte questions swirled in my brain. Why would Mindy hire a convicted felon? Did she know that Reggie had done jail time? Maybe she had found out about his jail stint and planned to fire him. If he had resorted to physical violence in the past, could he have killed her?

The plaza was starting to come to life. Business owners had placed sandwich boards on the sidewalk and the smell of bacon wafted in the air. A police car had parked in front of the Merry Windsor, blocking two spaces in front of the hotel. That must have been the siren that Lance and I had heard.

I slowed my pace. Richard Lord was spewing profanity at a uniformed officer. "You can't take spaces away from paying customers."

The officer spoke with his hands, obviously trying to calm Richard down. "Sir, I have my orders."

Richard adjusted his terry cloth bathrobe. "I want a word with your boss."

I ducked behind a propane heater when Richard looked

in my direction. As much as I wanted to stay and eaves-drop, I had to get back to the bakeshop.

Andy greeted me when I returned to Torte. "Hey, boss. We were just wondering if we should call out a search party."

"Sorry." I held up the empty delivery box. "I got stuck at OSF. You know Lance. He likes to chat."

Andy poured foam into a paper cup. "That's true. No worries. We've got everything under control here."

The pastry case had been stocked. There were a hand-ful of customers waiting for coffee and a few tables that looked like they might need refills, but otherwise Torte was running like a well-oiled machine.

"Good work, Andy." I squeezed past a customer and headed for the kitchen.

Mom was peeling apples and Stephanie was slicing bread. "Hey, you two," I called, walking straight to the sink to wash my hands after putting the delivery box back in its place. "Looks like everything is running smoothly."

"Did you think we were going to burn the place down in your absence?" Mom winked.

"No." I dried my hands and gave her a funny look. "I feel bad leaving you in the lurch. I got stuck talking to Lance."

Mom gave me a knowing smile. "I can't imagine how that could have happened."

"What are you working on and what do you want me to do?"

Stephanie stacked thin slices of bread. "I'm making French toast."

"Doesn't that sound good this morning?" Mom asked. "We had some leftover bread and I was in the mood to make my applesauce. We'll serve the French toast with sliced apples, cinnamon, and whipped cream as our breakfast special."

"Yum." I put my hand over my stomach. "Can I sign up to be the taste tester?"

Mom offered me an apple slice. "Do you need something to tide you over?"

"No, I'm fine. Should I start on lunch prep? Are we going to do another soup?"

"They've been selling so well. I was hoping that you would make your creamy chicken noodle soup," Mom said as she placed the sliced apples in a saucepan and sprinkled them with cinnamon and sugar.

"For sure. I haven't made that for a while," I replied. "We should also talk about the Chocolate Fest. Can you believe that it's next month? I started sketching out a plan but I want your input. You too, Stephanie."

Stephanie looked up from the bread. "What's Chocolate Fest?"

Mom lit the front burner on the stove and set the apples on it. She added water and a splash of maple syrup. "It's only the best weekend in Ashland. Weren't you here for it last year?"

Stephanie shook her head. "Nope. I don't remember it."

"Oh, that's right. You weren't working much last winter. You were taking extra classes."

"That term sucked." Stephanie shuddered. "I had three math classes," she said to me. "Someone told me to get them all out of the way together. Bad idea. Bad."

Mom stirred the apples. "Chocolate Fest takes place at Ashland Springs Hotel and brings in some of the best chocolatiers from all over the state. There are chocolate tastings, chocolate sculpture classes, presentations on sugar art, demos, and much more. Last year there were ten thousand people who attended over the course of the three days. We have to have tastings for everyone and this year we've been asked to be one of the presenting vendors. That means we'll have one of the biggest displays."

"Whoa, that's a lot of chocolate."

"It is," I said. "That's why we need to get started this week. It's going to be all hands on deck."

Mom nodded. "I'm so glad you're going to be here this year, Juliet. Last year I thought I could sleep for a week after the event. I can't even imagine what it's going to be like this year. It's such an honor to be named one of the presenting vendors, but it's going to be a lot of extra work. I hope everyone's up for it."

Stephanie cracked eggs into a mixing bowl for the French toast batter. "We'll all help, right, Jules?"

"Of course. I'm excited about it. I have some big plans. You guys might need to bring me back down to earth. I'm thinking chocolate fountains, chocolate pasta, chocolate art, chocolate, chocolate, chocolate. I could keep going."

"No, don't." Mom waved her hand in front of her face. "You're going to give me a chocolate rush."

"It's going to be absolutely delicious. Think Picasso in chocolate."

"Do you win anything?" Stephanie asked.

"I don't think so." I looked to Mom for confirmation.

"Not exactly. There's not a cash prize, but there are awards for different categories and some of the pastry chefs who've won in the past have gone on to do great things. It's a huge honor to win."

Stephanie added milk to the eggs. "Cool."

I pulled a stock pot from the top shelf for my soup. "Totally cool. We're going to win something. There's no better place on the planet than Torte and it's time everyone else learns that."

"I'm glad I raised such a humble daughter." Mom laughed.

"You have built an empire here in Ashland and I want everyone to know it, that's all."

"An empire?"

"A pastry empire."

Mom turned the flame on the burner down. "I like the sound of that. A pastry empire. Don't we wish, but empire or no empire the Chocolate Festival is always a highlight of the year. People come from all over Southern Oregon and other parts of the state. It's going to be fun, and exhausting."

I began dicing onions, garlic, celery, and carrots for my chicken soup. "Let's start thinking through each tasting and narrow down what we can realistically produce on a grand scale."

Mom agreed. "Right. We have to think about things that will hold up well and things that we can make in giant quantities."

"Oh, and I want to do a couple chocolate wedding cakes," I said. "If we're going to expand our cake business the Chocolate Fest is the perfect time to showcase what we can do."

"Good idea."

"Speaking of cakes, I need to create a booze cake for Craig at the Green Goblin."

"A booze cake?" Mom covered the apples with a lid.

"He said that his customers loved the cakes I brought

over yesterday. He wants both of them plus some kind of cake with alcohol. He's going for a bar theme."

"Smart man."

"That's what I said. I'm thinking of trying a marzipan cake with Grand Marnier cherry liqueur."

"How decadent." Mom looked at Stephanie "I don't know, what do you think, Stephanie? Are we sophisticated enough for marzipan and cherry liqueur cakes?"

Stephanie added vanilla to the egg mixture. "Doubt it. I don't think I've ever tried cherry liqueur."

"You are in for a treat," I said. My veggies were diced and ready to sauté. "I'll give you a taste as soon as I get this soup going."

The key to a flavorful chicken soup is the stock. We make all of our stocks from scratch at Torte. It's an easy process. Whenever we roast chickens we save the bones, skin, and any extra meat, then we simmer them in water with rough-chopped carrots, celery, corn, and onions for an hour. Once the stock is ready, we skim off the fat and store it in plastic containers. It will keep for a week in the refrigerator or can be frozen for months.

I stirred the veggies on low heat and added a container of our frozen chicken stock. Soon the veggies had sweated and the onions had turned translucent and the stock had melted down. Then I added heaps of shredded chicken, salt, pepper, a dash of oregano, and a little water. That would cook for another hour before I added the noodles and finished it off with some sour cream. The end result would be a slightly creamy soup bursting with healthy flavors.

While Mom and Stephanie grilled French toast and continually restocked the pastry cases, I started on my marzipan cake. I planned to soak layers of sponge cake in the Grand Marnier. Marzipan would be the glue for each layer and then I would finish the cake with a simple cherry liqueur glaze. Not only would it be a rich and unique taste, but it should hold up well.

Marzipan is an almond sugar usually used to form into the shape of fruits and vegetables or dipped in chocolate. It can be a beautiful medium to work with. I remember stopping at a candy shop in Germany that was famous for their marzipan displays. It was almost impossible to tell the difference between a real lemon and their artistic rendering of a marzipan lemon.

Marzipan paste can also be used in a variety of cakes, pastries, and baked goods. I pulsed almonds into a fine powder in the Cuisinart. Then I added powdered sugar, almond extract, egg whites, and rosewater. Rosewater is essential in making a good marzipan. The water helps bind the paste together and adds a slight hint of sweetness.

Once the ingredients had been incorporated, I placed waxed paper on the island and worked the paste by hand until it had a firm consistency. I reserved half of it for my cake and rolled the rest of the marzipan into a long roll that I covered in plastic wrap and chilled in the refrigerator. It should last for at least two or three weeks.

"Is that extra?" Mom asked as I walked to the fridge with the extra marzipan.

"You want a taste?"

She shook her head. "Not right now. I'm up to my elbows in apples." She wasn't kidding. Apple peels piled high in a mixing bowl. She worked the peeler like a pro. Coring and peeling each apple in one quick fluid motion.

"What if we do hand-dipped chocolate marzipans for the Chocolate Fest?"

"Great idea. Those will be easy to make." I paused and caught Stephanie's eye. She was topping an order of French toast with cinnamon apples and whipped cream. "When we get a break later I'll show you how to work with marzipan. In fact, we could get you started making candies for the fest. They'll keep for weeks in the fridge."

Mom tossed an apple peel into the bowl. "Check off one chocolate item. How many more to go?"

"Just a few." I smiled. In the front a crowd had begun to gather around the espresso bar.

Andy had talked to Mom and me about hosting weekly coffee tastings in the winter. We decided that Monday mornings would be designated for his "brewology class" as he called it. About fifteen people had shown up for Andy's demonstration on the difference types of grinds. "The kind of filter you use matters," he said holding up a flat-bottomed filter. "Paper, cone, flat bottom—they all require a different grind."

A woman raised her hand and asked Andy his recommendation for a gold filter.

I stopped and listened in for a minute. Andy chatted easily with each coffee connoisseur and he knew his stuff. I was impressed. I thought that he was going to offer customers tastes of different blends and coffee concoctions. He wasn't kidding about brewology. He was teaching a collegiate-level course on coffee.

How had Mom and I gotten so lucky?

I was about to return to the kitchen when I noticed Thomas crossing the plaza toward ShakesBurgers. I wanted to talk to him about Reggie, so I motioned to Andy that I would be right back and hurried across the street.

Thomas was clicking pictures of the front of the restaurant on his iPad.

"Morning," I called as I came up behind him.

He clicked off the iPad and greeted me with a bright smile. "Morning. What are you doing out and about at this time of the day? Shouldn't you be slaving away in the kitchen?"

"I'm always slaving away."

"Oh sure, we all know that you sit around and eat bonbons, Jules, come on. Come clean."

"You got me, officer." I threw my hands in the air. "Hey, speaking of coming clean, that's kind of why I came over here. I wanted to talk to you about something I found out that might be important in the case."

"Oh, yeah?"

"It's about Reggie, the cook that Mindy hired at Shakes-Burgers."

"What about him?"

I checked to make sure that no one was around. "Have you looked into his background? I heard that he was just released from jail."

Thomas nodded. "The Professor and I are on it. It's standard procedure to do background checks on every suspect."

"Even me?"

"Even you. Especially you." Thomas grinned. "No, but seriously, we have our eye on Reggie. He was arrested on assault-and-battery charges."

"Do you know what happened?"

"He got into a bar fight. Knocked a guy unconscious.

The guy lost hearing in one ear and suffered minor brain damage."

"Oh my gosh."

"Yeah, bad stuff, Jules. Stay away from him."

"Are you planning to arrest him?"

Thomas shrugged. "That's the Professor's call, not mine. But the Professor told me to keep Reggie in my sight. We've got a team staked out at the Merry Windsor where Reggie is staying. We're waiting for the coroner's report and a few other things to come in. Between you and me I think that we're close to making an arrest. I know the Professor is trying to tighten up Reggie's motive."

"Did Alan come talk to you?"

"Why?"

"He told me that Mindy offered him the job as head chef and a percentage of the business. If Reggie found out, don't you think that's motive?"

Thomas nodded. "It's possible. We need evidence, though."

Thomas stiffened. I watched his gaze shift from me to something across the street. I turned to see what or who he was looking at. I knew immediately—Carlos.

Chapter Twenty-two

Carlos caught my eye and started to saunter toward us. I said good-bye to Thomas and left as quickly as I could. The two of them hadn't exactly been on the best terms since Lake of the Woods. In a town the size of Ashland it was nearly impossible to keep them apart, but I'd been doing my best. It wasn't as if Carlos had anything to worry about. Thomas and I dated when we were kids. We were friends now, nothing more. I had told Carlos that repeatedly. He insisted that Thomas was still in love with me. There was a chance that was true, but I didn't see any reason to feed into Carlos's suspicions. We had enough to work out between us without adding Thomas to the mix.

"Julieta, you look lovely this morning. Did you sleep well?" Carlos reached for me the second I was within his grasp and pulled me into his arms.

I wondered if Thomas was watching us embrace.

"Not bad," I lied, returning his hug.

"You are a terrible liar, *mi querida*." Carlos kissed the top of my head. "When will you learn this?"

"Never." I pulled away from him. He was leaving tomorrow. How was that possible? It felt like he just arrived. Things were finally starting to feel normal between us. Maybe Lance was right. Maybe I couldn't have both. Was it Torte or Carlos?

"What is it?"

"Nothing," I lied again.

Carlos took my hand and kissed it. His lips lingered on my skin. I inhaled. "I will miss you too."

"How did you know?"

"It is in your eyes. They do not lie."

I leaned into his chest. "I don't want you to go, Carlos."

"I do not want to leave."

We stood together in a comfortable silence for a minute. People passed by. I didn't care. Being with Carlos felt right. Was I making a huge mistake?

Finally Carlos kissed my hand again and said, "Come. We must get to work. It is a busy day, *sí*?"

I sighed. "It is."

"Then we will cook and make some beautiful food in the kitchen."

"Let's do it," I agreed as Carlos led me toward Torte. I wasn't sure how I was going to concentrate for the rest of the day, but I would give it my best effort. "I didn't even ask how the rest of your night was."

Carlos shook his head. "It was terrible. That hotel is in terrible shape. It does not smell good. And Mr. Lord would not let me to my room without asking about Jose. He thinks we are planning something. He asked me again and again what I know about Jose's vineyard and wanted to know why Jose was at Torte yesterday. That man is horrible." He scowled and continued. "And the police, they were around all night and this morning. I got no sleep."

"I'm so sorry. We should have found somewhere else for you. Mom offered to have you stay at her place."

"No, no, it is fine. I wanted to be close to you. I look out my window last night and see the light on in your apartment. It made me feel good to know that I was so close."

I squeezed his hand and kissed his cheek before opening the door at Torte. "It makes me feel good too."

Andy had small paper tasting cups lined up on the espresso bar when Carlos and I walked inside. The crowd had grown. "Okay, give this a shot." He motioned to the tray. "This is my newest creation, the chunky monkey. It's not for the sweet of heart, as my mom likes to say. If you don't like sugar this one might not be for you, but I think it's pretty good and kind of funky." He laughed. "Get it, funky—chunky."

Carlos whispered in my ear. "He is a good teacher and he knows his coffee. He is so young to know this much, no? Did he learn this from your mother?"

I shook my head. "I don't think so. Maybe some of it, but he's self-taught. He's a very motivated student. Every time a new coffee vendor visits the shop he always sits in on the meetings and asks really good questions."

"Julieta, do you understand how special this staff is? We do not have staff this good on the ship. We do not have culinary graduates who are this dedicated and know so much at such a young age."

"I know. That's why I can't leave." I met his eyes.

His jaw flexed. "I understand this," he said quietly.

Andy's chunky monkey was an instant hit. "Is there banana in this?" someone asked.

"Yep. You like it?" Andy asked.

The woman held up an empty tasting cup. "Can I have seconds?"

"I can make you a sixteen-ounce if you want."

"Yes, please," the woman said.

"Me too!" someone else shouted.

Andy winked at me and started pulling espresso shots. I walked to the back. Carlos followed me. He stopped near the office where Mom was working on paperwork. "I need to talk to your mother for a moment. Will you excuse me?"

I nodded but as I continued on to wash my hands I wondered what Carlos wanted to talk to Mom about. Was he trying to get her on board with the idea of me returning to the ship with him? I hoped he wasn't putting her in an awkward position.

Whatever they were discussing they wanted to keep private. Carlos shut the office door behind him. I'd have to ask Mom later. I knew that she would speak for herself, but I didn't want her to feel like she was in the middle of my problems. She had enough to worry about. Which reminded me that I wanted to check in with her later and find out if she and the Professor had had a chance to talk too.

Right now I needed to assemble my marzipan cake. I sliced thin layers of sponge cake and soaked them in cherry liqueur. The alcohol permeated the light sponge.

Sterling showed up as I began rolling the marzipan into sheets. "It smells like a bar back here, Jules."

I reached across the counter to high-five Stephanie. "That's exactly what we're going for."

Stephanie and Sterling shared an amused look. "If that's what you're going for, I guess that's good." Sterling wore a gray hoodie with a retro peace symbol on the front. "Do you need any help with lunch prep or should I work the counter?"

"Why don't you work the counter? Andy's been doing his brewology class and it looks like all of his coffee students are sticking around."

"Works for me," Sterling said. Before he left to wash up and get an apron, he said something under his breath to Stephanie. She actually smiled. A genuine smile from Stephanie was almost unheard of. What had Sterling said to crack her sullen exterior? Maybe Carlos's advice was paying off.

I returned to my cake, placing the first layer of sponge. Then I covered it with a thin sheet of marzipan and piped almond–whipped cream between each layer. I continued to stack each layer this way until I reached the top layer. I had reserved some Grand Marnier and brushed it over the top and side of the cake. Once it had soaked into the sponge I piped the rest of it with whipped cream and decorated it with cherries. Craig would need to store this cake in the refrigerator.

"It looks good, Jules," Stephanie said when I showed her the cake.

"Yeah, I think it turned out well." I boxed it up. "I'm going to take this over to Craig. Be right back."

The coffee tasters had started to queue at the counter. Sterling was taking each order on the paper tickets we used and handing them back to Stephanie. That was something else I wanted to upgrade along with our ovens. It would be much easier and faster if we used iPads to take orders. That way Sterling—or anyone working the front counter—could log an order and a payment at the same time. I'd been doing some research into point-of-sale systems and they were surprisingly affordable. Plus, the vast majority of our customers pay with debit cards. Implementing a new payment and ordering system would allow them to swipe their cards and take a seat.

I stopped at the office on my way out. The door was still shut. I knocked lightly and called, "Hey, you two, are you still in there?"

Mom swung the door open. She held a crumpled tissue in her hand and her eyes looked red. Had she been crying? "We were just finishing up."

Carlos sat in a chair next to the desk. He stood. "*Sí*, your mother and I were having a nice talk."

Mom nodded and stuffed the wadded tissue into her pocket. She squeezed his arm. "We were." She sighed. "We were reminiscing about your father."

Or were they talking about me? I had a feeling that Mom was covering for something, but I didn't have time to ask.

"I'm heading out on a quick delivery. I think Sterling and Steph might need a hand. The lunch rush is starting."

Mom glanced behind her at the clock. "Oh, dear! I had no idea it was so late." She jumped back and nearly bumped her head on the filing cabinet. Carlos stepped aside to let her pass. She made a beeline for the kitchen. I heard her call to Andy and Sterling, "I'm here!"

Carlos stood in the doorway.

"What were you talking to Mom about?"

"Nothing." His eyes danced with delight. "She was telling me about your father and how they started this place. That is all."

"Right." I knew he wasn't telling me the truth. "I should go."

"I will be here."

For now, I thought. Tomorrow, Carlos would be gone and things would be back to normal again. Whatever normal was.

I was lost in my thoughts and didn't hear someone shouting my name.

"Juliet!" a voice boomed.

I startled and almost dropped the cake.

Richard Lord waved from the front porch of the Merry Windsor where one of his young staff members was scrubbing the wooden steps under Richard's watchful eye. He had changed out of his bathrobe, but the police car was still parked in front of the building. "I want a word."

"No time, Richard." I pointed to the cake box. "Highly perishable."

"Juliet! I'm coming over when you're back," he called after me as I continued along the sidewalk.

Great. It was too bad we didn't have a secret back entrance at Torte. I was going to have to hope that when I returned Richard would be berating his staff and not notice me slip back inside.

Craig practically did a backflip over the marzipan torte. "This is awesome, Jules. Thank you." He lifted the lid on one of the cake plates, revealing a quarter of a red velvet cake. "People are eating this up. It's barely noon and I've sold more than half of that cake."

"Cake for breakfast?"

"I guess. Breakfast beer and cake—who knew?"

"Let me know if you need a restock later."

"Will do."

As I started to leave, Craig stopped me. "Hey, before you go, did you hear the news?"

"No, what news?"

"About Jose."

"Jose Ortega?"

Craig started to answer when the sound of glass shattering reverberated throughout the room. A customer had dropped a pint glass. Beer and glass shards sprayed on the floor. "I better help," he said, reaching for a rag.

"Of course. We'll talk later. Be sure to keep the torte in the fridge."

Craig gave me a thumbs-up and went to mop up the spill. Two people had referenced Jose in the past couple of days. First Richard Lord and now Craig. I wondered what was going on with Jose.

Chapter Twenty-three

I tried to slink back to Torte. There was no sign of Richard on the porch as I passed the Merry Windsor, just his maintenance kid rubbing oil on the already shiny wooden porch slats and a uniformed police officer who appeared to be scanning the plaza. Carlos had mentioned that the police had been at the Windsor last night as well. I wondered again if it could have something to do with Mindy's murder and whether Richard could be involved.

Whew, what luck, I thought as I scurried past the hotel. At least I avoided a Richard Lord encounter.

At Torte the coffee crowd had dispersed to tables. Sterling took an order at the counter. Andy was working the espresso machine and Mom held a tray of sandwiches in her arms. "Jules, you're back. There's someone who wants to talk to you, but I need you to finish your soup." She nodded to the far booth. Richard Lord was seated with his arms crossed and a scowl on his face.

"I would have finished the soup myself, but I'm not sure what ratio you use for the sour cream."

"Not a problem. That will buy me a minute. Thanks for

the heads-up." I ducked between two customers waiting for coffee and made my way to the back. What was Richard's problem?

Carlos manned the Panini machine. "Julieta, it is busy today, no?"

"Mondays," I replied, lifting the lid on my soup. Since many restaurants in town are closed on Monday, it ends up being one of our busiest days. Mom had added noodles. It needed a quarter cup of sour cream to give it a nice tang and it would be ready to serve. I stirred in the cream and dished up four bowls. "How many more do we need?" I asked Stephanie.

She flipped through the order tickets. "Three."

I arranged the soup bowls on a tray. "I'll take these out and come back for the next round." Carefully holding the tray with two hands, I squeezed past Carlos and the customers waiting for coffee.

Most restaurants number their tables, that way any member of the wait-and kitchen staff can bring orders out with ease. On the cruise ship it was a much bigger production. Our waitstaff had specific sections they were responsible for. At Torte all of us lend a hand when needed. Mom took an Ashland approach to identify tables—she named them after Shakespearean characters. We had fun with her inventive names.

"There's a problem with Othello," Sterling would say. "They want more sugar. Classic."

My order tickets for the soup were for Macbeth, Brutus, and Caesar. I sensed a theme. I handed customers two of the bowls at Caesar, weaved my way to Brutus, and ended at Macbeth. "Here's your soup," I said, passing over a full bowl.

Mathew took the bowl from my hand.

"Oh, Mathew, I didn't know you were here."

He was dressed in jeans, a dress shirt, and jacket. A stack of real estate fliers, file folders, and pens were spread out on the table. "Doing a little business over lunch," he said. "I'm sure you know how that goes."

"Lunch *is* my business."

"Fair enough." He pointed to the empty chair across from him. "Do you have a minute?"

I looked toward the back. The line had thinned. Andy was wiping down the espresso machine and Sterling was restocking the pastry case. "Sure." I sat. "How's everything over at ShakesBurgers?"

Mathew clicked a pen on and off. "The police are still hanging around."

"Have they told you when you can reopen?"

"We could reopen now according to the police, but we're not ready. The place is a mess."

"Really? Usually the Professor and Thomas are good about that. Did they dust for prints? We had that happen here once and it was a pain to clean up. I have the name of a good cleaning company if you need it."

Mathew tapped the pen on the table. "I don't mean messy, I meant the restaurant is a mess. I don't know what Mindy was thinking, but we don't have any systems set up. Who knows where Reggie is. I can't find him anywhere and I'm not sure I want to."

"Why is that?"

He stirred the soup. "This smells great."

"Thanks. Don't mind me. You should eat while it's hot."

Mathew blew on his spoon and took a bite. "Wow, really good. Do you want a job?"

"I'm pretty set here, but I'm flattered."

"I can't figure out what Mindy was doing. She and I have worked together for so long that I trusted her when she said she'd found an ideal location here. What was she thinking, trying to open across the street from your place?"

"I don't know." I shrugged. "Didn't you two talk that through?"

Mathew shook his head. "No. Not this time. This venture was all Mindy's plan. She faxed me a few contracts to sign. I should have given them a closer look, but like I said, I didn't think I had to. We've done dozens of these deals."

"But ShakesBurgers has a very different menu than everything else in town. Maybe that's what she was thinking. She saw an opportunity and went for it."

"Maybe." He dove back into his soup. "We weren't going to compete with cooking like this, especially an established family business. Mindy knew that."

"She must have had her reasons."

"Or she was losing her edge."

"What are you going to do now?"

Mathew placed his spoon on his napkin. "I'm not sure. Find a cook. You have any ideas? Any of your staff need a job?"

I glanced at Sterling. Part of me wanted to offer his name, but I couldn't let him go. "Not really."

The doorbell jingled and Jose Ortega came in with a wooden box of wine. Before he even had a chance to place it on the counter Richard Lord was on his feet and stomping toward him. "I want a word with you!" Richard yelled. Customers stopped eating and turned to see what the commotion was about.

Richard had a way of bullying everyone in town.

Jose positioned the wine box in front of him, creating a barrier between himself and Richard.

"You betrayed me. Who are you working with?" Richard threw a beefy arm in the air and pointed back in the kitchen to Carlos. "Are you working with him?"

Carlos caught my eye and motioned for me to stay out of it. He wiped his hands on a dish towel and walked to the front counter.

Jose didn't respond.

Richard puffed out his chest. His cheeks flamed with anger. "Should I take that as a yes?"

Jose started to answer, but Richard cut him off. "I gave you my business when no one else in town would and this is the thanks I get?"

I wanted to tell Richard that that wasn't true. Mom gave Jose his start in Ashland and Richard, as always, was the one who copied her.

"I have not betrayed anyone," Jose said.

Carlos walked over to Richard and put his arm around Richard's shoulder. "What is the problem?"

Richard threw his arm off of him. "I know what's happening here."

Carlos kept his cool. If he was intimidated by Richard he didn't let it show. "My friend Jose here, he supplies to everyone in town, *sí*? This is how it works everywhere. There is nothing for you to be upset about. How about we go outside and talk this over so we don't disturb the customers?"

This only made Richard angrier. I thought he might lunge at Carlos or Jose. His face puffed up and turned the color of an overly ripe tomato. At that moment Mom came up to the front with a plate of pastry. Her clogs clicked on the floor. She tugged Richard's shirtsleeve. "Richard, come sit. I have something I'm dying for you to try."

Amazingly, Richard acquiesced, but not without a final warning to Jose. He shook a fat finger in Jose's face. "I'm going to find out who you're partnering with. I made you a great deal and you wouldn't take it. Now you're selling out? You haven't heard the last of me."

Jose frowned, but didn't say more.

What was Richard talking about? Jose selling out?

Mom led Richard back to the booth and sat across from him as he scarfed down the pastries.

Carlos handed the wine to Sterling and took Jose outside. Customers returned to their lunches. Chatter erupted in the dining room. Too bad Lance hadn't been here for this. He would have appreciated Richard's theatrics.

Mathew cleared his throat and gathered his paperwork together. "I have to go," he said, glancing at Richard and then outside to where Carlos and Jose were talking. "Thanks for the soup. It was great." He tucked his papers under his arms and power-walked outside.

I watched through the window as he stopped and whispered something to Jose before he crossed the street to ShakesBurgers. Richard had finished his pastries and was on his feet again. He huffed past me as I picked up Mathew's soup bowl and coffee cup. "You better find a new wine vendor. Your guy out there is selling out." He let the door slam behind him.

I watched to see if he and Jose would go head-to-head, but Richard stormed past Carlos and Jose.

Mom caught up with me as I took the dirty dishes to the sink. "What was that all about?"

"No idea. Richard is acting paranoid."

She grinned. "What else is new?"

"Good point." I set the dishes in the sink. "How did you do it?"

"Do what?" The overhead lights reflected the natural chestnut highlights in her hair. She didn't look anywhere near sixty. I hoped that I had inherited her genetics when it came to aging.

"Get Richard to calm down? I thought he was going to blow a gasket. Or worse—punch Jose."

Mom nodded. "Me too."

"How did you get him to calm down?"

She winked. "Never underestimate the power of pastry."

I laughed. "That's a good one."

"It's true."

"Obviously. I feel bad for Jose, though."

Mom glanced out the window. Carlos patted Jose on the back. "I wouldn't worry too much, honey. Jose can take care of himself. And everyone in town knows that Richard is all bark."

"Yeah, but his bark is pretty loud."

Mom ran hot water in the sink. "Don't let it get to you. I've known Jose long enough to know that he's not going to let Richard get under his skin."

"What do you think Richard meant about selling out?"

Mom shrugged. "Who knows? Richard likes to think that he owns this town."

Carlos came back inside. He looked worried. "Is everything okay in here now? The customers, they are not upset?"

"They're fine," Mom replied. "They're all used to Richard's antics. It's not the first time he's caused a scene around here and it probably won't be the last."

"This is not okay," Carlos said. "He cannot treat people like this. I will have a talk with him."

"Don't!" Mom and I both shouted in unison.

Carlos frowned. "But this is not the way of Ashland."

"I know, but talking to Richard will just make things worse. Trust us."

"I do not like this man." He looked to Mom for help.

She grimaced. "I'm with Juliet on this one. I appreciate your help, but Richard likes to hear the sound of his own voice. You'll only give him fuel if you try to get in the middle. Jose is a professional. He'll handle it."

"But I think Richard is treating Jose this way because he is of Mexican descent, no?"

"Richard treats everyone that way," Mom said. She shut the water off. "Let's get back to baking, shall we?"

Carlos agreed, but he didn't look thrilled about it. I hoped he would listen to our advice. The last thing I needed was for Carlos to have a confrontation with Richard Lord.

Chapter Twenty-four

Mom must have had the same thought about keeping Carlos occupied and away from Richard Lord. Once everyone had returned to their lunches, she pulled Carlos into the kitchen. "I could really use your help." She flipped through the notebook with our sketches for the Chocolate Fest. "Can you look this over and give us some feedback? We want to wow everyone who comes past our booth."

I mouthed, "Thank you."

She winked.

Carlos studied our plans. "This is original, yes. Chocolate pasta, how do you do this?"

Mom looked to me. "I was wondering that too."

I shared my vision with them. My idea for the chocolate pasta was to make thin chocolate crepes that we could slice with a pizza cutter into long pasta-like strips. Then we would cover them with a dark chocolate sauce and white chocolate shavings to replicate cheese.

"That sounds amazing," Mom said when I finished. "How will we serve it to so many attendees?"

"Good question. I was thinking about that this morning. What if we purchase red-and-white-checkered paper food boxes? You know, the kind that Alan used to serve his corn dogs in at the farmers' market?"

Mom nodded.

"We can get a case of a thousand of them for under twenty dollars. My thought was that we could serve the chocolate pasta cold and drizzle the sauce on as people come to the booth. It'll be like an Italian dessert to go."

"I love it!" Mom clapped her hands together. "We could even have extra toppings like cherries and chopped nuts to go along with the pasta."

Carlos didn't look as enthusiastic. "You will have to make this for me. Chocolate pasta, I cannot understand."

"Let's try it now," I said. "Why not? The lunch rush is done. We have time, let's experiment a little." There was nothing better than cooking to distract Carlos. And if I was being honest with myself, I knew that I needed something to focus on as well.

Mom interlaced her fingers. "Put me to work."

I had her start on the chocolate crepe batter. Carlos took on the dark chocolate sauce. Stephanie had to get to an afternoon class. "Do you want me early again tomorrow?" she asked as she showed me where she had left off on the afternoon's specialty orders. We had two birthday cakes and four pies to finish.

"Are you going to hate me if I say yes?"

She snarled her lip. "Nah. I'll be here."

"Don't sound so excited about it," I called after her as she sauntered to the front.

Sterling stopped organizing the order tickets and held the door open for her. He asked her something, which she responded to with a happy head nod. I wondered if he was finally asking her out. They obviously liked each other, but neither of them would make the first move. I had to resist the urge to play matchmaker.

The pie orders were for Parchment and Quill, a bookshop on the plaza. They were hosting a reading and the shop owner liked to offer readers pie and coffee. Mom worked on the birthday cakes and chocolate crepes while I filled our flaky pie crusts with lemon curd, chocolate crème, coconut cream, and vanilla cream. I boxed each pie individually in pie boxes with our Torte logo stamped on the top.

"I'm going to run these to the bookshop," I said to Mom and Carlos. "When I get back let's try and see if we can get this chocolate pasta to work."

Like the other shops on the plaza, Parchment and Quill was designed like an Elizabethan manor house. Inside, the bookshop was warm and cozy with benches and pillows tucked into corners for customers to curl up and read. It smelled like old books. When I was on the ship, I used to sneak away to the library when I had a free moment. Not many passengers frequented the library. They were more focused on their tans and soaking up the sun's rays on the pool deck.

I usually had the library to myself. I would pull a stack of old cookbooks and travelogues from the shelves and spend my break thumbing through their pages.

The bookshop had a similar welcoming vibe. "Juliet, thank you for bringing these over," the owner said as she made space on a card table she had covered with an emerald-green tablecloth near the cash register. There were fresh-cut yellow and white flower arrangements on either side of the table. A stack of paper plates, plastic forks, and napkins had been set out. "Can you put those right there?" the owner said, pointing to the empty space in the middle of the table.

I set the pie boxes down. "When does the reading start?"

She glanced at a watch with dangly book charms on her wrist. "In twenty minutes. People should be arriving any second." She pointed to a podium and rows of folding chairs.

"That should be fine. The cream pies need to be refrigerated, but they can be out for thirty to forty-five minutes."

"I'm sure they won't last that long. Our guest author is getting ready in the back. When she saw how many chairs I had set out, she was worried that we wouldn't fill them. I told her not to worry. People come for the pie!"

"Oh, no, don't say that. I'm sure they come for the books too."

She smiled. "This is a debut author. It's my little secret. I get them in with pie and they walk out the door with a new book."

"Glad to help." I made sure she didn't need anything else before leaving.

On my way back to Torte I passed ShakesBurgers. Reggie was hanging out by the shrine on the sidewalk. He was bending over, about to pick up a stuffed teddy bear.

"Hey!" I called.

He dropped the bear and whipped around to face me.

I stopped in midstride. Maybe I should have kept my mouth shut.

"What do you want?" Reggie said, rubbing his bald head. Now that I knew his background, he really did look like a criminal. His dark hair was shaved in a tight crop. Tattoos covered both of his forearms. Not tattoos like Sterling's hummingbird, but a skull and a dagger.

"Did you know that the police are looking for you?" What was wrong with me?

"Why do you think I'm here?"

"What?"

"That's why I'm here. I'm waiting for that cop, he hasn't showed." He kicked a plush pig that had fallen over.

"Thomas?"

Reggie rolled his eyes. "What's it to you?"

I scanned the plaza. People were milling around and thanks to the warm January sun many shop doors were propped open. I decided it was as safe a time as any to talk to Reggie. Plus, Thomas was meeting him and should be there any minute. "It's nothing, but there are a lot of rumors going around town right now. I don't know if you're familiar with Ashland or other small towns but news has a way of spreading and getting out of hand."

"So?"

"I thought you might want to know that people are talking about you."

"About what?" He twisted a black-and-white bandana in his hand.

"That you did jail time."

Reggie nodded. "That's out, huh?"

He didn't seem very fazed. "Is it true?"

"Yeah. It's not my proudest moment but what are you going to do?"

"What happened?"

He had twisted the bandana so tight that it looked like he had cut off circulation to his wrist. His wrist was turning bright red and starting to swell. "It was a stupid mistake. I got in a bar fight."

I waited for him to continue.

"I was drunk, I'll give you that, but I didn't mean to hurt the guy. He took a swing at my girlfriend. I protected her. Who tries to punch a woman? That's not cool. The guy was a total wimp. He couldn't handle one punch. It knocked him out. He hit his head on the bar. Idiot. If you swing at my girl, I'm going to knock you down."

He had a point, but I didn't tell him that.

"The guy pressed charges. He came after my girl and I'm the one who does time. The system is messed up."

"How long were you in jail?" I couldn't take my eyes off of his wrist. The bandana was still cinched tight and his hand was purple. It had to hurt.

"Two years."

"That's a long time."

"Tell me about it." He motioned to ShakesBurgers. "I was glad that Mindy gave me this gig. Not a lot of people want to hire a convict."

"Were you a cook before?"

"No. I guess that's the one good thing that came out of my time in prison. I learned to cook. A lot guys do their time, get out, repeat, land back in the cell. Not me. If I was stuck in there I figured I might as well make the best of it. Learned how to cook. Cooked for the inmates. Got a skill I can use now." He seemed to notice the bandana for the first time and unwound it.

"That's great."

He gave me a hard look. "Prison isn't great, lady."

"I mean that you learned a skill."

"Yeah. It's good. Except now the boss is dead."

"How did Mindy find you in the first place?"

"She knew the chef at the prison. Guess they went way back. He put in a word for me when he heard she was opening up this place. She told me she was willing to give me a shot, but that she didn't think it was a good idea to tell people about my past. I didn't care. She worked up a story about me training at some Portland restaurant."

Mindy had been friends with a prison chef. Was that a coincidence, or could she have had friends in prison? Did that mean anything? I wasn't sure. But knowing people in prison could have put her in with a dangerous crowd.

"So it was Mindy's idea to tell everyone that you were from Portland?"

"Yeah. Like I said, I didn't care. I wanted to cook. My girl left me. Some thanks. I defend her, do jail time for her, and she takes off with some other dude. Cooking is my way out, you know?"

I did know. Reggie had surprised me. He wasn't what I'd expected him to be. He seemed sincere, serious about wanting a career as a cook.

Thomas strolled up at that moment. He gave me a funny look. "Jules, what are you doing here?"

"Just talking to Reggie." I could tell that Thomas didn't believe that for one minute.

"Glad you made it here, Reggie," Thomas said. "Let's go talk inside."

Reggie nodded. I grabbed Thomas before he went inside with Reggie. "He seems like he's trying to turn his life around."

Thomas shook his head. "Will you never stop, Jules? Have you been pumping my suspect for information?"

"No. I bumped into Reggie and we got to talking, that's all."

"That's all?" Thomas raised an eyebrow.

"Well, I might have asked him a few questions about his past. Have you talked him?"

"That's what I'm here to do, but someone keeps meddling with my case."

"I'm not meddling. I am kind of surprised about Reggie and his attitude though."

"Thanks for letting me know. I'll make a note that Juliet Montague Capshaw likes my suspect's attitude." He pretended to write in the air.

I punched his arm.

"Ouch." He rubbed his arm. "Should I also make note that Ms. Capshaw is assaulting an officer of the law while I'm at it?"

"Be serious, Thomas. I'm simply telling you that Reggie seems like a decent guy."

"Jules, just because someone likes to cook as much as you doesn't clear him. But thank you for your input. I'll be asking Reggie about his past and I promise I'll keep an open mind. I always do."

"Fair enough." I walked back to Torte. I was more confused than ever. Reggie had a motive and a past, but after talking to him I wasn't sure. But I was also running out of suspects. Why was it that everyone in town seemed to have a reason to want Mindy dead?

Chapter Twenty-five

Mom was slicing beautifully browned chocolate crepes into thin strips the size of fettuccini noodles when I returned to the bakeshop.

Carlos greeted me with a wooden spoonful of his chocolate sauce. I took a taste and savored it for a moment. The creamy sauce was rich with flavor and had just a hint of bitterness from the dark chocolate.

"Did you add salt?" I asked.

"Of course." Carlos grinned as he watched me take another taste.

"It's perfect."

Mom bunched the chocolate noodles together onto four small plates. Carlos drizzled the sauce over the noodles and sprinkled shaved white chocolate over the top. The plates looked like pasta. I might have been fooled except for the fact that everything smelled like chocolate. Not a bad way to spend a Monday afternoon, I thought to myself.

Andy had left for class too. Mom called Sterling over as our other taste tester and handed each of us plate. "Honest answers only," she said, rolling a chocolate noodle around her fork. "Dig in."

We all tasted our noodles in silence. The texture of the crepes paired with the sweet and saltiness of the chocolate sauce was drool-worthy. I took another bite and let the flavors mingle on my tongue. It was a unique and innovative dessert. I was sold. We had to sample this at the Chocolate Fest and add it to our specialty rotation at Torte.

"What do you think?" Mom asked. She dabbed the corner of her mouth with a napkin.

Sterling answered first. He was the only one who didn't have a mouthful of chocolate noodles. "It's awesome. I could eat this for dinner or breakfast." He pointed to his plate, which was almost empty.

Carlos agreed. "It is not too sweet and has a good texture, but I do think it needs some toppings as you say, Helen. Some crunch and chewiness, *sí*?"

"I was thinking the same thing," I said. I walked over to the cupboard and pulled down a glass canister of walnuts. I chopped them and a handful of dried cherries. "Anyone want to add these?"

Everyone held out their plates. I sprinkled the nuts and dried cherries on the pasta and we all tasted again.

"Yes, this is it," Mom said. "Much better."

"I agree. It's amazing. Nice work, team." I added some more nuts to my pasta and took a bite.

"They will be a hit, *sí*." Carlos finished his noodles.

"We're rolling on this project. Marzipans, chocolate pasta, what's next?"

Mom laughed. "Can't we enjoy this for a minute longer before you make us work again? She's such a task master."

Carlos and Mom shared a look. "*Sí*, you should see her

on the ship. The sous chefs and line cooks they see her coming and they run and hide. She is terrifying."

"Knock it off, you two. I'm the nicest chef I know. Can I get a little help here, Sterling?"

Sterling took the dishes to the sink and tugged on the strings of his hoodie. "My shift is over. I'm getting out of here before it's too late. See you tomorrow."

"Wait," I pleaded. "I need moral support. You're my only hope."

"See ya." Sterling waved and ran for the door. Carlos followed after him. I watched as Carlos embraced Sterling and then whispered something in his ear. Sterling nodded twice and gave him a half hug.

"Good help is so hard to find," I joked to Mom. Internally, my throat tightened. I knew that Carlos was saying good-bye to Sterling. The fact that he was leaving tomorrow was starting to sink in.

Mom swatted me on the hip. "Tell me about it." She opened the sketchbook and made a note to include toppings and added cherries, nuts, and granola to our growing supply list.

"This is going to be an expensive endeavor, isn't it?" I asked, leaning over her shoulder.

"Yes, but I heard from a very wise pastry chef that we need to spend money to make money, right?"

"Right."

"Do you want to get started on a new chocolate offering for the Fest or should we call it a day?" Mom pointed to the clock. "It's almost closing time."

"Yeah. Let's call it a day. Knowing that we have two tastings nailed down is good, and we still have plenty of time to prepare. We're ahead of our game at the moment."

"Good." Mom untied her apron. "Because I have a date, and you two need to get out of here too."

"Why?"

Mom and Carlos exchanged another look. What was going on between them? Mom looked like she was about to say something. Carlos stepped forward and placed his hand on my shoulder. "I have a surprise for you, *mi querida*. You go home and take a shower and put on something nice. I will clean up here and meet you soon."

"Are you in on this, Mom?" I asked.

She winked at Carlos. "Me? I have no idea what you're talking about."

"Does this have anything to do with your hush-hush meeting in the office earlier?"

"I told you," Carlos said to Mom. "She cannot enjoy a surprise. She must know everything."

"It's true." Mom gave him a consoling pat as she slipped behind him and began rinsing the plates in the sink. "I blame myself."

He stopped her. "No, no, Helen you must go too. I will clean. You have done enough."

Mom protested, but Carlos wouldn't hear it. He shooed both of us out of the kitchen. Once Carlos has his mind set on something there's no stopping him. It's a quality we share. I linked my arm through Mom's. "We might as well go pamper ourselves. There's no way he's letting us back in the kitchen now."

"A chef doing dishes. That is love. Come to think of it, I like the sound of pampering. Maybe I'll go home and take a nice hot bath before dinner with Doug."

"Good idea, Mom." I switched the sign on the front

door to CLOSED and called to Carlos. "Do you want me to lock the door?"

"No, it is fine."

Mom gasped and stopped. "Oh, no, I just realized that I won't see him again before he leaves!" She unlinked her arm from mine and ran to the kitchen. I watched her embrace Carlos in a long hug. Tears welled in my eyes as she thanked him for his help this last week and told him to call when he was on the ship. Carlos returned her hug and kissed her on the cheeks. "Thank you, *gracias,* Helen, I will see you again soon."

Something had changed between them. When I'd brought Carlos home for brief visits in the past, I got the sense that they were both holding back. So much so that I had wondered if Mom thought I had made a mistake in marrying Carlos. They hadn't met yet, when Carlos and I tied the knot one spontaneous weekend in France. Mom was my biggest supporter and I knew she wouldn't say anything unless I asked her directly. I never asked. I was too worried that she'd tell me she didn't like Carlos.

It was clear to me in that moment that she liked Carlos—that she loved Carlos and that he felt the same about her too. It should have made me feel better, but watching them in a tender good-bye made my heart ache even more.

Chapter Twenty-six

A long bath sounded luxurious but I would have to settle for a hot shower. That was nothing new. I couldn't remember the last time I took a bath. We didn't have a tub in our cabin on the ship. We were lucky to have our own room. Most of the crew slept in bunk rooms with communal bathrooms. Life "down below" as we used to call it is a completely separate world from the swanky lounges, art galleries, and shops that passengers experience on board the ship. Rank mattered on the ship. Most cruise lines have a structured hierarchy. Higher-ranking crew members have access to the upper decks during their time off. They can grab a drink in one of the bars or sunbathe by the pool. Lower-ranking crew members, like the cleaning staff, aren't awarded the same privilege.

The same was true for living quarters. As head chef, Carlos was considered an officer, which meant that his cabin was on the upper deck of the ship. We might not have had a bathtub, but we had a window and after months at sea a window was much more luxurious and necessary for saving one's sanity.

I wondered what Carlos was planning. It had been a long time since we'd gone on a date. I felt like a teenager as I blew my hair dry. Typically, I wear my hair tied back in a ponytail. It's a quick and easy style when I have to get up before the sun and it keeps my hair out of my face while I'm baking. Tonight I decided to wear it down. After it was dry I used a straight iron to create soft curls. I took my time applying mauve eyeshadow that brought out the green in my eyes, blush, and lip gloss. I studied myself in the mirror and was pleased with the results. My hair looked wavy and sexy. I added a pair of dangling silver earrings and matching necklace, and then went to find something to wear in my meager closet.

My wardrobe was pretty basic. Standard attire at the bakeshop is jeans and a T-shirt. There wasn't much need for cocktail dresses on the ship either. I had a few dresses that I saved for special occasions like staff parties and going out when we were at port. Carlos had seen me in all of them. I wanted to wear something new for him tonight. Fortunately, Mom had forced me to go shopping for winter clothes back in November. Not that it mattered. Most of the sweaters, tights, and the pair of boots I had purchased were still hanging with their tags in my closet. Winter had been so mild I hadn't had a chance to wear most of it.

When I spotted a simple black dress on a sale rack that hit just above the knee and had halter straps and a fitted waist, I fell in love with it instantly. It was exactly my size and extremely flattering. Even though I had no use for it I bought it anyway. Now I was very thankful that I had splurged.

I found it in the back of my closet and slipped it over

my head. The fit was perfect. It clung to my hips and accentuated my chest. There was a thin layer of black taffeta under the skirt which gave it a slight swing when I walked. The dress made me feel feminine. I had a feeling that Carlos would like it. I finished the outfit with a pair of black flats and an ivory cashmere wrap.

The doorbell rang as I checked my appearance one last time. My stomach flopped. You're being silly, Jules, I told myself. This is your husband you're going out with.

Carlos stood on the landing holding a bouquet of fragrant white lilies. He oozed with sexiness. He wore a pair of tailored black pants, a crisp white dress shirt with the top three buttons undone, and a black sport jacket.

My breath caught.

"Julieta, you are so beautiful." He handed me the lilies and kissed my hand.

"You look great too, Carlos." My heart rate sped up. "Come in."

The scent of his aftershave blended with the floral scent of the lilies. I breathed it in. "Let me put these in some water. Then I'm ready to go," I said, walking to the kitchen to find a vase.

Carlos followed after me. "You do not need to hurry, *mi querida*. We have time."

We didn't have time, though. Tomorrow he would be gone and half a world away from me. My hands shook as I reached for a vase. Why did he have to leave? I filled the vase with water and stuck the lilies in it.

A knock sounded on the front door. Who could that be? I rarely got visitors to my tiny apartment. Carlos looked at me as I set the lilies on the counter.

"Are you expecting someone?"

"No." I walked to answer the door. "Just you."

I opened the door to find Thomas. He held his iPad in one hand and a winter bouquet of roses in his other. "Whoa, you look nice, Jules. Hot date or something?"

"Something."

"These are from my mom." He handed me the flowers. "She said to tell you thanks for the bread. She loved it."

"That's sweet of her." I took the flowers. Carlos had come up behind me. I could feel his breath on my neck and sensed that he was tense without having to turn around.

Thomas backed up when he noticed Carlos. "Oh, hey. I didn't know you were here."

Carlos stepped forward and put his arm around my shoulder. "Julieta and I are going to dinner."

"I won't keep you. I told Mom I would swing the flowers by and I was going to see if you had a minute to go over a few things on the case. We're watching a couple things across the street." He stopped and stared at me for a minute and then continued. "Never mind. It can wait. Have fun." He turned and jogged down the stairs before I could stop him.

The last thing I wanted was to be in the middle of the tension between Carlos and Thomas, but part of me wanted to run after him. What news did he have about the case? And by across the street did he mean at the Merry Windsor?

I stopped myself. I knew what I was doing. Mindy's murder had been a convenient distraction from keeping focused on the real problem I was facing. Tonight was my last night with my husband until who knows when. Stop sabotaging yourself and let the case go, I said internally. Tonight was about Carlos and me.

"Are you ready?" Carlos asked, holding the door open.

"Do I need anything?"

"Maybe you should bring a coat."

I grabbed my coat and took Carlos's extended hand. We walked down the stairs hand in hand.

The evening air was crisp and the sun had already begun to sink in the sky. We walked past a few shops to a black sedan parked on the street. Carlos beeped a remote and the locks popped open.

"Whose car is this?" I asked.

"It belongs to a friend. He let me borrow it." He opened the passenger door for me and helped me in.

Who did Carlos already know in Ashland who would let him borrow their car? I shook my head and buckled my seat belt. Of course Carlos would find a way to borrow a car. I wondered if whoever he had borrowed it from knew that Carlos had a need for speed.

The first time I drove with Carlos was when we were docked in Rome. He rented a convertible and took me outside of the city. I remember clutching the armrest and screaming as Carlos whipped the steering wheel and weaved through the crowded streets of Rome. It was like being on a roller coaster. He shifted gears and flew down alleyways where tourists were drinking Italian wine and eating gelato. I was sure that we were going to run someone over or take out a bistro table. But Carlos was an excellent driver. He laughed each time I let out a gasp of relief when we cleared a bicyclist by an inch or screeched around a corner.

Once we had escaped the throng of people downtown, Carlos hit the gas. We sped through hillsides and twisting roadways like real Italians. "Do not worry, Julieta, this is how we drive in Europe."

I trusted Carlos. He managed to get us back to the ship in once piece and without a scratch on the rental car, but my fingers were numb for two days after our adventure from clutching the armrest.

Carlos slid into the driver's seat and looked at me. "Shall we go?"

"My seat belt is buckled—tight."

He laughed. "*Sí,* okay, we go then." With that he reeved the engine and did a U-turn.

"Where are we going?"

"You will see. I think you will like this surprise."

We cruised up Main Street toward the surrounding hills. Within a few minutes of downtown, the streets rose to gorgeously wooded hills. Carlos speed past Southern Oregon University as the first stars began to make an appearance in the night sky.

"The stars have come out for you," he whispered.

I sat back and watched as we climbed a winding road. One of Ashland's premier vineyards was on my right. Its long rows of grapes sat in a silent winter's hibernation. We were headed toward the organic farmland surrounding the city.

After a few minutes, Carlos clicked on his turn signal and steered the car down a gravel road. I knew exactly where we were—Jose Ortega's winery.

"You're taking me to Uva?" I asked.

Carlos took his eyes off the road and looked at me. "You will see."

We drove down the bumpy road. It had wooden fences with electric wire on either side. I couldn't see the grape fields in the dark, but I knew that they stretched for acres in each direction. The gravel road led to an old red barn that Jose had converted into a tasting room. Behind the barn was a large house with an expansive deck that had a view of the vineyards and Mount Ashland. Jose and his family lived and worked on the property. Farther out in the fields were workers' quarters that housed migrant workers during harvest.

Carlos pulled up in front of the house and stopped the car. "We are here."

"We're going to Jose's?"

He held up one finger. "Wait, you will see."

I waited for Carlos to walk around the front of the car and open my door for me. He held out his hand. "This way, *mi querida.*"

My foot slipped on the gravel. Carlos caught me around the waist and steadied me. I was glad I had opted for flats.

He escorted me toward the house. It was lit from the inside with a warm glow. I could hear the sound of happy chatter between Jose's children.

"Are we having dinner with Jose's family?" I asked.

Carlos shook his head and laughed. "You will see. Come this way." He ushered me past the front door and around to the back porch.

My breath caught as I took in the sight. Torches lined the porch. Their amber flames danced against the black sky. A two-person table draped with a white tablecloth had been placed at the far end of the porch next to a built-in brick oven.

Carlos led me toward the table.

Heat and the scent of baking flatbread radiated from the oven. Maybe I wouldn't need my coat after all.

"Sit," Carlos said as he held out the chair closest to the brick oven for me.

I took a seat. Votive candles in a large glass Mason jars flickered. There were two place settings, a bottle of red wine, and two wine glasses.

Carlos sat across from me and poured the wine. "What do you think?"

"It's beautiful. But how did you do this? How did you talk Jose into using his house?"

He swirled the wine and stuck his nose halfway into the glass. "It is nothing. I told Jose I wanted to give you a romantic dinner. He said please let him cook for us. He and his wife are making you the most delicious, authentic Mexican dinner under the stars."

I had to give Carlos serious credit when it came to romance. He certainly knew how to sweep me off my feet.

The sound of an orchestra from speakers strategically placed on both corners of the house made me begin to sway. It was either that, the wine, or Carlos's dreamy stare. Our eyes met across the table. He reached for my hair and began to caress it. "Juliet, you are so beautiful tonight."

I didn't trust myself to respond. Fortunately, I was saved by Jose and his wife. They opened the sliding glass doors from their dining room to the porch and came outside with plates of food in their arms. The scent of spicy meat and grilled vegetables made my mouth water.

"Good evening, Juliet," Jose greeted me with a broad smile. "You remember my wife? We are so happy to have you join us for dinner tonight."

"Thank you." I returned his smile and waved a greeting to his wife. "Your place is beautiful and everything smells so amazing."

They placed the food in front of us. Jose explained each dish and gave us a quick overview of the recipe's origin.

No wonder he and Carlos hit it off so well. His wife removed wood-fired flatbread from the brick oven and showed us how fill it and roll it so that it could be eaten by hand.

Carlos stood and kissed them both on each cheek before they returned inside. "Thank you, my friends. Thank you so much."

Jose stoked the fire and refilled our wineglasses. "Enjoy! We will leave you to the stars."

I looked up. The sky was a kaleidoscope of brilliant white stars that flickered in rhythm with the flames on the torches and the votive candles. "I can't believe you arranged all of this," I said to Carlos.

He studied me. "I do this and so much more for you. I wanted to show you how much I love you before I must return to the ship tomorrow."

My throat tightened as he said those words. "Let's not talk about tomorrow. Let's enjoy tonight. The food looks incredible."

Carlos served me a scoop of grilled vegetables and seared beef. Jose and his wife had prepared five salsas to pair with our dinner. There was a traditional red salsa, a green—or verde as Carlos would say—salsa made from diced green chilies and cilantro, a fresh Pico de Gallo, a mango salsa, and one that was made from four different smoking-hot peppers.

"Go easy on that one, Julieta," Carlos warned. "It has real heat." He tasted it with his pinky and puffed out his cheeks. "Very good, but very hot."

I skipped the hot salsa and went for the red and green salsa and some additional Pico de Gallo. The flatbread was warm and crispy on the outside. It was the perfect vehicle for the Mexican meat and veggies. I scooped myself a helping of beans and a side of cilantro rice.

Carlos watched me as I ate. "You like it, no?"

"I love it."

A look of relief washed over his face. We finished our glasses of wine. He refilled my glass. I was starting to feel slightly dizzy. I knew it wasn't just due to the wine. Carlos hadn't taken his eyes off me all night. The evening felt surreal. I was having dinner under a canopy of winter stars with my husband on an organic winery in Ashland.

Carlos leaned closer. "Are you warm enough?"

I was. The bricks were like a heater against my back. "I'm good."

"Julieta, will you please consider coming back with me? I promise you there will never be secrets between us again. I am yours, *mi querida*. Only yours."

I swallowed hard, trying to clear the growing lump in my throat. We'd been through this before. Nothing had changed. I believed Carlos. I knew he was being sincere, but I knew that I couldn't leave Ashland either.

"It's not that I don't want to. I just can't. Not right now."

Carlos tried to keep his face neutral but I saw a sadness in his dark eyes as he smiled and said, "I know. It is okay. For now."

Chapter Twenty-seven

I tried to ignore the fact that we only had a few hours left together. We finished our dinner and the bottle of wine. Jose and his wife brought out dessert and another bottle of wine. The temperature dropped as even more stars erupted to life above us.

It was getting late and I was slightly tipsy. Carlos wrapped my coat around my shoulders. "You stay by the fire. I will help with the cleanup."

I didn't bother trying to protest. I knew that Carlos wouldn't let me help.

He stacked our empty plates and walked to the sliding doors. I scooted closer to the fireplace. I heard Carlos praising Jose and his wife inside and smiled to myself. How was I so lucky to have a man like Carlos who pampered me like this?

Jose came outside. "How was your dinner, Juliet?" He picked up the empty bottle of wine.

"It was incredible, Jose. Really incredible. Thank you so much. The food was amazing and the setting is like something out of a movie. Your vineyard is gorgeous."

I expected him to laugh at my gushing praise, but instead a shadow passed across his face.

"Did I say something wrong?" I asked.

Jose shook his head. "No. It's me. I'm sorry."

"It's you? Jose, is something wrong?"

He looked behind me to the kitchen where I could hear the sound of clinking plates and Carlos charming Jose's wife. "Do you mind if I sit?"

"Please." I motioned to the chair.

Jose sat. His shoulders sagged. "I don't think I'm going to be able to keep the vineyard and farm."

"What?" I sat up in my chair. "Why? You've put so much work into it."

He looked dejected. "I know. Thirty years. I started when your parents opened Torte. If it weren't for them I might still be working the fields. They made it their mission to get everyone in town to buy my wine. I owe your mom a lot."

"You don't owe her anything, Jose. You know that. She loves doing business with you."

He smiled. "Your mother is one of a kind."

"She is," I agreed. "Why are you thinking of selling? I don't understand."

"The recession hit hard. It hit everyone in Ashland hard. I don't have to tell you that, I'm sure."

"Yeah. Torte took a pretty big hit."

Jose nodded. "Many businesses stopped ordering from me. They went with cheap wines from bargain outlets. The kind with twist tops."

"Right." That was true on the cruise ship too. Sometimes cost trumped using the freshest or most locally sourced products. "Haven't things started to turn around and pick up though?"

"They have, but the weather hasn't. This drought has been terrible for my crops. I'm spending three to four times as much as I had to in the past for water. I can't keep up."

"Jose, I'm so sorry. I had no idea."

"Me too. I got an offer that I couldn't refuse. We talked it over this weekend. We're going to sell."

My heart broke for Jose. I knew how much work went into building a family business. "I guess it's good that you got an offer."

"It's a good offer, I think. You know Mathew the real estate developer?"

"Mathew as in Mindy's business partner at Shakes-Burgers?"

He nodded. "I had a few offers, but Mathew's is the highest. He wants to develop this land. He has plans to build a new gated community of luxury homes."

"You mean he's going to build out here?"

Jose twisted a wine cork in his hands. "I know it's terrible. I don't want to see my vineyard turned into homes, but I don't know that I have another choice. No one is interested in maintaining the grapes—no one who can afford it. It's too much work. It's too much water. You know what's happening in California. The water restrictions are hurting family farms and vineyards. It's starting here too. Every offer that I've had is to develop the land. At least Mathew has experience in real estate development. He wants to call the subdivision Farm Acres."

I felt sick to my stomach. That must have been what Richard Lord meant when he said Mom and I needed to find a new wine vendor.

"I'm sorry to tell you this, Juliet. I didn't mean to ruin your romantic night. Carlos was so excited to do this for you. He is a good guy. When you said such nice things about the vineyard it made me sad."

"It's okay. You didn't ruin my night."

Jose stood. "I will let you enjoy the fire and the stars."

I pulled my coat tighter over my shoulders and scooted my chair closer to the fire. It had started to die down. Smoke lingered in the air. The embers glowed in a final flush of red. Soon they'd be nothing more than a distant memory. Much like this night.

I couldn't believe that Jose was selling, and to Mathew. To Mathew?

Not caring about the cold, I threw off my coat. Mathew. What had the Professor said at Torte? Something about not letting my eyes deceive me. What if my first instinct had been right all along? What if I *had* walked in on Mathew right after he killed Mindy?

He'd told me that the business was broke, but he was offering to buy Jose out. Something didn't add up. Then I thought about my conversation with Alan. Alan had implied that Mathew didn't know anything about the deal he had made with Mindy. What if Mindy was planning to cut Mathew loose from the business? That could give him a very clear motive for murder—money.

I reached for my purse and pulled out my phone. Checking to make sure that Carlos was still in the kitchen, I hit Thomas's number. It rang four times. On the fifth ring his voice mail came on. "Thomas, it's Jules. I think you or the Professor should call Jose Ortega. I'm out here now and he told me that Mathew is buying his vineyard. *All* of his land. I'm worried that it could be connected to Mindy's murder."

As I hung up, Carlos and Jose came back outside with

a paper plate wrapped in foil. "For you." Jose handed me the plate. "You must take this to your mother."

"She'll love it, thanks."

Carlos kissed Jose on the cheek. "And you, my friend, you must come on the ship and I will cook for you and your wife."

Had Jose told Carlos that he was planning to sell Uva?

Carlos helped me back into my coat. There was a sting in the air. I wasn't sure if it was from the dropping temperature or the news that Jose was selling this beautiful land.

"You are quiet, now," Carlos said after we were in the car and driving back out the gravel road.

"I'm just thinking," I said.

"About us?"

"No. Well, yes. I'm always thinking about us, but at the moment I'm thinking about Jose. Did you know that he's planning to sell the vineyard? They're going to turn this organic land into a new housing development."

Carlos sighed and shook his head. "I did know. Jose told me when we were working on your surprise. It is terrible, no? This land belongs to the grapes. It should not become houses."

"I know, but it sounds like Jose has his mind made up. He said that the water bill has gotten too high with the drought."

"Maybe he will find an investor."

"Maybe, but he'll have to find one fast. It sounds like he's ready to sign the contract with Mathew."

Carlos removed one hand from the steering wheel and placed it on my knee. "Do not worry, *mi querida*. Jose he will find his way. This is not for you to worry about, *sí*?"

"Yeah." I looked out the window into a sea of blackness. There weren't any streetlights on this stretch of country road. "You're right. It's hard though. I've known Jose since I was a kid. Can you imagine building a life like that and then losing it?"

"I can." Carlos stared straight ahead. "It is terrible to lose something—*or someone*—you love."

"You haven't lost me."

Carlos gave me a quick smile. "*Sí*, but your heart it is now in Ashland."

Hearing him phrase it like that stung. It was true. It was what I had been thinking ever since Carlos had arrived in town. Part of my heart was in Ashland and part of it was about to return to the sea.

Chapter Twenty-eight

I invited Carlos upstairs to my apartment when we got back. "I know you have an early flight, but . . ." I hesitated.

"Julieta, I do not care about sleep. I will sleep on the plane." Carlos took my hand. It might have been the after-effects of sharing a bottle of wine, but my head spun a little as we walked up the steps together. I leaned into Carlos. His grasp was firm around my waist.

We barely made it to the top landing before Carlos's hands were sliding down my back and running through my hair. His lips were on my forehead, my cheeks, and then my lips. My body responded. I returned his kiss and massaged his muscular back.

His breath was shallow. I could feel his heart pounding against mine.

I fumbled through my purse for my keys. My fingers shook so much that I couldn't get it to turn in the lock. Carlos mumbled under his breath, "I will do it. Give it to me."

He unlocked the door. We tumbled inside. The apartment was as black as the night sky. The scent of flowers hung heavy in the room. Carlos kissed me again.

I bumped into the coffee table.

Carlos caught me. "Are you okay?"

It was hard to form words. My mouth moved but nothing came out. Carlos pulled me onto the couch. His lips brushed against my neck. We were so caught up in the moment that at first I didn't hear the knock on the door.

The couch felt like it was spinning. I held my finger to his lips.

"Hang on a second, Carlos." I pulled myself away. "Is that a knock?"

Another knock sounded on the door. This time it was louder.

"Someone's here," I whispered.

Carlos shook his head. "They will go away."

I heard a third knock and Mom's voice calling my name. "Juliet!"

In the darkness I couldn't make out Carlos's expression, but I was sure it matched mine. Mom wouldn't come to my apartment unless something was wrong. My heart rate slowed. I untangled my leg from Carlos's grasp.

"It's Mom."

"*Sí.*" He clutched my back and gave me one more kiss. Then he moved to let me get up.

I inhaled through my nose and pressed my dress back into place. Carlos flipped on the lights. I squinted as I opened the door. "Mom?"

Mom and the Professor stood on the landing. I wasn't sure if my eyes were playing tricks on me or adjusting to the light but it looked as if there were police lights on the street below.

I smoothed my curls. "Is everything okay?"

The Professor wore his standard attire of a tweed coat

and jeans, but Mom was wearing a pair of red-and-black flannel pajamas and wool slippers. Something was definitely wrong.

"Is Thomas inside?" The Professor peered around me.

"Thomas?"

"Yes. He told me he was stopping by your place, and I'm afraid I haven't heard from him for a while now."

I motioned for them to come inside. "He did stop by my place, but that was hours ago."

"Hmm." The Professor paused.

"Is something wrong?"

Mom shut the door behind her. "Sorry to barge in on you like this. We tried to call but you didn't answer your phone."

My cheeks burned with heat. I had a feeling that was because I didn't hear my phone ring while Carlos and I were caught up in the moment. "What happened?"

The Professor pushed his reading glasses up his nose. "I asked Thomas to check in with you. We were hoping to commandeer your apartment this evening. We have a team staked out at the Merry Windsor and your apartment has an ideal vantage point."

We all turned toward my front window.

"Why?"

"Our suspect has been on the move and we wanted 'eyes' on him, as we say in the business."

"But Thomas didn't ask to use my apartment. He dropped off flowers." I looked to Carlos to back me up. Carlos nodded in agreement.

"I'm afraid that's my fault." The Professor took off his reading glasses, blew on them, and wiped them on the sleeve of his shirt. "I asked him to be discreet. I should have told him to be up-front with you."

Mom touched his arm in a move of support. "You didn't know."

The Professor ran his fingers through his beard. His brow furrowed, revealing deep crevasses in his forehead. "Perhaps."

"So do you think that Thomas went out on surveillance himself? Maybe he's staked out in one of the businesses. Maybe he went downstairs to Elevation or something."

"I assure you that we've done a complete and thorough sweep of downtown. Thomas is nowhere to be found. He's not answering calls on his phone or the radio." The Professor paused and frowned. "That is not like Thomas."

That was true. Thomas didn't go anywhere without his iPad and cell.

"The last response I had from him was a text that he was heading to your apartment. We haven't heard from him since. That was before six."

"I called him from Jose's," I said. "Jose is selling Uva to Mathew."

Mom looked shocked. "What? Jose is selling the vineyard?"

"Yeah. Can you believe it?"

She shook her head. "No. That can't be true."

"It is." I nodded. "That's why I called Thomas," I said to the Professor. "I thought you might want to follow up with Jose. It seemed like there was a potential connection to Mindy's murder. Mathew told me he was broke. How is he putting an offer on Uva?"

The Professor looked thoughtful and then cleared his throat. "When did you call Thomas?"

"Maybe a half hour ago."

"I see. Excuse me please." The Professor opened the

door and went onto the landing. We could hear him on the phone.

Mom grabbed my arm. "Honey, I'm so sorry to put you in the middle of this. Doug called when he didn't hear from Thomas. He thought maybe Thomas was here, and then I couldn't get ahold of you. I panicked."

"It's okay."

Carlos kissed her cheek. "*Sí*, it is good that you were thinking of Julieta. Would you like some tea?"

Mom looked relieved. "Tea would be wonderful."

The Professor came back inside. "I have a team en route to Uva." His eyes traveled to my front window and across the street to the Merry Windsor. I followed his gaze. There were five or six police officers patrolling the front of the hotel. Two squad cars were parked on either side of the building. Both had their lights flashing.

Reggie stood on the porch, illuminated by the flashing red-and-blue lights.

"Are you looking at Reggie?" I asked.

The Professor returned his gaze to me. "The cook? No. Although I do believe that you and I have come to the same conclusion, Juliet. I've launched a full-scale manhunt for our killer and neither he nor Thomas are anywhere to be seen."

"Is there anything you can do? Can you ping Thomas's phone or track his police car?"

Carlos came out of the kitchen with a tray of mugs, tea packets, sugar, and cream. He moved the flower arrangements on my coffee table and made room for everything. "The water is heating."

Mom smiled at him and whispered thanks.

The Professor looked longingly at a packet of Earl Grey

tea. "We are working every angle, Juliet. I assure you of that. I intend to get back out there right now. I will knock on every door in town if need be. We will find Thomas and bring Mindy's killer to justice."

"I will help," Carlos offered.

"Actually, that would be appreciated. I have every man and woman on my team canvassing the streets as we speak. Having an extra set of eyes would be quite helpful." He tightened his scarf. "Shall we go?"

I looked to Mom. "What about us? We can help. We can spread out and search from both sides of downtown."

"No. You will be the most help here," the Professor said. He buttoned the middle buttons on his tweed jacket. "If Thomas shows up or gets in touch, please notify me immediately."

Mom held my arm and shook her head as I tried to protest. "Let them go, Jules."

They left together. The kettle whistled in the kitchen. I startled. Mom steadied me. She turned off the stove and returned with the steaming kettle. I poured myself a cup of lemon tea and sank onto the couch. How had this perfect evening ended up so wrong?

"Why did you stop me?" I asked.

Mom balanced her tea and sat next to me. "It's Doug's job."

"Yeah, but he let Carlos tag along."

"For physical support." She raised one eyebrow. "Like he said, he has the entire team sweeping each neighborhood. Every officer in Ashland is looking for Thomas right now. Doug doesn't usually participate in activities like this, but this time it's personal. Thomas is like a son to him."

"Do you think something happened to him?"

Mom reached for the sugar. She added a teaspoon to her tea and stirred it with a spoon. "I don't know, but what I do know is that Thomas is smart and resourceful. He's young and strong. If he is in any danger, I know that he can take care of himself."

Her words were comforting.

"This evening is a disaster." I massaged my temples and kicked off my shoes.

"I'm so sorry, honey. I shouldn't have worried. Like I said, when you didn't answer, I leapt to the worst-case scenario." She took a sip of her tea. "I know this was your last night with Carlos."

"It's okay."

She added a splash of cream to her tea and handed it to me. I did the same. "Does the Professor think that Mathew is the killer?"

"He didn't say."

"Why does he always have to be so tight-lipped about everything?"

"That's his job too." She gave me a knowing look.

"Fair enough." I took a drink of tea. It was hot and warmed the back of my throat. The slight buzz that I'd had from the wine and my romantic evening with Carlos had completely evaporated.

"Is something else bothering you?" Her eyes were kind and firm.

"Is it that obvious?"

"Only because I know you and because I know that Carlos is leaving."

I sat up. "Am I making a huge mistake, Mom?"

She reached for my hand. "I can't answer that for you." She sighed. "You know that."

"I know. I'm so confused. I don't want to lose him. I don't want to be apart from him, and yet I don't want to go back to the ship. I love being home."

"I love having you home." She squeezed my hand. "Does it have to be one or the other? Have you discussed the idea of Carlos living here with you? He's blended in beautifully. Everyone in town loves him."

"I know."

"He doesn't want to stay, is that the problem?"

"I'm not sure. I think he would if I asked him." My feet felt like ice cubes. I rubbed them on the carpet to try to warm them.

Mom dipped her tea bag in her mug. "Have you asked?"

"No."

"Is there a reason you haven't asked him?"

"I don't know. I don't know if he fits in here. I want him to—I think." I sighed. "I'm not sure. I'm confused. I think the right thing for the moment is for him to go back to the ship."

She nodded. "Sometimes the right thing is the hardest thing."

"Yeah." My eyes welled again.

"Let it out," she said, as she scooted closer and wrapped her arm around me. I sobbed on her shoulders the way I used to when I was a little girl. Carlos was leaving me, and as much as it hurt, I knew that it was the right thing—for now.

Chapter Twenty-nine

Mom's mantra was never underestimate the power of pastry. I decided after crying on her shoulder until my eyes were completely dry that my mantra would be to never underestimate the power of a good cry. Despite my scratchy eyes and runny nose, it felt cathartic to get all the intense emotions out of my body.

"Feel better?" Mom asked when I finally heaved my shoulders back and wiped the last tear from my eye.

"Much. Sorry."

"Never." Her voice turned serious. "You always have a shoulder to cry on." She patted her shoulder. "Always."

"Thanks." I sat up. "The same goes for you." I warmed my tea with hot water from the kettle and breathed in the steam. "I can't sit still. I have to do something—anything. I can't just sit here and worry."

Mom glanced at the clock. "It's after midnight." She motioned to her flannel pajamas. "I'm not exactly dressed for going out. What did you have in mind?"

"We could bake."

She refreshed her cup too. "We could bake. A little mid-night snack, perhaps?"

"It's better than sitting here worrying. Let's go see what I have." I stood and kissed her on the cheek. "Thanks, Mom. I don't know what I would do without you."

"I feel exactly the same way about you."

It had been a while since I had restocked my kitchen. I'd spent the early half of January at Lake of the Woods Resort catering a board retreat for Lance and then Carlos had come home with me. We'd been eating all around town for the past week. Carlos loves to dine out and sample other chefs' cuisine. He says that it inspires him to expand his palate. Often he'll create a delectable mash-up after going on a tasting tour at port. Some of his best creations came from blending unlikely regional foods, like his Greek and Cuban street tacos that he stuffs with marinated lamb and tops with a pineapple pepper salsa.

I opened the fridge and found butter, eggs, and butter-milk. "How do you feel about a coffee cake?" I asked Mom.

She already had rolled up her sleeves and was washing her hands. "That sounds great. Put me to work."

"Can you grab the dry ingredients?" I asked, preheat-ing the oven. One trick that works like a charm is to rest chilled butter on the stove as the oven is heating below. It's a quick way to bring butter up to room temperature. It's imperative to keep an eye on it so that it doesn't melt.

With the oven and butter warming, I measured butter-milk and beat the eggs with a fork in a separate bowl.

"What are you thinking about flavor?" Mom asked. She pulled a jar of cinnamon from the cupboard. "A good old-fashioned cinnamon crumble?"

"My favorite. Remember when you used to make that for Dad and me on Sunday mornings?"

"Your father loved that coffee cake."

"He had good taste."

"That he did."

"Speaking of good taste, did you and the Professor have a chance to have a heart-to-heart?"

She unwrapped a chilled cube of butter and began cutting it together with brown sugar, cinnamon, and oats. "What does that have to do with good taste?"

"He's in love with you. That's good taste—no, fabulous taste—in my book."

"You're biased."

"Maybe, but it's true."

She flicked me with her fingers. "We did talk last night, but I'm not sure that I feel any better."

"What did he say?"

"He admitted that he's stressed about the case. Not that investigating a murder is ever easy but this case has gotten under his skin."

"Did he say why?"

She shook her head. "No, he didn't. I don't think he knows. He mentioned that he's seriously considering retirement."

"Really?"

"He's been training Thomas." As she spoke Thomas's name she put her hand to her heart. "I hope they find him soon."

"Me too."

"Anyway, as you know, that's why he's been working so closely with Thomas. I thought he was still a few years away from actually retiring." She stirred the dry ingredients.

Watching her bake in her pajamas brought a flood of childhood memories. Since she and my dad both worked long hours in the bakeshop, she would wake extra early on the weekends and prepare a special crumble or casserole that she would leave with a note and baking instructions for me. Sometimes the smell of coffee or eggs would stir me. I would pad downstairs to the kitchen and watch her bake in her pajamas.

She caught me staring at her. "What is it?"

"Nothing." I shook my head. "A happy memory." I did a quick turn. "Plus I was thinking about how funny we must look. You in your pajamas and me in a black cocktail dress."

"Maybe this could be our new look at Torte."

I laughed. "Does the Professor think that Thomas is ready for that responsibility?"

"He thinks Thomas is an excellent and smart cop."

"Me too," I interrupted. "I didn't mean that. I just mean that it's a big jump to go from being an apprentice to running a full investigation."

"That's what Doug thinks too. Some of it comes with time. He said that when he was starting out, he had to learn on the job. He made plenty of mistakes along the way."

Thomas was a great cop. I'd seen how meticulous he was about following the letter of the law and recording every piece of evidence at a crime scene. However, I wasn't sure if *he* thought he was ready. He deferred to the Professor on every case. The Professor was more than Thomas's boss, he was a friend and a mentor.

Mom added the softened butter to a mixing bowl. The

muscles in her forearm flexed as she stirred it with a wooden spoon. I measured level cups of packed brown sugar and granulated white sugar and added them to the butter.

"How soon do you think the Professor will retire?"

"I'm not sure. I advised him not to make any decision now that he might regret later. If he can close this case then hopefully he can take some time to think about what he wants to do next."

"You don't you think he should retire?"

"Not necessarily." She reached for the eggs and incorporated them into the batter. I alternated adding dry ingredients and the buttermilk. "Doug's work has defined him for a long time. I'm worried that if he quits without a plan, and without thinking it through, that he'll be lost."

"He has his theater gigs."

"That's a hobby," Mom said, reaching for the vanilla extract. Her arm was too short. "Can you grab that?"

I leaned over her and pulled the vanilla from the top shelf.

"Dabbling in community theater and lecturing on Shakespeare's work around town every once in a while isn't the same as working full time. He's used to long hours—days and nights on the job. I know that we're getting older. Doug wants to travel while he's still young enough to enjoy it."

"That sounds good."

"Well, yes."

I suddenly realized what was happening. I understood why Mom wasn't fully on board with the idea of the Professor retiring. It wasn't about him. It was about her.

The Professor wanted to retire and take Mom on adventures around the world. Could it be that as I was beginning to put roots down in Ashland that Mom was thinking about leaving?

Chapter Thirty

"Mom, are you thinking about retiring too?" I asked as I greased an eight-by-eleven-inch pan.

"Not exactly."

"What does that mean?"

She used to a spatula to scrap the creamy coffee-cake batter into the pan. I was acutely aware of the fact that she wasn't meeting my eyes. "You know that I love Torte and I especially love it now that you're home and we're working together. This has been one of the best times in my entire life."

"I feel a 'but' coming on."

"You sound like your father."

"Do I?"

"He used to say that all the time. I can hear his voice right now." She sprinkled the butter, cinnamon, and oat mixture on top of the batter and slid it into the oven. Then she noticed me staring at her with an expectant gaze. "Don't look at me like that, Juliet."

"Like what?"

"That forlorn face. You inherited that from your father too."

"Mom, I'm not forlorn. I want to know if you're thinking of retiring, that's all."

"It's complicated."

"Is the Professor pressuring you to retire?"

She frowned. The lines on her forehead creased. "No. He's not pressuring me. He wants to travel and he made a good point that neither of us are getting any younger."

"And if he retires then he wants you to join him, right?"

"In a perfect world, yes. But we've talked about many options. For example, if you're here and running Torte I could leave for a few weeks at a time and take longer trips with Doug."

"Mom, yes, of course. You should go! You should travel. You've taken care of Torte, me, and everyone in town for decades. It's your turn now."

She brushed cinnamon crumbs from her hands. "I know that you feel that way, Juliet, but your life is in flux too. I don't want to put pressure on you. You don't know that you're going to stay in Ashland forever. Torte was your father's dream and my dream. It wasn't yours. I would never ask you to give up your dreams."

I set the timer on the oven. "Mom, I'm not going anywhere and you're not asking me to give up my dream. Torte is my dream now. I'm not saying that to make you feel better. I'm saying that because it's true."

She unrolled her sleeves. "We are a pair, aren't we?"

"We're a perfect pair." I pulled her toward the living room. "Let's go sit. I'm so exhausted."

"Sounds good, but we're not done with this conversation, you know. You're not kicking me out of the bakeshop that easily."

"We'll see about that." I grinned. My grin quickly evaporated. The living room looked like a disco. White, blue, and red lights flashed through my front window and off the walls in a sinister rhythm.

We ran to the window. Mom shielded her eyes with her hands. "What's going on down there?"

I had no idea that Ashland had so many police officers. Sirens wailed as three more squad cars sped to screeching halts in front of the Merry Windsor. Cops with their guns drawn had surrounded the hotel. Between the blinding lights and officers spilling out of the cars that had just arrived on the scene, I couldn't tell exactly what was happening except that I was very glad not to be at the Merry Windsor at the moment.

"It looks like something out of a movie," I said to Mom.

She nodded and yanked me away from the window as a loud boom sounded.

"What was that?" My heart lurched in response.

Mom ducked. We both crouched on our knees and peered out the base of the window. Someone was shouting in a bullhorn. Was it the Professor? "Come out. We have you surrounded. Let's bring this to a peaceful resolution."

"Is that the Professor?" I whispered to Mom.

"Yes," she whispered back, and then gave me a funny look. "Why are we whispering?"

"I don't know."

Another bang sounded. Mom and I flinched and scooted closer together. The Professor shouted the command, "Move" into the bullhorn. Pandemonium broke out below.

Police officers with flashlights, guns, and batons spread in every direction around the hotel. It was so surreal I almost expected Lance to stroll over, take the bullhorn out of the Professor's hand, and yell, "Cut."

Only this wasn't a staged production. Mom's fingernails dug into my skin as the sound of gunshots reverberated through my tiny apartment. "Was that close?" I asked.

"No. I think that was across the street." She loosened her grip on my arm and sat up a bit to get a better look.

Another shot fired. We both ducked again. It was impossible to tell if the cops were shooting or being shot at.

I could feel my heartbeat in my head. Where was Carlos? Please don't let him be in the middle of this, I prayed silently.

Mom sat up and took another look out the window.

"Can you see anything?"

She shook her head.

Heavy footsteps thudded up the stairs and on the landing. Someone pounded on my front door. I let out a little scream. Mom clutched my arm. "Don't move."

Was it Mathew? Could he have a gun?

"Police!" a voice called from outside.

Mom squeezed my arm tighter and put her other finger to her lip.

My heart beat so fast I couldn't catch my breath.

"It could be anyone," Mom hissed. "Don't answer it."

Another knock pounded on the front door. "Police! We have an active shooter outside. Do NOT leave the premises."

Mom put her hand to her heart. I tried to breathe through my nose.

"Should I answer it?"

"No." She kept her voice low. "They told us to stay inside. That's what we're going to do."

I nodded. The officer didn't knock again, but I didn't hear footsteps heading back down the stairs either. Mom was right. We needed to stay where we were and to stay quiet. The person outside was probably a cop, but it could also be Mathew in a ploy to trick us into opening the door.

More shots were fired. Someone was on the ground. Someone shouted, "We got him!"

A group of officers surrounded the man on the ground. It was too dark to make out anyone.

Another bang sounded on my door. "Stay inside. Keep your door locked until further notice."

"I think he left," Mom said as footsteps thudded down the stairs.

"It sounds like it." I glanced out window again. Someone in handcuffs was being led to a police car. "Do you think it's over?"

"We can only hope." She squinted. "I can't see Doug or Carlos. It's too dark."

I'm not sure how much time passed. It felt like everything was happening in slow motion. My body began to quiver. I grabbed a blanket from the couch and wrapped it around Mom and me. We huddled together trying to figure out what was happening.

Mom's purse, which was hanging by the front door, began to vibrate and buzz. "My phone!" She jumped to her feet and hurried to answer it. "It's Doug," she said.

"Answer it," I said, tossing the blanket off. My foot bounced on the floor. Please let Carlos be okay.

I couldn't sit still as Mom listened to whatever the

Professor was saying. Her face stayed passive and serious as she nodded and inserted a "mmm hmm" every so often.

She held up her index finger when I whispered, "What's he saying?"

"Okay, then. We'll be here, yes," she said and hung up.

"What did he say?" The floor vibrated as I continued to shake my foot.

"It's good news. They've captured the killer and they've found Thomas."

"And?"

"He's been in an accident, but he's going to be okay. They're taking him to the hospital right now."

"What kind of an accident?"

"A car accident."

"How? What did the Professor say?" I was on my feet and pacing in front of the couch.

"Relax. Everyone is okay. Doug and Carlos are heading to the hospital. Then they're coming back here."

"Carlos is okay?" My heart beat of out rhythm.

"He's fine. Sit down, honey. Everyone is okay."

I followed her advice. She sat next to me and placed one hand on my knee. "That's better. Keep breathing."

"Was I not breathing?"

She laughed. "You were looking pretty blue in the face for a minute there."

"Sorry. I guess I didn't realize how nervous I was."

"Me too." She patted my knee.

"What else did the Professor say?"

"That's it. He said that Thomas had been in a car accident. Not to worry. He was going to be okay, and that he and Carlos would be here as soon as they could." She looked at the clock. "Oh my goodness, it's late."

According to the clock it was almost two.

"What did he say about the gunshots?"

"He didn't. I'm telling you word for word exactly what he told me."

"Right. Sorry."

"Let's finish our tea," she said. Her eyes widened and she sniffed. "Do you smell that? Is something burning?"

"The coffee cake!" we shouted in union.

I ran to the kitchen and pulled the cake from the oven. "It's well-done." I held it up for Mom to see.

Mom shrugged. "Maybe we can scrape some of the burnt topping off and salvage it."

"It's worth a shot." I rested the cake on a cooling rack and returned to the living room. I sunk back onto the couch and cradled my mug in my hands. A sense of relief washed over my body. Everyone I loved was okay and accounted for. Thank goodness.

Chapter Thirty-one

The next hour passed slowly. Mom attempted to distract me by talking about our plans for the Chocolate Fest. She gathered a few of my vintage cookbooks and brought them over to the couch. "Ooh, what about a chocolate lava cake?" she asked, flipping through their well-worn pages. "Or chocolate fondue. Could we make that work?"

"That would be pretty messy, don't you think?"

She turned the page. "Yeah. Scratch that."

A knock sounded on the front door. We exchanged a look and practically knocked each over down as we ran to open it.

The Professor and Carlos stood on the landing. They looked weary. The Professor had his jacket draped over his arm. Carlos's hair was slightly rumpled, his shirt was un-tucked, and his jacket was slung over his shoulder. I threw my arms around him. He responded by wrapping me in a sturdy hug. After a minute we broke apart.

"Sorry," I said, realizing that I was blocking the door. "Come in."

Mom reached for the Professor's hand. "We have some

questionable coffee cake waiting for you. Should I brew a pot of coffee as well?"

"If it isn't too much trouble," the Professor said. He came inside. "I have a long night of paperwork ahead of me. This is but a brief resting stop for me. I wanted to make sure to return your most helpful husband in person, Juliet." He extended his hand to Carlos. "My deepest thanks."

Carlos returned his handshake. "It is nothing. I was happy to help."

"You two sit." Mom pointed to the couch. "I'll bring you slices of coffee cake. I can't promise it's our best effort. It got a little burned with all the action outside."

"How's Thomas?" I asked.

The Professor hung his coat on the rack next to Mom's purse. "He suffered a mild concussion, but the doctors assure me that he'll make a full recovery. They're keeping him overnight to monitor him, as a precaution."

Carlos sat in one of the kitchen chairs that Mom had brought out into the living room. The Professor sat on the couch. The long lines on his face revealed his age.

Mom placed plates with generous slices of our coffee cake in front of each of them. "I'm going to grind some beans. Give me one second. I want to hear about Thomas and what's happened too."

"I assure you that I will savor this delightful dessert and await your return, Helen." The Professor picked up his fork and dug into the slightly charred coffee cake. Mom had done her best to scrape off the blackest parts of the crumb topping.

Carlos stabbed his. "Very nice."

"You don't have to lie," I said. "We know that it's overdone."

"But flavorful, no?"

Mom wiped her hands on her pajamas and sat next to the Professor. I opted to stand, even when Carlos offered me his chair. Adrenaline pumped through my body. I wanted to get outside and walk it off.

"What happened out there?" Mom asked. "Juliet and I were watching from the window. It sounded like there were gunshots."

The Professor nodded and swallowed a bite of coffee cake. Then he crossed one leg over the other and scratched his head. "It is a puzzle how the events of the past week have unfolded. I do believe that the Bard could have used it for inspiration for one of his works. Although in this particular case, I think we must turn to Sir Arthur Conan Doyle."

Carlos looked confused.

I walked over to him and whispered into his ear. "Just go with it. The Professor enjoys theatrics."

"Why?" Mom asked.

The Professor rubbed his beard. "Sometimes it is the most obvious clue, isn't it? One of Sir Arthur Conan Doyle's most famed quotes is, 'There is nothing more obvious than a deceptive fact.'"

"Are you saying that we—you—missed an obvious clue?" I asked.

"Ah, I can always count on your quick wit, Juliet."

"What clue?" I crossed my legs, wishing that I was in my pajamas like Mom.

"Think back to the morning of the murder."

I nodded. "Okay."

"Walk us through what you observed."

I repeated how I had found the front door at Shakes-Burgers open and Mindy's body on the floor.

"And?" The Professor urged me to continue.

"And Mathew was giving her first aid."

The Professor watched me.

"Or was he?" I said aloud.

A somber smile spread on his scruffy cheeks. "A-ha. That is the question. Was he? Or perhaps is that what he wanted us all to believe?"

"So it was Mathew?"

The Professor nodded. "It is sometimes the most obvious suspect. What was your initial reaction at the crime scene?"

I thought back to that terrible morning. When I spotted Mathew I had backed away as quickly as I could. I was scared. Why hadn't I focused more on Mathew?

As if reading my mind, the Professor continued. "In the vast majority of cases I've been involved in it's our intuition—that first instinct—that we must trust. Of course, Mathew played his part perfectly."

"Why did he do it? I thought he and Mindy were successful business partners."

"Ah. Again, another trick of the hand. Mathew wanted us to believe that he was distraught to lose his business partner and friend, when in reality the opposite is true."

The coffeepot beeped. "Hold that thought," I said to the Professor. My mind tried to replay every interaction I had had with Mathew as I poured fresh cups of coffee for the Professor and Carlos. Why hadn't I trusted my intuition?

I handed them cups of coffee. "How did you find out that it was Mathew?"

"Evidence never lies."

The Professor must have seen the confused look on my face. "Mathew's prints and DNA were all over the crime scene. We ran a background check and thanks to your phone call earlier this evening were able to connect all the dots. It seems that Mathew was out of cash. His investments had been terribly unsuccessful. Mindy intended to sever ties with him. The paperwork for the buyout had already been drawn up. There was nothing Mathew could do. His funds were completely dry."

"But with Mindy dead he would become soul owner of ShakesBurgers and have the cash to buy Uva."

"Exactly. He needed Mindy's cash. We found paperwork that her lawyer had drawn up. She intended to cut Mathew out of the business. She was a smart businesswoman and had diversified her investments. She had a number of properties and assets that he didn't have access to."

"Let me guess," I said. "If she died then those assets would become part of the company and he would have access to the money."

The Professor turned to Mom. "I told you she was quick."

Mom smiled. "I can't take credit for that."

"But what about Thomas? How is he connected? Did Mathew attack him? How did he get in a car accident?"

"Yes, yes." The Professor drank his coffee. "When Thomas received your call about Jose, he decided to follow up directly on that lead. He drove out to the vineyard."

"And Mathew came after him?"

"No." The Professor shook his head. "A case of bad luck. Thomas popped a tire on the gravel road and rammed into the fence. The impact knocked him out. When he came to, he called me."

"What about Mathew?"

Carlos cleared his throat. "So many questions, Julieta."

Mom pointed at Carlos. "Exactly! I was thinking the same thing. It's almost like she thinks this is her case."

I gave them a sheepish smile.

The Professor chuckled. "I'm quite happy to have your assistance anytime. You were most helpful in informing Thomas immediately when you learned that Mathew made an offer to purchase his vineyard. We believed that Mathew was on the hunt for other investments, but hadn't had confirmation as to where and with whom. We had enough evidence to make an arrest, but Jose's statement will add to the case the DA will bring against him. Your husband was so kind to wait while I took his statement after we saw to it that Thomas was safely in the ambulance and en route to the hospital."

"What happened at the Merry Windsor?" Mom asked again. "We saw the lights, all of the police force, heard you on the bullhorn, and then we heard shots."

"Oh, of course, I got off topic, didn't I? One of the reasons I asked Thomas to come pay a visit to you was because I suspected that Mathew was getting nervous. He had become less and less talkative in each subsequent interrogation. That is usually a clue that a suspect is about to make a move. I had the entire Ashland police force on alert. Two of my officers have been staked out at the Merry Windsor for the past two days. Our friend Richard Lord was less than pleased with the arrangement."

"Ha!" Mom laughed. "Karma."

"Mathew disappeared earlier this afternoon. I called in

the order to make an arrest, but he was gone. My team found airline tickets and cash that he had drained from ShakesBurgers' accounts so we knew he couldn't have gone far. We launched what I believe might be Ashland's biggest manhunt for him. I sent extra backup to the Merry Windsor, since we knew he would have to come back at some point for the cash." The Professor paused and nodded at Carlos. "Thank your husband for spotting him."

"Carlos?" I caught his eye.

Carlos waved us off. "It was nothing."

"I assure you it was something," the Professor continued. "Carlos noticed someone in a burger costume near Lithia Park. I pulled my team back and we waited for him to make a move."

"Did he have a gun?" Mom asked. "We heard shots."

"He fired but no one was hurt. I think it was an attempt to scare us off." He glanced at the clock. "He's in custody as we speak. I'm quite proud of the Ashland police force and Carlos for your invaluable help this evening. In fact, I need to be on my way. I have a long night ahead of me, but I believe we'll all sleep easier knowing that a killer is behind bars. Many thanks for the coffee and cake. It will sustain me."

Mom got to her feet. "Let me wrap up another slice for you."

"That would be lovely, Helen. I can take you home and then return to my office." He gave Carlos and me a half bow and they left together. Carlos and I were free to pick up where we had left off, except he had a flight to catch.

Chapter Thirty-two

The clock ticked on the wall as if it was taunting me. Each second was a reminder that our time was limited. "Do you have time for coffee before you have to go?" I asked as I picked up the tea tray and walked to the kitchen. I started to put the dishes in the sink.

Carlos reached for my arm. "Leave it." His voice was husky. "We do not have much time."

Tears welled in my eyes. "You're leaving. Tonight was perfect. It was magic and now it's all going to end." I wiped my nose with the back of my hand.

He handed me a dish towel. I dabbed my eyes. "I don't want you to leave, Carlos."

"I do not want to leave either. We will be together again soon. You will see."

My eyes felt grainy. I wiped them on the towel again and took in a long breath through my nose. "I'm okay."

He took the towel from my hand, placed it on the counter, and kissed my tears. "Come with me, my love."

"I can't."

We collapsed into each other's arms. Being apart had

made the passion between us feverish. Finally, Carlos pulled back. "I must go. My flight leaves soon. I do not have my things. I had not planned that the night would end like this."

I followed him into the living room. "Do you really have to go?" Moonlight shone through the window. His silhouette filled the frame. I sucked in my breath at the sight of his muscular arms and tight abs underneath his white shirt.

Carlos hugged me so tight I thought I might break in half. "*Mi querida,* it is time. I will call you as soon as I can and we will make a plan to see each other soon, *sí*?"

I reached for his hand.

He kissed my head. I breathed in everything I could, trying to create a sensory memory of how he smelled and the caress of his warm skin against mine. "I will see you again very soon, you will see. You must trust me. I will not leave you for good, Julieta. This is temporary."

We kissed. I knew that he had a flight to catch but I didn't care. I couldn't let him go. Finally we pulled apart. He touched his lips to his fingers and placed them on my forehead. "Do not cry, I will see you soon, my love. My heart." He touched his heart, turned, and walked out the door.

I stood frozen for a second, then ran to the window to watch him go. Part of me felt like it was leaving with him. Why did it have to be like this? I watched him walk across the street and into the Merry Windsor. That was it. Carlos was gone. He had breezed into my new world in Ashland, turned everything upside down, and now was gone again.

In a half daze I washed the dishes and dumped the burnt coffee cake in the trash. There wasn't much point in trying to sleep. It was nearly time to start my day, but I padded into my bedroom and crashed on the bed anyway. My alarm shook me from a happy dream of Carlos and me dancing on the bow of the ship. I must have dozed off.

Had it really only been last night that Carlos and I had been having a dreamy, romantic dinner under the stars? I dragged myself out of bed. I considered running to the airport and begging Carlos to stay. Then I realized that his flight had already boarded.

I took a long shower, trying to wash away the craziness of the past few days. I wondered what would happen to Mathew and to ShakesBurgers. Maybe there was a chance that Alan would be able to bring back the Jester after all.

The empty sidewalks and dark storefronts on Main Street seemed lonely as I walked to Torte. I knew that Carlos was on an airplane headed south, but I couldn't help but stop in front of the Merry Windsor and stare longingly at it. What if he had changed his mind at the last minute? What if he hadn't gotten on the plane?

Stop, Jules. I gave my body a quick shake and continued on to the bakeshop. I went through the motions of making coffee, rising yeast, and warming the oven. It was time to stop worrying about the mistakes my heart had made and move on.

Stephanie arrived as I was sliding the first batch of bread into the oven. "Hey," she said, tucking her purple hair behind her ears.

"How are you doing this morning?" I asked.

"Fine. Why?" She narrowed her eyes.

I threw my hands up and chuckled. "Don't bite my head off."

She grinned. I couldn't believe it. Stephanie was grinning and it wasn't even dawn.

"Late night?"

She reached for an apron. The red Torte apron with our Torte logo clashed with her hair. "Huh?"

"Were you up late studying for your midterms?" I repeated.

"Yeah. Kind of." She twisted a strand of violet hair around her index finger, which was painted jet black. "Hey, is there any kind of dating policy here?"

"What do you mean?" I tried to play it casual.

"Like—uh—is it cool with you and your mom if employees date?"

"I take it this means that your late night involved more than studying." I smiled.

A blush matching her cherry-red apron spread across her face. "Sterling and I kind of hung out, that's all."

"That's great, and no, we don't have a dating policy. You're free to date anyone you want." If hanging out with Sterling meant that Stephanie was happy and smiling this early in the morning, that was great with me. However, I hadn't ever considered a dating policy. I would have to talk to Mom about it. I wanted to see both Stephanie and Sterling happy, but if it didn't work out and they broke up things could get awkward in Torte's tight quarters. I'd have to keep my fingers crossed.

I changed the subject. "You probably haven't heard the news yet."

"What news?"

"They made an arrest in Mindy's murder last night."

"Really?" She washed her hands in the sink and came over to the island.

"Yep. It was Mathew."

"Weren't they in business together?"

I nodded.

"Good thing they caught him."

"My thoughts exactly," I said, handing her a mixing bowl. "Can you start on cookie dough?"

Stephanie had become so well-versed in our morning routine that she could have made the dough with her eyes closed. In fact, at one point when I checked on her, it looked like her eyes were halfway closed. I couldn't blame her. It was early and she was getting the job done—eyes closed or not—I couldn't ask for more. And I was glad for an extra set of hands. I wanted to get the morning deliveries out the door and the pastry case stocked so that I could sneak out later to visit Thomas in the hospital.

I left Stephanie in charge and headed out to drop off the bread and cake orders. The sun had begun to rise and birds sang overhead. I didn't feel like singing. How long was I going to stay in a funk? If Carlos had stayed away I might have been able to keep my feelings at bay, but having him here had changed that. My passion had been reignited. And now he was gone again.

My delivery route took a bit longer than usual. Everyone wanted to know what happened last night. They had heard the sirens and seen the flashing lights on the police cars in the plaza. News in Ashland travels fast. I filled everyone in on what I knew. There was a sense of solidarity. Everyone was relieved that Mindy's killer had been caught and was behind bars. Life in our sweet little town could return to normal.

As I finished my deliveries I passed the Merry Windsor. To my disappointment Richard Lord stood on the front porch holding a giant ceramic mug of coffee—probably straight from a can—in his hand. "Juliet, come over here," he boomed as I tried to duck out of his line of sight.

"Hey, Richard," I said, holding the delivery box in front of me like a shield.

"Have you heard the news?" His silk bathrobe barely covered his portly waist.

"About Mathew?"

"It all went down here, you know. I'm having my marketing gal send out a press release this morning. The Merry Windsor had a hand in bringing down a killer. That should bring in more business."

"Good for you, Richard."

"Have you talked to that friend of yours, Jose?"

"No, why?"

"No reason." He raised his coffee mug. "I heard that he might have reason to celebrate, that's all."

"What does Jose have to celebrate?" I could feel irritation mounting inside.

"Rumor has it that he found a few new investors for the vineyard." Richard winked and pointed to himself.

"*You're* going to invest in Jose's vineyard?"

"Don't look so surprised, Juliet. I like to diversify my investments."

"What do you want with an organic winery? You don't even use organic products."

Richard puffed out his chest. I was worried his bathrobe might come undone. "I'll have you know, young lady, that the Merry Windsor uses the freshest products in town. Now we'll have a direct link to only the finest wine. You might want to start looking for a new vendor. Who knows if Jose will have anything left after we do a revamp?"

I didn't know what Richard was hinting at and for the moment I didn't care. I did know one thing and that was that the Merry Windsor used only processed food. Richard was up to something, and it wasn't investing in an organic vineyard. I'd have to find a time to talk to Jose and get the real story.

"I've got to get back to the shop, Richard," I said, shifting the box in my arms.

"Don't let me keep you." He gulped his coffee and gave me an evil grin.

Ugh. Richard Lord knew how to get under my skin. I whipped around and crossed the plaza. Mom, Andy, and Sterling were all hard at work prepping for breakfast.

"Morning," I greeted Andy and Sterling. Andy had a Southern Oregon University baseball cap on backward. He offered me a latte before both of my feet were even inside the door. "Hey, boss, I heard that you could use this." He handed me a creamy white latte.

"You are a dream." I took the latte. "Nectar of the gods."

Sterling stopped wiping down the pastry case. "How are you doing, Jules? Your mom told us about last night. That's insane."

"I'm fine, thanks, you guys. Especially with this." I nodded a thanks to Andy.

He flipped his cap around. "It's what I do, boss."

"You do it well."

Andy blushed and returned to pulling shots. Sterling motioned me over to the pastry case. He dropped his voice. "How did it go last night?"

"With Mathew?"

"No, the surprise dinner. Did you like it?"

"With everything else that happened, I completely forgot about it."

"Completely?"

"Maybe not completely. It was amazing. Is that what you two were conspiring about?"

"I can't say. It's bro code, you know?"

"Bro code? Since when are you a bro?"

Sterling smiled. "Once a bro, always a bro. That's what Carlos says."

I flicked his wrist. "There is no way that Carlos says that."

He laughed. "True."

Mom waved me back to the kitchen. "Juliet, can you come take a look at this?"

"You missed a spot," I said to Sterling.

He scrubbed the already spotless counter. "Don't fire me." He pretended to beg.

I laughed and walked to the back. "Something smells amazing." I peered into the oven. "What do you have baking?"

Mom frowned. "I thought I had a sponge cake, but look at it. It's not rising. I'm having a moment of panic. You don't think we're about to lose this oven too, do you? The temperature gauge says that it's at three hundred and fifty, but feel in there. It doesn't feel hot enough to me."

"Oh, no." Working with one oven had been hard enough. But without a single working oven it would be impossible to keep our doors open. I reached inside. Mom was right. The oven was warm, but certainly not up to temp.

"Did you try turning it off and on again?"

Mom shook her head. "No. I was hoping that it was all in my head."

I clicked the oven off, waited for a second, and then turned it on again. "Cross your fingers. Maybe it's a weird glitch."

We waited, staring at the glass window. I could tell that Mom was holding her breath. I crossed my fingers on both hands. The temp gauge stayed at three hundred and fifty. After a few minutes I looked at Mom. "Should we give it a try?"

She winced and closed her eyes. "Okay. You do it. I can't look."

This time when I opened the oven a blast of warm air hit my face. "We're good!" I shouted.

Mom clapped and exhaled. "Thank goodness."

I shut the oven. "We can't put this off any longer, Mom. I'm putting in our order for new ovens right now."

She nodded. "I agree. Even if it means things might be tight for a while we have to do it. I had visions of having to go beg Richard Lord for oven space."

"No way! We're doing this. Richard Lord can keep his expensive and never-used ovens, we're getting our own." I marched to the office, pulled out the industrial kitchen equipment catalog, and placed a call. Within a matter of minutes our order was complete.

"It's done," I announced, returning to the kitchen. They're coming in three weeks."

"Three weeks?" Mom said. "What about Valentine's Day and the Chocolate Fest?"

"What about them?"

"How long is it going to take them to install?"

"They do it during off hours. They'll come in the evening when we're closed. Don't worry. They do this kind of install all the time. In fact, the Chocolate Fest could be the perfect time to have this done anyway. Downtown is going to be dead that week. What if we have Sterling, Andy, and Stephanie rotate shifts at the fest and here? We can close for a couple days to paint and to shift some things around."

Mom rubbed her temples. "That's a good idea. Do you think we can pull it off?"

"Don't worry. I know we can." I squeezed her hand to reassure her. Then I called a team meeting. We mapped out a schedule. Sterling and Andy were excited to paint. Stephanie wasn't quite as thrilled, so they agreed she could work the fest. They would help at peak times but otherwise would be in charge of Torte's face-lift.

New ovens were going to take us to the next level. They'd been a nagging concern in the back of my head ever since I'd come home. If we were going to do this, we might as well do it right.

Then I walked Andy and Sterling through my vision for the kitchen. The dining area was in good shape. The paint was still bright and the tables and booths were in excellent condition. The kitchen, though, hadn't been painted for years. A new coat would help spruce it up, and I had some ideas for moving existing shelving and building new shelving that would help streamline production.

After we had everything arranged I felt lighter. Torte was getting a fresh start and so was I.

Chapter Thirty-three

Later in the morning I packaged up a box of cinnamon rolls, jelly-filled doughnuts, and chocolate croissants for Thomas. A long walk was exactly what I needed to clear my head. I took my time walking past Southern Oregon University, where students were reading on the lawn and tossing Frisbees. Rosalind had been right. ShakesBurgers would have done well in this part of town that catered to hungry and usually broke college students with chain sandwich shops and fast-food joints.

When I arrived at the hospital, the nurse at the reception desk showed me to his room. I knocked lightly on the door.

"Come in," Thomas said. His bed was in an upright position and aside from the bandage around his head he looked alert and happy. "How's it going?"

"I was going to ask you that." I handed him the pastry box.

"Sweet. You're the best." He nodded at an uneaten tray of gray oatmeal and dry toast. "You don't even want to know what that was like." Sticking his finger in his mouth, he pretended to gag. "Bad. So bad. I think I might have nightmares about it."

"Happy to help. I brought you one of everything. I wasn't sure what you would be in the mood for."

He reached for a cinnamon roll. "I'll eat every one of them before they let me out of here."

I sat in the chair next to the bed. "You better pace yourself. Otherwise they'll have to pump all of that sugar from your stomach."

"Good point." He took a bite of the soft roll. "This is awesome."

"How are you feeling?"

"Fine. It's nothing. A bump. I don't know why they kept me. I think the Professor made them."

"He was worried about you. We all were."

"Stupid sedan. I've been trying to convince the Professor to put in a request for a four-wheel drive. Maybe now he'll do it."

"You might as well try to work it. You could say that you're seeing double or something."

"I like it." He rubbed his head. "Come to think of it, did you grow an extra head?"

"Oh, no, I think I've created a monster." I handed him a napkin. "Did you talk to the Professor?"

"Last night. Why?"

"Has he said anything to you about retiring?"

Thomas shook his head. "No. Did he say that to you?"

"No, but my mom hinted that he was talking about it, but she also said that he was stressed about the case."

"The Professor doesn't usually get stressed."

"Exactly."

Thomas frowned. "I hope he's not serious. I don't

know what I would do without him." He chuckled and pointed to the wrap on his head. "I got this just driving around town."

"You should come up with a good story—tell people that you were chasing a suspect and speeding through the streets."

"Trust me. I'm already working on it. The guys are not going to let me live this down." He finished his cinnamon roll and reached for a strawberry doughnut.

"Have they told you when you get to leave?"

"Hopefully before lunch." Thomas took a bite of the gooey doughnut. "I heard that Carlos left. How are you doing?"

I sighed. "I'm okay."

He cleared his throat. "You don't have to play tough around me, Jules. I've known you too long."

I smiled. "It's complicated."

"If you want to talk, I'm here."

"I appreciate that. Thanks."

Thomas pushed the box of pastry toward me. "Can you put those over there? I am going to eat the entire box if you don't take it away."

I made space on his bedside table for the box. "Is there anything you need?"

"Nope. I'm good now that I have Torte by my side." He wiped his fingers on the napkin. "You know what I was just thinking? Remember the last time we were both here? You were in the bed, and I brought you flowers. That can be our thing."

"How about if our thing is that neither of us end up in the hospital again?"

"Yeah. I like that plan better." Thomas grinned.

"Did you suspect Mathew the whole time?"

"The Professor did. He thought it was too convenient that Mathew was on the scene. You helped confirm that. That's why he wanted me to go over the timeline with each suspect and witness multiple times. You arrived on the scene, minutes after Mathew killed Mindy."

I shuddered.

"I know," Thomas said. "It's a good thing you didn't get there sooner. You might have caught him in the act and who knows what might have happened."

"You're not making me feel better."

"Sorry. Anyway between you and the coroner's report we were able to determine that Mindy was killed right before you got there. She made a call to Alan fifteen minutes earlier. The Professor said this is one of the tightest timelines he's ever worked. Usually the time of death is a window of an hour or more. This time it was literally minutes."

"I can't believe Mathew did it."

"He had financial motivation. The tech department was able to recover the digital contracts on Mindy's laptop. She was cutting him out. That's usually one of the number-one motives."

"It's so sad."

"Murder is sad," Thomas agreed.

A nurse tapped on the door. "I'm going to need to check his vitals," she said, wheeling in a cart.

"That's okay, I should get back to the shop anyway." I stood. "I'm glad to see you looking good. Feel better. Let me know if you need anything."

Thomas pointed to the pastry box. "I might need another round of sustenance later."

"Consider it done." I waved and made way for the nurse.

Torte was a straight shot down Main Street. Seeing Thomas had made me feel better. He looked fine and was obviously his normal, upbeat self.

I continued past the library. The closer I got to downtown the more the shop façades began to resemble an Elizabethan village. When I arrived at ShakesBurgers, Alan and Rosalind were standing in front of the restaurant. Rosalind had a notebook in her hand and was making notes as Alan pointed to the front window.

"You two look like you're plotting something," I said, slowing my pace.

"Good morning, Juliet," Rosalind said. She tapped the notebook. "Guilty as charged. Alan and I are going over the new design for the Jester."

"The Jester?" I asked Alan. "You're going to reopen? Is that why you're back in costume?" I noted his purple-and-green jester outfit, complete with a cap with dangling bells.

He smiled. "Yep. Thanks in part to Rosalind. I don't have to work for the man. The city is going to offer grant money to downtown businesses to help offset the cost of redesigning any modern buildings to be in line with Ashland's Shakespeare corridor. That's what you're calling it, right, Rosalind?"

Rosalind nodded. "Yes. Not only did the council pass the ordinance, but they found grant money to help businesses in the process. I'm going to be overseeing the program."

"That's great news."

"Having some financial support should help me get it right this time," Alan said.

"Tell me about it," I said. "Running a small business is costly."

Rosalind perked up. "Maybe we can find grant money for you and your mom, Juliet. Your storefront is already up to our high standards, but what about inside? Perhaps you could add some additional Elizabethan touches. The council is highly motived to roll this program out before the start of the new season."

"Do you think they want to offer grant money for new ovens?"

"I don't know about that." She flipped through the notebook. "You know what? I have an idea for you! An amazing idea. Why didn't I think of it sooner?"

"What?" I looked at Alan. He shrugged.

"The space below you has been vacant for years." Rosalind started sketching something on the notebook. "Have you consider expanding? I'm sure we could get you a city loan or grant to develop that space."

The space Rosalind was referring to was on the back corner of Torte. Many of Ashland's downtown storefronts have back-alley spaces as well. There's a cobblestone walkway around the corner that parallels Lithia Creek. Some restaurants have back decks and patios for alfresco dining. The basement shop underneath Torte used to be a bookstore. Customers would access it from back stairs on the alley. The bookstore went out of business five years ago, and had been vacant ever since.

"Are you serious?" I asked Rosalind.

"Very serious. We are committed to ensuring that our downtown Shakespeare corridor is a world-class destination. Torte is an institution on Main Street and your family has led the charge in keeping the spirit of the Bard alive."

"I don't know. Let me talk it over with Mom."

She reached into her purse and pulled out a business card. Placing it in my hand, she said, "Talk to your mother and get back to me. I'd love to help see this idea to fruition."

"Okay." I tucked the card into my jeans pocket. "I will."

Her foot slipped as she shifted her purse. Alan caught her arm and steadied her. "Are you okay?" I asked.

"This old hip." She patted her hip. "I took a bit of a tumble walking down the steps on the stage at the Black Swan the other night. Threw my hip out. It flares up sometimes."

"You fell at the theater?"

"More like slipped. Why do you look so surprised?"

"It's nothing. It's just that I heard a rumor that you and Mindy had a fight that night and then you were limping and bruised. I thought maybe . . ." I trailed off.

Rosalind tapped Alan with her purse. "She thought that I could be a killer. Well, Juliet, I have to tell you I'm actually flattered by that."

"I didn't really think that you could have killed Mindy." I felt color rising in my cheeks.

Alan scratched his head. "Hey, what about me, man? I'm feeling left out."

"Oh, no, don't. Remember our conversation at Shakes-Burgers?"

"Yeah." He flashed the peace symbol with his fingers. "The hippie and grandma."

"I guess that's why it's best to leave murder investigations to the Professor and Thomas."

They returned to sketching out a Shakespearean façade for ShakesBurgers. I crossed the plaza. Who would have thought that my parents' obsession with Shakespeare might lead to cash to help expand Torte?

Expand Torte! I couldn't wait to tell Mom. We were excited about new ovens and a kitchen paint job. Taking over the vacant basement would be a major undertaking, but my mind was already running through designs. We could knock through the floor and build stairs. We could even move the entire kitchen downstairs and expand the coffee bar and dining room upstairs.

I practically skipped across the plaza. Mom and I could expand Torte! My vision of owning a pastry shop and restaurant could come true sooner than I'd ever imagined. I was home. I was where I wanted to be and about to take a big leap forward.

Recipes

Chocolate Molasses Crinkles

Ingredients:
- ¾ cup butter
- 1 cup sugar
- ¼ cup molasses
- 1 egg
- 2 cups flour
- 2 teaspoons baking soda
- ½ teaspoon salt
- 2 teaspoons cinnamon
- 1 teaspoon cloves
- 1 teaspoon ginger
- 1 teaspoon nutmeg
- 1 package chocolate chips
- ½ cup granulated sugar in extra bowl

Directions:
Cream butter, sugar, and molasses together. Add egg. Then slowly incorporate dry ingredients and spices. Once

batter is firm, add chocolate chips and chill in the refrigerator for one hour. Spoon batter into 1-inch balls and bake for 15 minutes at 350 degrees.

Immediately roll in granulated sugar when cookies are hot from the oven.

Creamy Potato Casserole

Ingredients:
   6 medium russet potatoes
   ½ onion
   ½ cup butter
   1 pint sour cream
   2 cups grated cheese—Jules uses a blend of Colby
      Jack and sharp cheddar
   1 teaspoon salt
   1 teaspoon pepper
   2 tablespoons chopped fresh chives
   ½ cup parmesan cheese

Directions:
Scrub potatoes and cook in skins in boiling water until tender when forked. Allow potatoes to cool, then peel and grate cooked potatoes into a large mixing bowl. Chop onions and sauté in butter until translucent. Add butter and onions to grated potatoes. Mix in sour cream, cheese, salt, pepper, and chopped chives. Mix well and add to a greased casserole dish. Sprinkle with parmesan cheese. Bake at 350 degrees for 45 minutes. Serve hot.

Tomato-Orange Soup

Ingredients:
- ½ cup butter
- 1 medium onion
- 10 fresh tomatoes or two (14.5 oz.) cans of diced tomatoes
- 1 teaspoon salt
- 1 teaspoon pepper
- ½ teaspoon baking soda
- ½ teaspoon fresh rosemary
- ½ teaspoon fresh thyme
- 1 cup fresh orange juice
- ¾ cup half and half

Directions:

Melt butter in a saucepan. Add chopped onion and sauté until translucent. If using fresh tomatoes, wash and cut slits in the tomato skins. Boil for 5 minutes. Remove from water. The skin should easily peel away. Dice tomatoes and add to the onions, or add cans of diced tomatoes. Then add salt, pepper, baking soda, and chopped rosemary and thyme. Bring to a boil, reduce heat to low, and simmer for 10 to 15 minutes.

Use an immersion blender or food processor to puree. Once the mixture has been pureed, return to saucepan and whisk in orange juice and half and half. Bring to a simmer and serve hot.

Red Velvet Cake

Ingredients:
- ½ cup butter
- 1 ½ cups sugar
- 2 eggs
- 1 teaspoon vanilla
- 2 tablespoons cocoa powder
- 3 oz. red food coloring
- 2 ½ cups flour
- 1 teaspoon salt
- 1 cup buttermilk
- 1 teaspoon baking soda
- 1 ½ teaspoons vinegar

Directions:
Cream butter, sugar, and eggs together. Add in vanilla, cocoa powder, and food coloring. Mix flour and salt in a separate bowl. Alternate adding flour mixture and buttermilk to butter mixture. Fold in baking soda and vinegar last. Bake in two 8-inch greased round pans for 30 minutes at 350 degrees. Once cooled, cut cakes in half crosswise to frost.

Flour frosting

Ingredients:
- 6 tablespoons flour
- 1 cup water
- 1 cup butter
- 1 cup sugar
- 1 teaspoon vanilla

Directions:

Heat flour and water in a saucepan on medium high. Be sure to continually whisk the mixture as it begins to thicken. Once the paste is opaque, remove from heat and allow to cool.

Beat butter, sugar, and vanilla in a mixer. Add in cooled flour-and-water paste and beat until the frosting is light and fluffy. Spread a thin coat of frosting between each layer of red velvet cake. Use remaining frosting to ice the top and sides of the 4-layer cake.

Bacon-Wrapped Dates

Ingredients:
- 25–30 pitted dates
- 1 ½ pounds of bacon—sliced thin
- 25–30 toothpicks

Directions:

Preheat oven to 400 degrees. Wrap each date with a slice of bacon and secure with a toothpick. Place on a cookie sheet. Bake dates for 20 minutes. Turn halfway through so that the bacon is cooked on both sides. Serve warm.

Lemon Olive Oil Cake

Ingredients:
   1 large lemon (juice and zest)
   1 cup sugar
   4 eggs
   ½ cup olive oil
   1 teaspoon vanilla
   ½ teaspoon baking powder
   ½ teaspoon salt
   1 cup flour
   Powdered sugar to dust the top of the cake

Directions:
Zest lemon and then squeeze juice. Beat sugar and eggs on high for 5 to 10 minutes until they become fluffy and pale. Add in lemon juice, zest, olive oil, and vanilla and mix on low. Sift dry ingredients together and fold into the mixture by hand. Pour into a greased springform pan and bake at 350 degrees for 45 minutes.

   Allow cake to cool for 30 minutes, then remove from springform pan and dust with powdered sugar.

Chunky Monkey

Andy's latest funky coffee creation. It's like dessert in a cup.

Ingredients:

    Good quality espresso (Jules and Mom serve
        Stumptown at Torte, but are always open to
        trying new blends.)
    2% milk
    2 tablespoons dark chocolate sauce
    1 teaspoon banana extract
    Whipping cream
    Macadamia nut shavings

Directions:

Prepare espresso and steam milk. Mix chocolate sauce and banana extract in the bottom of your favorite coffee mug. Add steamed milk and stir. Pour over espresso. Top with whipping cream and macadamia nut shavings.

Read on for an excerpt of the next installment
in the Bakeshop Mystery Series

Fudge and Jury

Available January 2017 from St. Martin's Paperbacks!

They say that chocolate makes everything better. I agree. Torte, our family bakeshop, looked as if it had been dipped in chocolate. Every square inch of counter space was filled with chocolate tarts, chocolate eclairs, chocolate cakes, chocolate cookies and chocolate truffles. Chocolate posters were plastered on the bakeshop's front windows and the scent of chocolate simmering on the stove permeated the cozy kitchen.

Every March, Ashland, Oregon, my hometown, hosts an annual Chocolate Festival. This year Torte had been chosen as one of the showcase vendors. That meant we would have a prominent booth in the center of all the delicious action and have an opportunity to showcase our chocolate artistry. Being recognized as a showcase vendor was a huge accolade, but also meant that we had to prepare double—if not triple—the amount of chocolate samples. Our staff had been working around the clock.

Torte looked like a scene from *Charlie and the Chocolate Factory*. Chocolate bubbled on the stove and cooled in long thin sheets on the butcher block island. We drizzled white, dark, and milk chocolate over marzipan, dipped shortbread cookies in vats of it, and baked with industrial-sized containers of cocoa powder.

In addition to the bakeshop being taken over by chocolate, we were in the middle of a remodel. After months of skimping and saving, Mom and I had finally managed to amass enough cash to purchase new ovens we desperately needed. Since the Chocolate Festival would take place over a four-day weekend, we decided to close Torte for the duration of the Fest. Andy, Stephanie, and Sterling, our small but mighty staff, would focus on the kitchen upgrade while Mom and I dazzled guests with our chocolate confections at the Fest.

I had worked out a schedule that would allow enough time to clean and prep the kitchen, paint, reorganize and inventory our stock, and (fingers crossed if everything went as planned) to install the new ovens just in time to reopen for business on Monday. The Chocolate Fest kicked off on Thursday afternoon, which meant that the team had two and half days to complete all the prep work before the installers arrived with our ovens on Sunday morning. It was going to be tight, but I was confident we could pull it off. No one at Torte was afraid of hard work or a little elbow grease. I had a feeling that was due to Mom's incredible work ethic. She set an example for our young staff. Despite the fact that she was in her mid-fifties she was still one of the first people to arrive and last to leave.

That was one of the many things that she and I needed to talk about. I knew that part of her wanted to scale back, and I also knew it was time. She had been at Torte's helm since my dad died and thanks to her tireless effort, kind listening ear, and delicious bread and pastries, Torte was thriving. I wanted her to be able to thrive too. She and the Professor, Ashland's resident detective and Shakespeare buff, had been getting serious. The Professor wanted to travel. Mom had been reluctant to commit, and I had a sneaking suspicion I knew why: me.

When I returned to Ashland last summer my heart was broken. I'd left everything I knew, including my husband, at sea. Being back in Ashland surrounded by warm and welcoming familiar faces and Torte's bright and cherry red and teal walls was exactly what the doctor ordered. My heart had finally started to mend. It helped that Carlos, my estranged husband, had made a surprise visit to Southern Oregon last month. Seeing his sultry Spanish skin and romantic dark eyes had been unsettling, to say the very least. When we parted ways we agreed that we would take a hiatus. He was the last person I expected to show up in Ashland.

At first the distraction of having him underfoot was too much, but after a few days we fell into our old rhythm. I guess in some ways it was inevitable. Food was our love language. We didn't even need to speak when we were in the kitchen together. We had worked together for years on the cruise ship and it was if our bodies remembered. We moved in a comfortable easy cadence just like we had on the ship. But things we different now. Carlos had lied to me. He had hidden the fact that he had a son for the duration of our marriage. I hadn't been sure that I could forgive him for that. Maybe it was the time we had spent apart, or maybe it was because I had carved out a new life for myself in Ashland, but either way I had found a way to forgive him.

When he first arrived I was angry, but that had begun

to dissipate. Of course I was sad and disappointed that he had kept something so important from me, but I had also begun to understand why. He was trying to protect his son, Ramiro. I couldn't blame him for that. I felt fiercely protective of Mom, and came to realize that was how Carlos felt about Ramiro.

It would have been so much easier if I could have stayed angry with him. When Carlos was oceans away I had concentrated my time and energy on Torte and let thoughts of our time together slip into the recesses of my brain. He became more like a fuzzy dream until he showed up in real life and flipped everything upside down again.

Even though things were healing between us and even though I knew that Carlos loved me and would do anything for me, I didn't want to leave Ashland. My life on the ship was a distant memory. My future was at Torte, and only time would tell if Carlos was part of that future. For the moment he was back on the ship and sailing under sunny Caribbean skies, and I was late for a date with chocolate.

I shook myself free from my thoughts and concentrated on my immediate surroundings. Mom and Dad used to tease me about living in my head too much when I was growing up. I blame them; after all, they named me Juliet Montague Capshaw. A name like Juliet requires time spent in your head.

The clock on the far wall signaled that it was a few minutes before noon. I needed to get moving. Brushing cocoa powder from my hands, I untied my apron and folded it on the island. "Back in a few," I called to Stephanie and Mom and headed for the front door.

The sky dripped like a leaky faucet as I stepped onto Main Street. Many tourists are surprised to learn that Ashland gets very little rain. People tend to think that Oregon is one giant mud puddle in the winter months. There's some truth to that. Portland and the surrounding valley west of the Cascade Mountains tend to get waterlogged, but Ashland is much more Mediterranean. It's one of the sunniest cities in the Pacific Northwest with a relatively mild climate.

I pulled my rain jacket over my head and ducked under the red-and-white striped awning at Pucks' Pub. In addition to boasting a serene climate, Ashland is also known around the world as being home to the Oregon Shakespeare Festival. Our quaint downtown plaza could be mistaken for an old English village. Most of the buildings are themed after Shakespeare with ornate façades and gables, and witty Bard-inspired names. In fact I was on my way to meet with Rosalind Gates, the president of the downtown business association. Rosalind had been working with the city to preserve Ashland's old world charm. The city (thanks to Rosalind's persistence) had recently passed new design ordinances in order to ensure that businesses in the busy plaza adhered to the historical esthetic.

Rosalind had even found grant money to help small businesses, like Torte, expand. That's why I was meeting with her today. I tucked a white paper bag with our Torte logo stamped on the front into the inside pocket of my jacket and hurried along the wet sidewalk.

Hearth and Home, the brokerage firm where I was meeting Rosalind, was located just outside the plaza. I headed toward Lithia Park and took a right at the end of Main Street. Rain splattered on my jeans and soaked through my tennis shoes.

I pushed open the glass door and stepped inside.

Rosalind was waiting for me near the reception desk. Her silver hair was tucked behind her ears revealing plastic earrings in the silhouette of Shakespeare's bust. She wore a purple t-shirt that read, "Ashland: Such Stuff as Dreams Are Made On." The last time I'd seen Rosalind she had been sporting a "Save our Shakespeare" shirt when a chain restaurant threatened to move into the plaza.

"New shirt?" I asked, taking off my rain coat and hanging it on a rack by the door.

She glanced at her chest. "Do you like it? I'm testing out a new tagline for the plaza. I'm not sure if this one is going to stick."

"But you made a shirt."

"My son bought me a screen press for Christmas and I figured I'd give it a whirl."

"That's great." I walked toward her and handed her the bag. "Sorry if I'm a couple minutes late, but I come bearing chocolate."

"Lateness is completely excusable if it involves chocolate." She removed a dark chocolate-covered cherry from the bag. Her eyes sparkled. When she smiled the deep crevasses formed on her cheeks. "Come on back. I have the paperwork for you to look over."

She led me to an empty office. Blueprints and maps were tacked to the walls. I noticed one that outlined plans for a railroad terminal and station. "Is this for a railroad?" I pointed to the far wall.

Rosalind's smile broadened. "Yes. It's not public knowledge yet, so let's keep that between us."

I studied the sketch. "But the railroad tracks have been abandoned for years."

"Exactly." Rosalind walked behind the oak desk and

took a seat. She motioned for me to sit too. "Do you remember the sound of the train whistle when you were a girl?"

I nodded.

"We've been cut off from the rail line for too long. I intend to change that. Not only will freight deliveries return with my plan but we're also negotiating with Amtrak to bring passenger trains to Ashland again." She nodded to the wall. "The Siskiyou Summit Railroad Revitalization Project is set to resume train traffic early next year. I can't wait to hear those lovely whistles again."

Rosalind explained that the railroad had abandoned service to Ashland in 2008. Since then freight had to be hauled by big-rig trucks. In the winter when the mountain passes were snowed in that meant that goods and supplies couldn't be delivered until the roads were cleared.

"I didn't know there were any plans to reopen the rail lines," I said to Rosalind.

She nodded. "It's been a long time coming, and a vital step for our local economy. Per-mile costs are much less by rail. That's a good thing for you as a business owner."

"Right," I agreed.

Pushing a stack of blueprints rolled up with rubber bands to the side of the desk, Rosalind picked up a file folder and handed it to me. Her hands trembled. "Here are the loan papers. You'll need to fill them out and return them to me no later than tomorrow at noon. That deadline is firm. The city council will be making all of their decisions on granting funding. I've already submitted your preliminary application. This is the final paperwork, and Juliet, as we discussed, I think you're a sure thing. Would you and your mother like to do a walk-through this afternoon?"

"I think that's probably a good idea." I could hear the hesitation in my voice. Everything was moving so fast. It had only been a couple of weeks since Rosalind approached me about the city's grant program. The space below Torte had come available for lease, and we were seriously considering an expansion. It was rare for property on the plaza to open up and when it did there were usually multiple offers from businesses vying for a spot in Ashland's prime retail market.

Mom and I had discussed expanding Torte someday, and suddenly that dream was becoming a reality. We both had reservations about more than doubling our square footage though, especially as she was starting to think about scaling back. At the same time we knew that opportunities like this didn't come very often.

Having help from the city would be paramount. Renovating the basement space was a much bigger project than our kitchen remodel and new ovens. We couldn't afford that kind of undertaking on our own, but with grant money or a low-interest loan from the city, the idea was one step closer to a reality. The only problem was that this was a temporary offer.

"Juliet, I can't stress this enough. If you're serious about moving forward you have to be ready to go. This is unprecedented. Thanks to your friend Lance we have secured an art development grant, but that money has to be spent before the first of July. If Torte is awarded a grant, construction must start immediately."

"I understand." I nodded. The final loan papers felt heavy in my hands as I thanked Rosalind for her time and left. Outside the sky continued to drip. I took a different route back to the bakeshop, along the Calle Guanjuato, a brick path complete with antique street lamps that paralleled Lithia Creek. The trees lining the path revealed the first signs that spring was on its way. Tiny green buds bent the tips of their branches. I tightened my rain coat and smiled at the thought of cherry blossoms and fresh-cut grass.

The basement space we were considering was at the far end of the cobblestone path. Steep concrete steps with a black iron railing led down to the shop. I couldn't resist peeking in the window for the hundredth time. The steps were slippery. I held tight to the railing as I made my way down the slick moss-covered steps. Water had pooled in a large puddle about two inches deep in front of the door. That couldn't be a good sign.

I bent down to see if it was spilling under the rusted old door. Power had been cut off to the empty space months ago, so it was too dark to tell. I'd have to mention that to Mom and add potential flooding to our "con" list. The plaza sat in the middle of a flash-flood zone. When heavy rains fall (which fortunately doesn't happen very often) they spill down the city's surrounding hills and funnel straight into the plaza and Lithia Creek. I remember one summer when I was in high school a thunderstorm erupted over the city and dropped three inches of rain in less than an hour. Every business on the plaza, including Torte, was inundated with water. We ended up better than most, with only a few inches of water flooding Torte's dining room. It took weeks to pump all the water out.

Was this a sign not to move forward? I pressed my face to the wet glass and peered inside. As far as I could tell the basement looked dry. At least for the moment.

I sighed and walked back up the stairs. A contractor would know what to do about potential flooding. We were scheduled to meet with the city's building inspector tomorrow. Keeping the space dry was going to be my first question, but for the moment I had a date with some delicious dark chocolate . . .